Born in 1905, H. E. Bates was educated at
Kettering Grammar School and worked as a
journalist before publishing his first book, *The
Two Sisters*, when he was twenty. In the next
fifteen years he won a distinguished reputation
for his stories about English country life. In 1941, as
'Flying Officer X', he wrote his two famous books
of short stories – *The Greatest People in the World*
and *How Sleep the Brave* – which were followed
in 1944 by *Fair Stood the Wind for France* (published in Penguins). These, and his subsequent
novels of Burma, *The Purple Plain* and *The
Jacaranda Tree*, and of India, *The Scarlet Sword*,
stemming directly or indirectly from his war experience in the East, won him a new reputation
and, apart from their success in Britain and
America, have been translated into sixteen foreign
languages. Of his later books *The Feast of July*
and four of his humorous books about the Larkin
family are amongst those which have already appeared in Penguins.

H. E. Bates lives in Kent.

H. E. BATES

A Moment in Time

PENGUIN BOOKS

Penguin Books Ltd, Harmondsworth, Middlesex, England
Penguin Books Australia Ltd, Ringwood, Victoria, Australia

—

First published by Michael Joseph 1964
Published in Penguin Books 1967
Reprinted 1969

—

Copyright © Evensford Productions Ltd, 1964

—

Made and printed in Great Britain
by C. Nicholls & Company Ltd
Set in Linotype Granjon

Give them their life :
They do not know how short it grows;
So let them go
Young-eyed, steel-fledged, gun-furious,
For if they live they'll live,
As well you know,
Upon the bitter kernels of their sweet ideals.

Give them their wings :
They cannot fly too high or far
To soar above
The dirty-moted, bomb-soured, word-tired world.
And if they die they'll die,
As you should know,
More swiftly, cleanly, star-defined than you will ever feel.

I

'Do come and look, Elizabeth,' my mother said. 'The swans are making a hole in the lake.'

I shall remember for ever, sometimes with joy and pride and at others with sadness and utter dread, but no longer with bitterness, the year 1940, more especially a winter evening deeply entombed in snow, when my mother stood at the big bay window in the drawing-room of our house and said these words to me, in her usual lost and fluttering fashion, as she stared at the lake below. I was then a very young nineteen and I remember, as I started to move over to the window, looking at the illuminated wrist-watch my grandmother had given me for my birthday and seeing that it was exactly five o'clock. It was, though I didn't realize it then, an important moment in time.

My mother was tall and gaunt. Her eyes were dark and never looked well. The skin of her neck was like a piece of chamois leather that had been wrung out and left to dry in brownish, uncomfortable, awkward folds. The flutter in her speech was not so much nervous as indecisive. When she spoke she always seemed to be chasing her words as if they were a brood of recalcitrant chickens she was trying to get to roost and when she finally spoke to them they were nearly always the wrong ones. Hence the hole in the lake.

'A very big hole?' my grandmother said. She was sitting by the big open fire-place, her skirt up to her knees, her brilliant dark head erect, her legs rosy in the light of a great flaming fire of ash-boughs. In contrast to my mother her voice was firm. Its tone was level, with a certain controlled acidity about it. Her question mocked my mother, but lightly and without cruelty. My mother in any case was quite incapable of being hurt by it for the simple reason that in her absent-minded way she was wholly unaware that the words carried with them any such purpose as mockery. In the same way my grandmother could have flattered her and she wouldn't have been aware of that either. She was a human duck off whose back even the most sereing of words flowed like harmless rain.

I reached the window and stood by her side. After a week of frost and snow the lake had become one with the land. Only a crest or two of frozen reed sticking up through billows of snow marked the line of the banks, beyond which copses of hazel and alder stood like a low petrified forest, the intense whiteness of it fired by the savage carmine ball of the setting sun.

Below us the swans, five of them now, were swimming slowly round and round, occasionally breasting the thick edges of snow and ice, keeping open their clear dark circle of water. My mother, in her funny way, was right after all. It really did look like a big black hole, a bottomless grave in the glistening sepulchral whiteness of snow.

'I could have sworn there were seven of them,' she said.

'There were,' I said, 'yesterday. But they had a great fight. I watched it. The other two were strangers and the five drove them away.'

'That was very cruel,' she said. 'Why couldn't they be sociable.'

'Swans,' my grandmother said, 'have no idea what it is to be sociable.'

'Oh! don't they? I always think they look so neighbourly. I suppose it's the shape of them. Did anyone give them bread today?'

'I gave them bread,' I said, 'three times.'

'That was nice. They look sort of in prison, don't they?'

Again, in her odd way, she was right. The clear circle of water was their prison. In the great friendly embalming stretch of snow it looked curiously dark and sinister.

'Is there any more toast?' I said. 'I'm simply ravenous still.'

'We shared the last piece ten minutes ago,' my grandmother said. 'If you really want more ring for Edna.'

'Oh! I'd love to make it myself. Couldn't I? I adore making toast by the fire.'

'Ring for Edna.'

The war was still young. The notion of making one's own toast by the fire was, for our family at any rate, still an unthinkable one.

8

I crossed over to the fireplace and pulled the bell-pull and rang for Edna. As if by some sort of magic the door opened instantly and my Uncle Harry came in.

It would be truer to say that he exploded in. He came sweeping in like a big hairy whirlwind. His heavy reddish-brown tweed suit matched his thick coarse hair, which not only came down low over his forehead but sprouted in lush gingery watch-springs from his ears and nostrils. At some distant date, before I was born, he had broken his right leg in a fall from a horse and the resulting lameness caused all his physical acts to be done, as it were, at double strength. The ferocity of his clumsiness was that of an unbalanced bull.

'Tea finished? Doesn't matter. I'll have a whisky-and-soda.'

In the act of pouring himself a whisky and soda at the table by the window he twice dropped the stopper of the decanter and once spouted soda on to the carpet. At the first of these explosions I actually saw my mother jump. At the third she merely crept away, after the fashion of a whipped dog, and sat down on a low claret-coloured needlework chair away from the fire.

'They say whisky's going to be damn scarce. Any toast left?'

'We're just about to ask for some,' my grandmother said.

The soda siphon, suddenly caught by a ponderous elbow, spun like a lop-sided top on the polished surface of the table. My Uncle Harry, grabbing at it with a meaty hand, promptly bashed it over .

'I occasionally wonder,' my grandmother said, 'why you don't use a hammer and chisel for mixing your drinks.'

That the arrow of her words was too subtle for him hardly mattered. A moment later Edna knocked on the door. My grandmother called for her to come in and presently she was in the room, a thin, grey-haired, round-shouldered woman, half at attention and dressed in black, with white lace cap and apron. I had once heard my Uncle Harry call her – not in the presence of my grandmother – 'ninepenny worth of scrag-end,' and the description, rather like some of my mother's, was an oddly apt one. There was more bone than flesh on Edna and such bone as there was seemed to creak as she limped along.

'You rang, ma'am?'

'Of course she rang,' my Uncle Harry said. 'If she didn't ring why are you here?'

'Bring toast for two, please, Edna,' my grandmother said.

It seemed to me that Edna trembled. Her already ash-pale face seemed to grow whiter. I was still trying to wonder why a simple request for toast should have had this devastating effect on her when she actually said:

'I'm sorry, ma'am. I can't.'

'What do you mean, you can't?'

'We've no bread, ma'am.'

'Good grief,' Harry said. '*No what?*'

'Bread, sir. The baker couldn't get through today. Nor yesterday.'

'Stale will do perfectly well for toast,' my grandmother said. 'Haven't you any stale?'

'No, ma'am. Miss Elizabeth threw the last of the stale to the swans.'

At this shattering announcement my Uncle Harry's mouth dropped open, as if either in the beginning of prayer or protest, but not a sound emerged.

'If there's no toast I'll have a piece of my birthday cake,' I said.

'Yes, miss. Will that be all, ma'am?'

'That will be all, Edna. Thank you.'

Edna backed dumbly out of the room. The door hadn't been shut more than ten seconds before my grandmother whipped herself to her feet, turned on Harry and said in a seething voice:

'I will not have Edna spoken to in that fashion. What in Heaven's name has got into you?'

'I – I –'

'Don't slobber,' Some few drops of whisky and soda had fallen from my Uncle Harry's lips in the course of a brief mono-syllabic protest. 'And don't say it's the war getting on your nerves. I've heard that before.'

'I had a row with that beggar Mitchell. I threatened to sack him.'

'Then you'd better threaten to unsack him. What was the reason for this magnanimous gesture?'

'I told him to dig the snow away from the gates. The drifts

are all of twelve foot deep there. He went damned insolent all of a sudden and said he had only one pair of hands.'

'You could have made them four.'

'I've been cleaning my guns.'

'To shoot what? The approaching enemy?'

'There are still a good few wild duck. I thought of going out tomorrow.'

My mother, woken as if out of a dream, now uttered the first words she had spoken since the shattering episode of the decanter. As usual they were strangely mixed and wrong and yet right at the same time.

'I don't think,' she said, 'wild duck ought to be shot while the Red Cross are so desperate for things.'

'I suppose if we keep them alive they'll drive ambulances,' my grandmother said. 'Is that it?'

Suddenly, as if this part of the conversation had never taken place, my mother said in her fluttering, amiable way:

'Mr Hudson always clears the snow away. He always brings the snow-plough.'

My Uncle Harry went over to the fire and kicked an ash-log into flame. Ash, they always say, burns like a candle and suddenly it was as if the whole room became filled with a great glow of candlelight. The reflection of the brilliant yellow flares on the darkening lake outside startled me and I almost expected to see the swans, startled too, get up and fly away. But when I looked down again they were still there, swimming round and round in the twilight, imprisoned in their clear sinister ring of water.

'That's another damn fine thing,' Harry said. 'Where's the snow-plough? Days and days of snow and no snow-plough. Nothing ever gets done since this damn war started.'

'Started?' I said. 'When did it start?'

This bright remark of mine drew no comment from anyone; nor did its empty triviality, together with that of the rest of the conversation, strike me at the time. I remember, on the other hand, thinking that the business of the bread was very bad. There really ought to have been bread. There was no excuse for that. The baker really ought to have got through. And the snow-plough too. I thought Harry was right about the snow-plough.

My grandmother suddenly went back to the fire to warm her knees, ending her acid attack on Harry as swiftly as it had begun. She might well have sensed the return of Edna, who in fact knocked on the door some few seconds later and came into the room bearing the remaining half of my birthday cake, together with a plate and a silver cake knife, on a *papiermâché* tray.

'Oh! good,' I said. 'I'm raging ravenous.'

My school-girl words and crow of delight were as trivial as my remark about the start of war had been. After I had made it Edna put the tray on a little walnut side-table and asked me if I would cut the cake myself or if I would rather she cut it for me?

'Oh! you cut it,' I said. 'And a good big old wedge too.'

Edna, having cut a thick dark segment of cake, then stood decorously by the door, hands folded in front of her apron.

'Yes, Edna?' my grandmother said. 'Did you wish to say something?'

'Mr Hudson has called, ma'am.'

'Which Mr Hudson, Edna? Young or old?'

'The young one, ma'am. He would very much like to speak to you.'

'Ah! the jolly old snow-plough johnny,' Harry said. 'And about time too.'

My grandmother instantly gave him a glare so brilliant with the reflection of ash-flame that he shut himself up immediately, mouth first dropping open and then closing again like a trap.

'Show Mr Hudson in.'

For some reason or other I suddenly felt unaccountably shy. The evening was rapidly growing darker every moment but when my grandmother suddenly asked Harry to switch on the lights I immediately begged him not to.

'Oh! no. Not yet. Let's keep the firelight. The firelight's so beautiful.'

So we kept the firelight. If the swans were imprisoned in their ring of water I now felt equally imprisoned by the bright ring of ash-flame. I stood withdrawn against the big bay window and for the next several minutes – there might equally well have been five or fifty of them for all I knew – I didn't speak a word except to say 'Good-evening' when Tom Hudson came.

Tom was a big, fair, muscular boy of twenty who, I now saw, was wearing glasses. I had never seen him in glasses before and it made him seem suddenly very much of a stranger. Something about the glasses seemed to make him nervous too and for the most of the time he kept rolling a pair of big sheep-skin gloves round and round in his hands.

He began by saying he'd come to apologize about the snow-plough. He was very sorry about the snow-plough. His tractor had broken down. But everything was in order now and if all went well he would be out at first light tomorrow, getting the roads clear.

During the course of his saying all this Uncle Harry broke in to offer him a whisky and soda but he refused, out of sheer nervousness I thought. And presently, nervousness being infectious, I started to feel impossibly nervous too. It wasn't that Tom was a stranger to me. His father had farmed a hundred and fifty acres of our land on the far side of the lake for as long as I could remember. As a child I had ridden on hay carts with him and as a girl I had ridden side by side with him at hunt meetings. When we met we called each other by Christian names.

The growing feeling that something about him was wrong this evening, in some way disjointed, was suddenly confirmed by a remark of my grandmother's. She, in her shrewd way, had sensed it too.

'Tom, do forgive me if I seem exceptionally personal but I don't ever recall seeing you in glasses before.'

'That's right. I've only just had them.'

From the way he said this – he sort of tried to throw the words away, over-casually – it might have been that he was ashamed of the glasses. The fact of them was a physical humiliation.

'Your eyes,' my grandmother said, 'always look so bright and healthy.'

'Blue eyes always do,' my mother said.

'I went to join up,' Tom said. 'Air Force. They turned me down because of the eyes. Not a hope, they said.'

'Ah! well,' Uncle Harry said. 'We'll need grub. We'll need you on the land. Every bit as important.'

As if these few words solved not only Tom Hudson's problems but those of the war in general, Uncle Harry went over to the fireplace and started to bash about with his pipe, hammering it first on the heel of his shoe, then on the bricks of the hearth and finally digging noisily at it with his knife. The racket of all this apparently not being enough he then took a running kick with his good leg at an ash-bough, knocked it clean off the fire and then threw a fresh one at it, scattering wood-ash everywhere and generating more sparks than any anvil.

Fresh flames shot into the air. The room was as bright as day. I saw my grandmother scowl and then Tom Hudson said:

'I'm sorry, but isn't it about time for black-out?'

'Good grief,' Uncle Harry said. 'I'm always forgetting.'

He stumped across to the window. I stepped aside. The big bay had been difficult to screen. Ten inch strips of black paper were pasted round the edges of the glass. The heavy crimson velvet curtains were thickly lined with black too and as Uncle Harry wrenched at them there was a mad overhead jangling of brass rings on the curtain pole.

'I suppose you want to drive one of those things up there?' Uncle Harry said. He now proceeded to switch on the lights, once again crashing into the soda siphon in his thumping course across the room. 'Fighters or bombers?'

'Is there a difference?' my mother said.

Even I winced at this, though I hadn't the vaguest idea what the difference was either.

'Fighters,' Tom said. I thought he seemed acutely embarrassed, under the revealing glare of electric light, by the whole affair. I thought it also seemed impossible that his very bright blue eyes were any sort of handicap and they merely looked restless as he said: 'Tony Jackson's in fighters. He was home from France the other day. Went back yesterday.'

'Not young Johnson from Egerton Court?' my grandmother said. 'Robert Johnson's son?'

'Yes. Seems impossible that he's only ten minutes flying time away.'

'But he's only a boy,' my mother said. 'He doesn't look strong enough.'

'He was telling me about a fight he had not long ago. He and a Hun just went round and round, glaring coldly at each other before he shot him down.'

'Good grief,' Uncle Harry said. 'He always looked a bit of a dreamer.'

I suddenly felt as if I were in a dream too. It wasn't merely that the aspect of war suddenly presented by Tom Hudson was unreal. The war seemed unreal anyway. I was a girl and I wasn't part of it. It was outside of me somewhere and I didn't understand it. It didn't seem necessary for me to understand it either.

'Of course they just hate this snow. They just long for the spring. He says there'll be fun and games in the spring.'

I found myself listening uneasily. Into the woolly recesses of my dreamy vacuum there slowly penetrated the delayed echo of his voice. It was strangely full of longing. It was also painfully youthful and perhaps for that reason I was embarrassed too.

Later that same year I was to hear that same echo, in varying degrees, in other voices, but that evening I didn't know this. As I look back on it I realize that everything, in spite of the extraordinary sharpness of my memories now, was very vague. I suppose the best way of putting it is to say that I really wasn't awake. Even that doesn't quite explain my feeling of being immersed in unreality, partly shut away.

Presently Tom Hudson stopped fidgeting with his gloves, put them down on the back of the chair, turned up the collar of his overcoat and said he ought to be going. 'Have one for the road?' Uncle Harry said. Tom thanked him, shook his head and said he wouldn't really. He had the tractor outside. He had a feeling it was going to snow again.

Then he started to say good night to us, first to my grandmother, then my mother, then to Uncle Harry and finally to me. Between the first of these good nights he interposed to tell us once again that he would be back with the snow-plough, early, the following morning. He said he would try to clear the whole of our avenue for us, from the front door to the gates at the road. The double line of horse chestnuts, about a hundred and fifty yards long, had been pollarded the previous winter, more for safety than anything else, after three massive boughs had split and fallen in a gale, and now they looked strange and gaunt in the snow, like objects from a slightly sinister fairy tale.

'Have you a torch?' my grandmother said. 'It must be quite dark now.'

Up to that moment he had been altogether very serious but now he smiled, for the first time.

'Funny thing,' he said, 'my eyes are all right in the dark.'

With that he turned and said good night to me. His eyes were briefly but directly focused on me and he used my Christian name. It wasn't the first time he had used it by any means but suddenly for the one and only time that evening the feeling of vagueness left me. I stepped momentarily out of my vacuum. So much was I awake suddenly that I actually smiled back at him, at the same time lifting one hand and throwing back a loose strand or two of my hair.

'Good night, everyone,' he said.

'See Mr Hudson out, Elizabeth,' my grandmother said.

'Oh ! no, no. Please. I'll manage. I can find my way.' he said and in a hurried burst of embarrassment was gone.

The ensuing two or three minutes were largely taken up by Uncle Harry starting an untidy personal conflagration with his pipe. Matches were too simple a medium for the purpose and special yellow and crimson spills, which he got from some shop in Bond Street, had to be used instead. The room filled rapidly with smoke. Harry struck with a heavy boot at the heart of the fire, rousing it into flame and saying how cold the night was. My grandmother scowled again and said it was time for a glass of sherry and would Harry stop rampaging about and be good enough to get it for her? Harry blundered across the room like a hippopotamus, finally fetching up against the chair by which Tom Hudson had stood.

'Good grief, young Hudson's left a glove.'

'I'll take it,' I said. 'He can't have got far.'

I snatched up the glove and went out of the room and down the long tiled dimly-lit hall to the front door. It was very chilly in the hall and harshly, bitterly cold as I opened the door. A row of icicles like the crystal drops of a chandelier hung from the roof of the porch and beyond them I could just make out the spectral black outlines of the first of the pollarded chestnuts. 'Tom !' I called and waved the glove. It was an utterly useless gesture and in another instant my voice froze on the snowy darkness.

Far beyond the avenue gates a searchlight, and then a second and a third, threw faint swinging foolscaps of light to the stars. I thought for a moment I heard the sound of a plane. In time I remembered the black-out and pushed the door shut behind me. Then I realized that what I could hear was the sound of a tractor driving away down the road and suddenly, in a strange moment of utter isolation, I was overcome by the oppressive notion that for some reason I was never going to see Tom Hudson again.

It was a notion that couldn't have been more wrong but it was enough to drive me, shivering, back into the house. In that moment all the unreality of war encompassed me completely again and presently, still carrying the glove, I was back with my grandmother, my mother and Harry, imprisoned with them as securely as the swans were imprisoned by their dark ring of water.

2

OFTEN, in the late winter, we heard the ghostly growl of distant artillery fire. It seemed always to come from the direction of the sea. We were not more than twenty miles from the sea in a straight line but the fact merely seemed to increase, rather than lessen, the unreality of the gunfire. We also heard, almost every day, the sound of air-raid sirens but the wails no longer drove us to the cellar, where six months or more before my mother had been accustomed to sit for hours in breathless and dreadful tension while my grandmother played ice-calm games of patience and Harry moodily swigged at his whisky.

The cold left us very reluctantly. A long succession of white savage weeks brought us to a March in which there was no sign of spring. The banks of the lake were still wrapped in white marble waves. Bitter winds rattled the dry reeds and always when the swans took to flight you heard the strange whine of their passage, like the wind's echo.

All at once summer began in April. Orchards suddenly offered a rich and shining feast of plum bloom. In sheets of almost unbearably brilliant emerald young wheat rose from under the snow and soon primroses, together with crowds of white anemones, spread themselves everywhere about the copses, the lakeside and the banks of the little river where Harry had already started to cast for trout. It was really warm at last and there was a great chorus of bird-song everywhere.

In this new idyllic atmosphere I woke late one morning, had my bath and then, looking out of my bedroom window, saw my grandmother in the paved courtyard below. She was talking to two men. They were wearing blue uniforms and peaked caps of the same colour and one of the caps was resplendent with thick gold braid.

My grandmother looked dominant and peremptory. Her head was high. It was a very fine head in any circumstance, with its wide arresting forehead and exceptionally bright black hair, but that morning, in the brilliant April sun, it looked positively queenly. She looked like a woman half her age.

All at once it struck me that her manner wasn't merely peremptory. She was stiff with anger. The fact that she hardly made a single gesture as I stood there watching her merely increased the magnificence of her tension. I couldn't think for the life of me what it was all about but after watching for another minute or two I dressed hurriedly and started to go downstairs.

At the head of the staircase I was passed by a glassy-eyed figure who half-fell up the last three steps and then staggered blindly past me, stuttering out the frozen words :

'We must pack. We've got to pack.'

It was my mother. With another broken cry she disappeared into her bedroom.

The staircase, built of heavy oak, was splendid and wide. My grandmother was intensely proud of it. Rich carvings of grapes, wheat ears, roses and water-lilies – all, I suppose, symbolic of the bountiful countryside surrounding us – adorned the head and foot of it. But that morning, as I groped my confused way down it, I felt it seemed curiously barren. Vague as my mother, I felt a sense of doom.

In the hall below I bumped into Harry, or rather Harry, even more clumsily directionless than usual, bumped into me.

'What on earth,' I said, 'is happening?'

He barged against the door of his study, crashing it open.

'Requisitioning the place.'

'Requisitioning? What? Who?'

'Air Force johnnies. I've got to ring Partridge.'

Partridge was the family solicitor. With a further crash but no further word of explanation Harry disappeared.

I went outside, into the courtyard. The two Air Force officers, preceded by the rigid figure of my grandmother, were coming towards the house. The elder of the two, the one with gold braid on his cap, was rather rubicund. He looked, I thought, something like a sea-dog of Drake's time; there was something robustly Elizabethan about him. The other was taller and slighter. He sported a tremendous barley-eared moustache, the colour of dark sherry.

I suddenly felt intensely shy. I half-turned to scurry away but my grandmother halted me in a voice that I can best describe as salty. But that I mean that it somehow sounded dry, white and bitter.

'Don't go, Elizabeth. I'm sure you will be most interested in what these gentlemen have just said to me. This is my grand-daughter, Elizabeth. Elizabeth, this is Group Captain –'

The two officers saluted me. I felt myself blushing and their names were lost on me.

'They are proposing,' my grandmother said, again in that salty voice, 'to take the house away from us.'

'Now that isn't quite true, Mrs Cartwright.'

My grandmother turned on the elder of the two officers with a look of regal scorn.

'Are you suggesting I am suddenly hard of hearing? If it isn't what you propose then what do you propose?'

'I said that we were looking for a house for use as an extra Officers' Mess. This is the sort of house we're looking for and I think we should like to take it over.'

'And by what authority?'

'We have every authority, madam, as I explained before.'

'And who delegates authority to rob people of their property?'

'There is a war on, madam.'

'I am perfectly well aware of it.' She gave the two officers, their caps and the white wings above their breast pockets calm and separate glares of scorn. The elder of the two officers had a double row of brilliant medal ribbons across his chest and she reserved yet another separate glare for them too, her eyes flashing like magnifying glasses. 'And I might add that since there is a war on I regard it as your duty to protect us, not to fleece us of our rights and privileges and property.'

'Even an Air Force flies on its stomach.'

'So you propose to descend on us like' – she waved a contemptuous, regal arm – 'like an army of locusts and strip us bare!'

'We –'

'My family has lived in this house for four hundred years. Even Cromwell couldn't turn us out. And what Cromwell couldn't do I'm certain no one else is going to do.'

'I very much hope you will see sense and reason about this, Mrs Cartwright. I hope you will co-operate.'

'I have every intention of doing so.' All of a sudden she gave him the most disarming of smiles. 'Perhaps you and your colleague will come in and have a glass of sherry?'

The officers half-bowed their thanks. The four of us went into the house. On the way the elder of the officers ran his hand in silent approbation over the carvings at the foot of the stairs and my grandmother noted it acidly.

In the big drawing-room she herself poured out the sherry. I withdrew to the window and stared at the lake below. Many new water-lily leaves covered the surface of it now and the sun was brilliant on the gold-green circles of them. On the near bank a pair of swans were nesting, not twenty yards from where, in winter, they had kept open their iceless ring of water, and I could see the cob, the male, majestically swimming about the same circle, wings slightly aggressive, watching for intruders.

'Is the lake very deep?'

I turned to find the younger of the officers standing at my side. I found his physical presence intensely disturbing and merely said :

'Oh ! I believe so. In places.'

'Looks wizard. Tempting to go in for a swim.'

Wizard? Curious word, I thought, and said :

'You wouldn't make a stroke. The swan would see to that.'

'Oh ! so the swan resents us too.'

'I didn't say I resented you.'

'No? Awfully sorry.'

He ran an over-polite and consequently rather mocking hand across the barley-ears of the moustache, so that I felt even more disturbed.

A moment later Harry exploded into the room with the shattering news that Partridge was out of town for two or three days and that we were all ruddy well done like dinners. My grandmother greeted this last expression with a withering stare that halted even Harry, though not for long. He had clearly been working up a private rage of his own and now suddenly shook his fist at the elder of the officers and half-shouted :

'You won't get away with this, I tell you ! You won't get away with it !'

'We are not trying to get away with anything, sir. But if Air

Ministry decides to requisition this property then it will have to be requisitioned.'

'You damn well won't get away with it, I tell you !'

Suddenly I was powerfully struck by the fact that Harry in his civilian clothes looked bloated, untidy, shabby and in some curious way unmanly. Beside the well-pressed uniforms of the two officers his baggy tweeds looked horribly and hopelessly wrong.

'You said something just now about *if* Air Ministry decided,' my grandmother said. 'Does that mean there is some uncertainty ?'

'Frankly, Mrs Cartwright, no. We desperately need more room. We must have it.'

'Haven't I some right of appeal in this ?'

'I'm afraid there isn't time. We need the house in forty-eight hours.'

'Good God ! Good grief !' Harry said.

'You mean you would turn me out of my home in two days ?' my grandmother said. 'Just like that ? I never heard of anything so brutal.'

'War is rather apt to be brutal.'

'I've always understood it also had its decencies.'

The officer said nothing. I felt sick. Harry did a complete blundering circle of the room and finally fetched up by the window, hammering his fist on the frame.

'And where,' my grandmother said, 'do you suppose we are going to live ?'

'That's something I'm afraid I can't arrange, madam. I wish I could. I know it's all very painful for you –'

'Painful.' Even she, in that moment, looked utterly bewildered. The one word, neither question nor protest, was full of despair. I was full of despair too and suddenly said what I suppose must have sounded like an exceedingly puerile and stupid thing :

'But you can't do such a thing. It will kill her.'

Instantly she was her old self again.

'I'm not so easily killed, thank you.'

'My adjutant is due back from leave this afternoon,' the

Group Captain said. 'I will send him and Flight-Lieutenant Ogilvy over to arrange final details.'

I saw my grandmother wince at the word final but beyond that, in her stiff way, she showed no sign of further emotion.

'I suppose we get some ruddy pittance for letting the place, eh?' Harry said. 'And what about damage? There'll be a hell of a lot of careless bastards rampaging all over the place I suppose. What about that?'

The Group-Captain clearly didn't like the word bastards and it was now his turn to be stiff.

'I said, sir, that the house was for use as an *Officers'* Mess.'

Harry had no word of answer and the Group-Captain, with a cold gesture, turned to my grandmother.

'That's a very magnificent staircase you've got, Mrs. Cartwright. I'll have it boxed in.'

She thanked him, acidly. Oh! yes, it was very good of him, really very considerate, to think of the staircase.

'You couldn't by any chance box us in? Or spare us an inch or two of attic?'

'I think we must go, Mrs Cartwright. Thank you very much for the sherry.'

Half a minute later the revolution was over. Harry stormed back to his study and my grandmother stood with deceptive calm by the window, arms folded, looking out. I wanted desperately to say something to comfort her but there was a great lump in my throat and I knew very well I should cry if I started to speak.

Instead I went upstairs. On the landing a door opened and was banged shut again. It was my mother once more and this time she greeted me with the tearful, fluttering announcement 'I shall go to Malvern! I shall go to Malvern!' as if that hilly haven of refuge were heaven itself.

That afternoon I walked slowly along the lake and then along the banks of the little river that fed into it at the southern end. There were woods for half a mile along one side of the river and you could smell the deep glorious scent of the first bluebells.

I longed desperately, that afternoon, to talk to someone; but that wasn't all. I longed desperately to talk to someone of my own generation. The revolution of the morning had had a curious effect on me. With alarming clarity I suddenly saw my mother as a figure of pitiful futility and Harry hardly less so. What was more I felt I saw my grandmother with something like adult objectivity for the first time. She seemed to me almost like some female Canute, trying to stem the waters of war.

But what had affected me most was that brief and not exactly pleasant interview with the younger of the two officers, by the window. I was, as I have said, a very young nineteen and I suppose I fancied that what I had said about the swans was very clever. Now I had already started to regret it. I would have given anything to have been able to make some sort of redress.

There was another thing. Although I wasn't fully aware of it at the time I was already on the verge of an attack, and a very bad one, of hero worship. The intense physical disturbance of the morning had become amazingly persistent. I couldn't get those handsome, barley-eared moustaches out of my mind.

Two hundred yards along the river there was a small white bridge that led to a path through the woods that, in turn, led to the land the Hudsons farmed. I started walking through the woods and heard, presently, the sound of a tractor. When I came out of the woods I could see Tom Hudson chain-harrowing the field beyond. After a minute or so he saw me and waved his hand and I waved in answer.

Then he drove the tractor over to me and stopped it and said hullo and what a beautiful day it was. For some unaccountable reason I suddenly started feeling mightily superior and said:

'I hoped I'd see you. I've got some rather terrific news.'

'Oh?' he said. 'Peace been declared or something?'

This frivolous remark rather set me on edge.

'Not exactly. The Air Force is going to requisition the house. Our house, I mean. For an officers' Mess.'

'Good God. Amazing thing.'

'Why amazing? Even an air force flies on its stomach.'

I said this as if it were some highly original remark I'd thought up on my own.

'You mean they're actually turning you out?'

'They are. And in forty-eight hours.'

'But where on earth will you live?'

'Mother's moving to Malvern to live with Aunt Rosemary, and my grandmother and Harry and I are moving into the bailiff's house.'

'Good God. I think that's pretty rough.'

'Oh! do you?' I said. 'I think it's rather wizard.'

I aired the word wizard with what I thought was splendid nonchalance and he looked very hard at me.

'Of course grandmother's terribly upset and mother's in floods of tears and Uncle Harry's bouncing about like a lunatic but after all you've got to see it the other way.'

'The other way?'

'The officers, I mean. The Air Force. Oh! we had two officers over all morning. Absolutely charming, both of them. I had a long talk with one of them and after what he said I must say I rather saw it their way.'

My despicable part in this conversation wasn't exactly deliberate. Perhaps it was merely my way of rationalizing the situation. I don't quite know. But the words came out as if premeditated. Moreover I was so young and impervious and obtuse that it didn't ever occur to me remotely that I might be causing him pain. I had utterly forgotten the desperation of his disappointment about the eyes.

For a moment or two longer he looked rather crushed. He was wearing an open-necked blue shirt and an old pair of yellowish corduroys and I remember suddenly thinking the same thing about him as I had thought about Harry – that the civilian dress looked untidy and shabby and somehow all wrong.

'What about moving the furniture and all the stuff?' he said presently. 'If it's any help I'll bring the tractor over.'

'Oh! I think that's all arranged,' I said. 'Well, I must go now. Two of the officers are coming over again about four o'clock and I rather want to be there. It's all rather exciting.'

'Yes,' he said.

As I turned, tossing my hair back, I had a final glimpse of him sitting steadfastly on the tractor, the large blue eyes transfixed behind his spectacles, and again it didn't occur to me that he might have been in pain.

The courtyard of the house has a stone balustrade running

along one side of it; from it there is a drop of six feet or so to a long bed of roses, beyond which a lawn slopes down to the lake edge. I was walking rather dreamily along this lawn on my way home that afternoon, not really taking much notice of anything, when a voice said:

'Careful of the swan.'

Very startled, I looked up to the balustrade and there were the barley-eared moustaches leaning over.

'My goodness,' I said, 'you frightened the life out of me.'

'Sorry. Came at you out of the sun.'

I couldn't think what on earth this curious expression meant and he gave no hint of an explanation but merely grinned. It was a very engaging grin and he followed it by saying:

'Glad I saw you. Fancy I put up a bit of a black this morning.'

I couldn't think what on earth that meant either and I merely said 'Oh?'

'The bit about the swan, I mean. I thought you took rather a dim view.'

I might have been listening to a foreign language. I stared, open-mouthed, and he said:

'I suppose the business about the house and all that rather shook you.'

'We didn't find it exactly pleasant.'

'Oh! I say. *We* are *not* amused.'

Before I could think of a reply to this he suddenly did an extraordinary thing. He put one hand on the balustrade and with the ease of a circus performer vaulted clean over it and landed at my feet. He then gave a cheeky sort of mock salute and said:

'O for Ogilvy presents his compliments, ma'am, and begs permission to make amends – if that's the right phrase, which I doubt.'

He spread out his arms and for one awful moment I thought he was about to take me in his embrace and kiss me. I felt and must have looked absolutely stony. No one had ever behaved to me in this astounding fashion before and my emotions were somewhere between excitement and outrage.

'Oh! don't look at me like that, please. I can't be as bad as all that, for Pete's sake. Am I really in disgrace with fortune and men's eyes?'

He made a sudden grimace of mock pain and I tried, in turn, to look as dignified as possible.

'Shall I call you Liz, Lizzie, Liza, Elizabeth, Beth, Betty, Bess or plain ma'am? State the alternative preferred, with reasons for your choice.'

'I'm not sure I want you to call me anything.'

At this he made another mock gesture, at the same time sweeping a hand across those magnificent moustaches, and said :

'You know, I rather think I shall have to introduce you to Chloe. '

I was foolish enough to ask who Chloe was and he said :

'Ah ! who is Chloe? What is she, that all her swains commend her? Wizard job, Chloe. If you can spare the time I'll introduce you.'

'Can *you* spare the time?' I said. 'I thought you came over to make arrangements about the house.'

'Oh ! the Adj is doing that. That's his pigeon.'

We started walking. I was half way to being in a flat spin, as I should have called it only a little later, and I was hardly conscious of mounting the steps that led to the courtyard or of crossing the courtyard into the avenue beyond, where the double row of pollarded chestnuts were now sprouting fresh short growths of the vividest April green.

There we halted. Why I remembered it at that particular moment I don't know, but suddenly I recalled the snow. For a few seconds it imprisoned me again, so that I only half heard him say :

'Liz – Chloe. Chloe – Liz.'

I woke to see him patting with elaborate affection the bonnet of the oldest and oddest little two-seater sports job I had ever seen. Chloe had been done over in yellow and black and looked something like an enlarged tin wasp with eyes – her headlamps – out of all proportion to her size.

I suppose there is nothing quite so infectious as banter and already I was learning fast from Bill Ogilvy.

'Does it actually go?' I said .

'*It? It?* Oh ! what a wounding thing to say.'

'My apologies.'

'Offer them to Chloe. She's highly sensitive in these matters. Highly sensitive.'

'How old is she?'

'Hell!' he said. 'How *what*? – Age cannot wither nor custom stale – Oh! Liz, Liz – please, please.' All of a sudden he wrenched open the door of the car. 'Hop in!'

'No thanks,' I said. 'I don't want to be killed. I'm too young.'

'Madam, I beg you. I entreat. Prithee,' he said and suddenly, with a gracious bow, lightly held my hand.

It was utterly impossible to resist these charming blandishments and I got into the car. Several seconds later a major explosion tore the air and we were away down the chestnut avenue like a yellow sky-rocket, my black hair streaming out in the wind.

At the end of the avenue we skidded out into the road with a calamitous scream of tyres and a white blast of dust. Behind us an elephantine snarl rose, fell and then rose again as we went through the gears. I was frightened and excited. A new physical pain shot through me, at once hurting me and giving me pleasure. The force of the wind wrapped my hair round my face and then whipped it back and then scrambled it away again, so that half the time I was seeing the road, the verges and the hedgerows through a black tangled veil.

Once we narrowly missed an army truck and once a farm wagon – drawn, incredible as it now seems, by two horses. The driver shook his fist at us and Bill Ogilvy grinned.

If anyone had been there to have told me that only an hour before I had been walking dreamily through the calm of a bluebell wood I should have called him crazy or a liar.

We climbed a hill. Beech woods hid the sky and occasional big creamy balloons of hawthorn blossom went flying past like driven clouds. The noise of Chloe's exhaust, louder than ever now, was a siren of exhilaration that finally stopped like the burst of a bomb, setting up a frightened cackle of jackdaws from the emerald skein of beech-leaves overhead.

I lay back for some time and gazed up at these beech leaves. They looked almost transparent in their fresh young tenderness. The oasis of which they were part was now as unreal as

28

the bluebell wood of an hour before and I could only lie and gaze at them in stunned disbelief, wondering what sort of planetary excursion had brought me there.

A few minutes later Bill Ogilvy called me Liz and, with a gravity I'd never expected in him, kissed me. Nobody had ever called me Liz before; nor, incredible as it also seems, had anyone ever kissed me.

I lay there in a strange vacuum. I couldn't believe anything of what happened. I heard a blackbird scream down the road, clearly frightened by something. A remotely distant sound of planes humming across the sky like bees gradually grew louder and louder and finally screamed over us, not more than a quarter of a mile away.

'Spits,' Bill said. 'Coming home to tea.'

I shut my eyes and let the sound of the Spitfires die away; then I opened my eyes and stared up at him and said in a whisper :

'Do you know what you just did to me?'

'Incredible as it may seem, I believe I do.'

I slowly held up my lips and then, again with that altogether unexpected gravity, he kissed me for the second time. It was a moment quite rapturous enough in itself but he crowned it by a remark that suddenly had me caught, in exquisite suspense, between laughing and crying.

'I think I like you even more than my Chloe,' he said. 'Again? Once more? Wizard girl. Good show.'

And there was I, gaily flying upside-down.

3

YES: it was a good show. Everything, slightly ridiculous
though it may now sound, was absolutely wizard. What was
more I wanted it to last for ever and was quite sure, in my very
young heart, that it would .

Two days later we scrambled. Ordinarily, of course, I should
have said we moved – my grandmother, Harry and I – into the
bailiff's house. This was a former dower house in almost orange
brick standing a quarter of a mile beyond the other side of the
lake, with a small pretty garden and a fine dove-cot, in that
same lovely shade of brick, with a white weather-vane and a
big magnolia growing up the side. I mention this magnolia
because later that summer, when it flowered in August with its
huge creamy chalices of blossom that might well have been
carved from marble, it had ceased, for me, merely to be a tree
in flower; but I will tell more about that later.

Meanwhile my mother moved to Malvern where, as I said to
my grandmother with gay laughter, I hoped the waters would
comfort her. I laughed a good deal in those first days of up-
heaval, often without really being aware of it, and my grandmother noted it shrewdly. She for her part had no cause for
laughter; nor had Harry, who blundered about like a big lost
sheep dog unable, after years of living in a big house, to find
his bearings in a little one.

By contrast I found the smaller house delightful. I felt infinitely more free in it than I had ever felt in the older, far larger
one. The feeling of being imprisoned by walls and black-outs
and snow and sheer size left me completely. My great happiness didn't arise, of course, simply from this. It stemmed directly
from Bill Ogilvy, the beloved and fantastic Chloe and those even
more fantastic moustaches. It was nurtured by the new and
wizard language I had to speak. It thrived because everything
was wizard. The weather was wizard, as it was to be all summer.
The mad drives in Chloe up to the big beech woods on the hills

were wizard. The hours Bill and I spent drinking shandy in small secluded pubs were wizard. The laughter and the utter foolishness of our talk was wizard. To be kissed by Bill with that curious combination of gaiety and gravity was wizard. Above all the very fact of being young and alive and loved was the wizardest thing of all.

I really believe I also thought the war was wizard, even though in a sense it still hadn't begun. That strange sense of unreality still hung over southern England. It was impossible to believe that that lovely pastoral landscape of ours was under any sort of shadow. Every day, it's true, we heard the growl of distant artillery fire; every morning, as regularly as a milkman calling, the Luftwaffe made its reconnaissance flights, though I was blissfully unaware of it at the time. Air raid sirens screamed and all clears sounded. Planes buzzed about the sky, sometimes at great heights, often invisible, like hornets. Bill frequently flew sorties, at the same time countenancing me with considerable seriousness not to ask about them. My grandmother knitted considerable numbers of long white hospital socks and Harry growled for hours beside the radio, again like a dog suspicious of every sound, grumbling that authority never told you anything and what a way it was to run a war.

But the greatest piece of unreality was the big empty house. Having been thrown out of it in little more than forty-eight hours we waited expectantly for the new merchant adventurers, as my grandmother sometimes rather acidly called them, to move in. Nothing happened. Almost every day I walked over to look at it. I peered in at the windows, looking at the boxed-in staircase, the carpetless floors, the billiard table shrouded in sheets. Dust had started to gather everywhere. Big dead blow-flies lay about the window sills. Cob-webs were beginning to skein themselves about the cornices. Sheets of old newspaper lay about, growing yellower every time I looked at them.

At first I felt keenly about this. I thought it to be, as my grandmother did, callous and inhuman and really cruel. Then I got it off my chest by asking Bill about it. He said it was just the way it was. Nobody ever blasted well knew what was going on. He supposed some dim chair-borne clot of a type at Air

Ministry had forgotten to pull his finger out. There was too much frigging about and bumf and so on to get things done. You never got the gen.

Apart from this I was really very good about not asking about things. My seclusion had been such that I then had only the very vaguest idea where the nearest air-field was; it was, in fact, four miles down the railway line. When Bill spoke of Ops. and scrambles and Maggies and Mae Wests and gen and Brown Jobs and flaps and gremlins and kites and so on I was thrilled by the new syntax but innocently unaware of what most of it meant half the time. My needs and their accompanying ecstasies were really, in a sense, very simple. I didn't want to know too much. There wasn't any need for too many questions.

But one afternoon, as we lay on the hills, under the beeches, staring up at the expansive fragmentary pattern of blue and emerald, I did ask a question. Out in the distance I could hear a solitary plane coming in from the direction of the coast and something suddenly made me say :

'If that was a German plane would you know?'
'My dear Liz !'
'But would you really? I mean what sort?'
'They'd throw me out on my 'ear-'ole tomorrow if I didn't.'
'What sort of plane is that one?'
'A Maggie.'
'Do you fly Maggies?'
'Little girls mustn't ask questions.'
'Where do you suppose it's coming from? France?'
'Hardly.'

The question I really wanted to ask had still to come and in my innocence I now asked it.

'Will you ever have to go away?'
'You're just a load of offal when it comes to posting. Just a bod.'
'I mean would you ever have to go to France for instance?'
'Might.'
'Nothing much seems to be happening over there, does it?'
'Not much.'
'Would you like to go to France?'
'Like Hell I would !'

He said this with enormous vehemence, like a boy being offered a vast plum cake, and I felt a great chill go through my heart. The shadow of a terrible thought also crossed my mind and for a time I lay absolutely quiet, without a word.

'Something the matter?' he said.

'No.'

'You're very quiet all of a sudden.'

'Am I?'

'France,' he said. There was tremendous relish in his voice. 'Champagne three and six a bottle. Wizard.'

I lay very quiet again.

Perhaps this makes clearer what I mean by asking too many questions. It was asking questions that brought me face to face, that afternoon, with the first of many substantial realities. The trouble was that I wasn't ready, in my innocence, to face them in return. Instead I simply asked another question and a pretty silly one it was.

'Do you really love me?'

'My mother once overheard a woman ask the same question and her man said "You know cuss well I do".'

He laughed and leaned over and kissed me.

'You're very sweet,' I said.

'You too. You too.'

'Flatterer. That's all you are. Just a big, big flatterer.'

'Wounding words. Very wounding words.'

'I don't think you could be truly serious if you'd tried for a month of Sundays.'

'Try me.'

'If you did by any chance go to France would you love me just the same when you came back?'

'I'd bring you oceans of champagne and Chanel and Camembert and silk panties and all things nice.'

'I can't wait for the day,' I said and lay very quiet again.

Just before we walked out of the wood to walk to the road, where Chloe was parked, I did another foolish thing. As if I hadn't already asked enough questions that afternoon I now asked yet another. Something made me say:

'Do you know a boy named Tony Johnson? A pilot. He comes from here. He's in France. Flying Spits, I think.'

33

'Not in France.' If it was a careless word it was almost the only one I ever heard him utter. 'Because there ain't none there.'

'Well, he's over there anyway. Flying something.'

In reply he looked up at the sky, lost in a remarkable rapture of his own.

'Lucky bastard,' he said, 'lucky bastard.'

When I got home, half an hour later, there were cucumber sandwiches for tea. The mention of cucumbers may sound slightly ridiculous too but it is also significant. Authority, in its magnanimity, had allowed us to keep our glasshouses, so that to the long string of useless slogans urging us along the path of war, such as *Digging for Victory* and *Lend to Defend Whatever It Was*, we were able to add our own, which might well have been *Peace Through Cucumbers*. But this wasn't all. I read somewhere, much later, that when you eat cucumbers there is a taste of Spring in your mouth. But the taste of Spring isn't always sweet, and the taste I felt in my mouth that day was a cool, sharp one.

I had made a rapid drop, in fact, from extreme exhilaration to chilling doubt, and my grandmother wasn't slow to notice it. In her wisdom and shrewdness she hadn't asked much about my absences from the house, some of them long and late, but now she said.

'Lately you've been so gay. Now you're surprisingly quiet all of a sudden.'

'Am I?'

'You're not by any chance in love, are you?'

'As a matter of fact I am.'

'I suspected it.'

'You sound as if you disapprove.'

'On the contrary.'

'You actually mean –'

'I think it's high time,' she said.

Considering that these were the first words we had exchanged on the subject it was uncommonly acute of her to detect a change in me that day. But that was typical of her and she went on :

'May I know who he is?'

34

I told her. 'Perhaps you remember him from that morning when the officers came to take over the house.'

'Ah! yes. The one with the very large moustaches? By the way has he any explanation as to why they still haven't moved in?'

I said he hadn't. He could only suppose that some clot of an Air Ministry type had forgotten to pull his finger out.

'What an extraordinary expression. What on earth does it mean?' she said and looked very hard at me.

I said it was just a figure of speech and helped myself to another cucumber sandwich.

At this point Uncle Harry came exploding into the sitting-room, which was hardly large enough to accommodate my grandmother and me with ease, let alone Harry, who had just been to the village to buy an evening paper, which he now struck loudly with the flat of his hand as if he were slapping a recalcitrant horse.

'Nothing in the damn thing as usual. I'm blessed if I know why I buy the wretched thing every evening. It merely repeats what you've already heard on the radio and then the radio repeats what you've read in the paper.'

My grandmother countered this remarkable piece of logic by saying 'I suppose you won't really believe the war has started until we all wake up one morning to find ourselves bombed in our beds.'

Heavily ironic, Harry said: 'Ah! but we won't. Our great Air Force friends will see to that. The great takers-over of other people's property. What a farce.'

'There's no need to throw insults about,' I said, 'even if it is.'

'Ah! so we're on our high horse, are we? We're on our high horse.'

'Yes, we are,' I said and glared at him with what I hoped was some of my grandmother's own imperious scorn.

With that he struck the back of a chair with great fierceness with his paper and stalked out.

'He does lose his temper so,' I said. 'He does bang about.'

'You were not exactly sweet-tempered yourself.'

'Oh! there's nothing wrong with me.'

35

She made no comment on this. She knew perfectly well there was. I was irritable, uncertain of myself and wanted someone to quarrel with. I was in consequence aggrieved that Harry should have walked out and taken the opportunity away from me.

A few minutes later I walked out myself. It was a very beautiful evening, full of a high sea-washed light, and in a field down the road some farm hands, helped by two soldiers in khaki shirts and trousers, were tossing rows of hay with pitch-forks. The evening air was delicious with the fragrance of hay but my mood was dark and when one of the soldiers whistled at me as I passed I tossed my head in great indignation and strode scornfully on.

Greater experience would have told me that evening that I wasn't in love, but the experience wasn't there. I was bold with the conviction that I was in love and nagged by a doubt that I wasn't really loved in return. In this mood I started to quarrel with myself as I walked along, occasionally breaking off to quarrel with a too persistent cuckoo whose mocking, aggravating voice was hardly ever quiet across the fields.

In this way I walked across to Hudson's land and finally saw Tom and his father and two oldish farm-hands making hay too in one of the smaller meadows by the river. Everything was very early that year and farmers were trying to wrest as much from the land as quickly as they could.

The four men had just knocked off for tea and were sitting with their backs against a hay-cock in the centre of the field. I sat for a time on a gate and watched them before Tom at last happened to turn his head and saw me sitting there. At that he put down his tea mug and brushed his hand across his mouth and walked across the field to talk to me.

'Hullo,' he said. 'Haven't seen you for donkey's years.'

That expression irritated me too and I merely said 'No?' rather archly.

'Well, I say I haven't seen you –'

'Make up your mind.'

'I meant I'd seen you quite a few times from a distance but not to talk to.'

'Oh ! really.'

The pastoral scene of the hay-field in the evening sun mocked my ridiculous mood just as surely as it mocked the notion that war was a reality about to burst on us.

'Quite a smart little job, that sports car.'

'Yes, it is rather wizard, isn't it?'

'I see you speak the language.'

'Yes.'

'I hear them quite a lot of an evening. Down in the pub. Quite a gay lot. I've seen your friend with the moustaches there a time or two. He seems to be the gayest of the lot.'

'Bang on.'

'Have you seen him stand on his head and down a pint? That wants a bit of doing.'

'Things like that are a piece of cake to Bill.'

We went on talking in this fashion for another minute or two before he said he thought he ought to be getting back and then added, almost as a casual after-thought :

'They've moved into the house, I see.'

'They've *what*?'

'Been moving since crack of dawn.'

'I don't believe it.'

'I had to go down to the forge about nine o'clock to have a repair done on a coupling and they were moving in then. Truck loads of stuff.'

'All I can say is you're better informed than we are.'

'I went down and picked the coupling up about an hour ago and it looked as if they were really in. The place actually looked civilized.'

'Well, thanks for telling me. It's nice to know.'

The coolness of that last remark, like the rest of the conversation, must have given him some pain but I was too obtuse, too wrapped up in my own private vexations, to notice it. Grieved and irritated as I was by the suspicion that Bill might not be in love with me it never once remotely occurred to me that Tom Hudson might have been in love with me instead.

Tangling in fresh irritations, I walked slowly home, feeling like a child turned out in the cold. You might have thought, I told myself, that the business of moving into the house was some monstrously important official secret that couldn't be divulged for fear of betraying the country. It was security gone mad and I felt as if I had been soundly wounded and betrayed myself.

'Bill,' I told myself, 'I hate you. I hate you. I really hate you,' and finally dragged myself to bed and inconsolably wept myself to sleep.

Only three days later my grandmother opened an envelope at the breakfast table, took a card from it, peered at it for some moments with keen black eyes and then said:

'Well, I must say the Air Force moves fast when it does move.'

'That's the nature of the beasts. What is it now?'

She read from the card: 'Group-Captain L. T. P. O'Brien, A.F.C., O.B.E., D.F.C., requests the pleasure of the company of Mrs Catherine Cartwright and Miss Elizabeth Cartwright to the Officers' Mess, Bracehurst, on May 2nd. Cocktails 7–9 p.m.'

I suddenly felt very excited.

'Wizard. Will you go?'

'Of course I shall go. You know I adore parties.'

'May I have a new dress?'

'You had one for your birthday.'

'Oh! let me have another. A ravishing new one, please.'

'We'll see.'

'Oh! I wonder what sort of party it will be,' I said. I wrapped my arms about myself in excited anticipation. 'I wonder what sort of a party it will be.'

'I wonder.'

And we may well have wondered too.

4

I WENT to that party with two intentions firmly fixed in my mind : to look, in the first place, as ravishing as possible and to be as cool as was humanly possible to those too handsome barley moustaches. My intention, in fact, was to wither them. I inherit a great deal of pride from my grandmother and for three days I had kept myself apart, self-pitiful, angry, aloof, stubborn, and thoroughly wretched. I hadn't even answered a hastily scribbled note from Bill which simply said : 'Busy as a bee. But not too busy to see my lovely Liz. Meet you at *The Olive Branch* at 8 tonight.' Olive Branch, my foot ! I thought and didn't turn up.

In the matter of beauty I succeeded, I thought, rather wonderfully. My new dress, sleeveless and cut rather low at the neck, was of a curious and haunting shade of green, a sort of smoky Chinese jade colour. My skin is very slightly sallow and my eyes and hair, like my grandmother's, are very dark. For about a year my figure has been losing its puppiness and was now everywhere as firm as an apple. My breasts were neither too large nor too small and were moulded so well that I even scorned support for them.

The party began, as parties are sometimes apt to do, rather decorously. Our big drawing-room had been transformed into the mess ante-room, with a bar at one end and various squadrons' coats-of-arms adorning the walls, together with coloured pictures of Hurricanes and Spitfires and Gloster Gladiators. A big shining wooden propeller hung over the bar and a glistening silvery model of a Spitfire stood on a shelf underneath it, guarded by a positive palisade of bottles. The only hint of indecorum at that early stage was the sight of a dumpy and very pink *padre*, already pleasantly drunk, sucking at a quart silver tankard of beer as he leaned against the white napery of the bar-front, a sight at which no one but myself seemed in the least surprised.

When we entered the room Group-Captain O'Brien came

to greet us with what was almost old-world charm, shaking hands with us and bowing with much politeness.

'I hope you won't faint, Mrs Cartwright, at what we've done to your lovely old house,' he said.

'I am not,' my grandmother said, 'in the habit of fainting.'

The ante-room was full of blue uniforms and youthful faces. Large moustaches and young girls were scattered among them in about equal proportion but when the largest of the moustaches started to bear down on me like some swaying brown outrigger I contrived a sudden air of coolness and what I thought was distant hauteur. It simply wasn't any good. I needn't have bothered. My avowed intention of withering the Ogilvy emblem went for a heavy and immediate Burton.

'My dear old Liz. My sweet, long lost Liz.'

'Not so much of the old and not so much of the long lost.'

'My sweetest Popsie.'

'I am not your Popsie.'

'What will you drink? Sherry, gin, wallop, whisky, wine?' He grinned all over his face and I felt myself start grinning too. 'Punch? Admirable punch. *Specialité de la Maison*. Origin unknown. Monks or something. Pleasant and quite innocuous. Which will it be?'

I was about to say sherry when I changed my mind and said 'Punch.' A white-coated mess steward was passing and Bill stopped him and gave the order and said :

'Must introduce you to the chaps. Who's about? Ah! Splodge, old boy. Splodge – Miss Cartwright – our dearly beloved Liz, in whom we are well pleased. Liz – Pilot-Officer Miles Bannister, otherwise Splodge. Bad type.'

I shall never forget that first meeting with Splodge. Anything less like a bad type it would be hard to imagine. Splodge was modest, slight, soft-mannered, smooth-cheeked, very fair and almost heart-breakingly young. His wings were up but on the other hand it looked as if hair would never grow on his face at all.

'Good evening, Miss Cartwright,' he said in a treble voice so soft that it half gave me the impression that it hadn't even broken yet.

'Liz and her grandmother lived in the house,' Bill explained,

40

'until us shockers pinched it. Grandma tore us off a strip, I fear.'

'It must have broken your hearts,' Splodge said.

'My heart,' I said, in imitation of my grandmother, 'doesn't break so easily,' and the words, so casually thrown away, might well have been my own epitaph.

Curiously enough they seemed instantly to endear me to Splodge and it was he who took the glass of punch from the steward's silver salver when it came. The punch was a strange green shade and Splodge, as he handed it to me, was quick to notice that it almost matched my dress.

'What a beautiful combination,' he said and gazed with shy approval at my neck line.

'Beware of this type,' Bill said. 'Behind that innocent exterior lurk dark Satanic motives.'

'Cheers,' Splodge said and gave me the slightest of smiles as he raised his tankard of beer.

'Cheers,' I said.

'Cheers,' Bill said. 'Good show.'

Presently Bill left us. He was going to gather up more chaps, he said. Splodge and I half-looked at each other for fully a minute before I said :

'Funny man.'

'Hell of a good bloke.'

That cured a bit of my vanity and merely for want of something to say I said :

'What did you do before the war?'

'I didn't. I came practically straight from school.'

'What did you want to do?'

'Play the violin, actually.'

'Well, there's still time.'

'Is there?'

There wasn't time, though I didn't know it at that moment, and the question hung above us, unanswered.

'Do you like it here?' I said.

'Yes. I like the lake. I think the lake is very beautiful.'

'Soon the water-lilies will all be in bloom. It looks at its best then.'

I thought for a moment that he was going to say something

more about this but he merely looked past me with those heart-breakingly young, almost juvenile eyes, just as if he hadn't heard.

Bill, ever jovial, now came laughing back into our company, bringing with him a short wiry man a good ten years older than Splodge. His hair was thinning noticeably at the temples but it wasn't this that I noticed so much. What really struck me most about him was his immensely powerful wrists, almost out of proportion for so small a man.

'Flight-Lieutenant Burnett,' Bill said. 'Matters to you.'

'I sincerely hope it matters.'

A triple explosion of laughter almost blew down the chandelier in the ceiling above us as I said this.

'Good show, good show. Dear Liz. Damn good show.' Bill waved a jocular, approving tankard. 'Bless your splendid little heart.'

I begged that my heart should be left out of it and wanted to know, if possible, what black I'd put up now?

'Oh ! no black, Liz dear.'

'Then perhaps you might explain.'

'Mountaineering type.' Bill put his hand on the Flight-Lieutenant's shoulder with a sort of tender irony. 'Crazy man. Matters is merely short for Matterhorn, off which mountain he once fell when young.'

'Slanderous words. Duels have been fought for less.'

'He wakes i' the night and babbles o' South cols and crevasses.'

Once more we all exploded with laughter and again I thought the chandelier would come down. After this, without really knowing it, I drained my glass, whereupon the Flight-Lieutenant peered politely into it and asked if he might know what my poison was ?

'Oh ! yes – I see. Punch. Nice ?'

'Delicious.'

'Then I shall bring you another.'

'Good party,' Bill said. 'Going to be a good party,' and took a long exploratory glance round the now-crowded, babbling room and finally said, almost under his breath :

'Beautiful two-engine job over there, old boy.'

I wanted so much to be in the conversation and suddenly wanted to know which were the two-engine jobs? Spitfires?

Bill was instantly struck with a sobbing attack of apoplexy and leaned in a state of half-collapse on Splodge's shoulder, to be comforted there by a mock-tender hand.

'I cannot bear it. I cannot bear it. It's more than the jolly old frame can bear. Liz, my precious, please –'

The Flight-Lieutenant now came back with my glass of punch and, confronted by the sight of the helplessly muttering Bill, demanded to know :

'What? Already?'

'Tell him. Tell him, Splodge, old boy. He must be told.'

Feeling mildly foolish and bewildered I waited for Splodge to whisper in the Flight-Lieutenant's ear. Tears were running down Bill's cheeks, even as far as the moustaches, and I demanded to know at last what my latest black could be?

'Tell her, Matters old boy,' Bill said, 'As doyen of the party you must tell her. Tell her, please. Quickly. If 'twere done, 'twere well 'twere done quickly.'

The Flight-Lieutenant took me aside and whispered in my ear. I felt still more foolish as I listened but somehow, in those few moments, I also grew up a little. And finally I turned to them and said :

'May this little two-engine job rejoin the squadron now?'

'You're in !' they said. 'You're in !' and I felt that all of them could have kissed me.

This incident was hardly over before Bill was breaking out into mock protestation once more.

'Oh ! no. Oh ! no. Oh ! no. Go away, go away ! Cover her face, Splodge, she's too young. She mustn't be exposed to this. Not this, please. Not this.'

The officer who had now suddenly joined us was very tall. His long face was both bony and bone-coloured. The cheek-bones were high and the jaw lean and oblong. The proud slate-grey eyes were somehow both pained and painfully hand-some. His fingers were long and bony too and the left hand held in it a long amber-green cigarette holder.

'Go away !' they all said. 'Go away ! This is England. Foreigners not admitted.'

'Good evening, gentlemen. I profoundly beg your respective pardons.'

'Not granted ! Go away !'

'May I be introduced?' he said and with the most unflickering and penetrative eyes I had ever seen looked straight through me.

'This, unfortunately,' Bill said, 'is the Count. Count Dimitriov Mihail Sergei Zaluski. Miss Elizabeth Cartwright – the Count.'

He now gave me the most enchanting of smiles, bowed, and kissed my hand.

'Flannel !' they all said. 'Flannel !'

'I am most honoured, delighted and charmed to meet you, Miss Cartwright.'

'Flannel ! Flannel !'

'You do not look typically English, Miss Cartwright, if I may say so.'

'Why? I am very English.'

'You look more as if you might come from my country.'

'And where is that?'

'Poland.'

'No : I am very English,' I said.

'Which is better. Much, much better.'

A great insincere and collective sigh went up from the other three officers. It was a very beautiful performance, they would have him know. A very beautiful performance.

'I am very glad to know I am appreciated.'

'Flannel ! Flannel !'

'And if I may say so,' the Count said, 'beauty is not always in performances' and looked straight down at my partly bare bosom, so that I felt I had no dress on at all.

So we bantered our way through the first part of the evening. I am not sure now how many glasses of punch I drank or how many more officers I met but as the spring darkness came on I began to feel that innocuous green mixture roving its way inside me in twisting, simmering spirals. I began to feel very gay and from time to time, across the crowded room, I caught glimpses of my grandmother, very gay too, holding court with other officers. The laughter she aroused seemed to be even louder than the laughter I aroused. There was, in fact, great laughter everywhere. We might have been celebrating the end and not the beginning of war.

As the late dusk came down the party was buzzing like an over-turned bee-hive. An occasional glass crashed to the floor. I lost all count of time. At irregular intervals the moustaches of Bill Ogilvy mysteriously disappeared and were just as mysteriously replaced by other moustaches. Once Bill returned and with a rush of overpowering sentimentality kissed me full on the lips and declared himself for ever to be true and promptly left me for the little two-engined job, blonde as oat-straw, in a tight black dress, sitting on a bar stool. This prompted two other officers I didn't know at all to kiss me too, but merely in passing, on the forehead. In turn this prompted the Count to run a light exploratory hand down my right thigh and ask if I wouldn't do him the great honour of having dinner with him the following night? I thanked him and said I had six invitations already and that I would try to sort out my diary the following morning, though in fact at that time I didn't keep one.

'I have never seen anything more beautiful,' he said and pinched the softer parts of my thigh and pressed his face against my ear. 'Never, never more beautiful.'

It must have been eleven o'clock or more when I realized that Bill and Matters were no longer with us and that there was a sudden wild shouting and cheering from outside the house, as from a game of football.

'Going to be fun and games,' Splodge said and grabbed me away from the aggrieved Count and bore me outside and along the terrace, where a crowd of twenty or more officers had gathered, some of them standing on the stone balustrade and all of them looking up at the front façade of the house.

I looked up too. It still wasn't really dark and we could see what was happening by the light of a thin, faint moon. Bill had already climbed up to just beyond the first floor windows and Matters was close behind him. There seemed to be no kind of foothold on the wall except that from the window sills and I saw that Bill, to make things more difficult, was climbing it with a pint silver beer tankard balanced on his head. Matters had a pink enamel chamber-pot on his, worn like an air-raid

45

warden's helmet. In strict mountaineering style the two officers were roped together.

'On to the south col !' a wag shouted.

The tankard on Bill's head swayed, quivered and almost fell. Bill waved a cheerful right hand, then steadied the tankard with an almost elegant hand, like a man with a topper.

'Is it full ?' I asked, again in my innocence.

'Well, the tankard is,' Splodge said.

Slowly Bill drew himself up by his finger tips, groping up the wall. Above him the sky was full of stars and once or twice I could have sworn that some of them were dancing on the chimney pots. At every inch of Bill's progress the tankard quivered and swayed and there were many hoots and much laughter from the terrace below. Every few moments my heart came into my mouth and once I groped too, feeling for Splodge's arm as my head went round.

All the time I knew that the tankard must fall but that Bill never would. If it isn't too ridiculous a word to use of that slightly mad situation of horse-play, laughter, chamber pots and stars I will say that I carried a conviction in my heart that Bill was immortal. If he fell from the wall he would simply bounce. But I knew quite confidently and simply that he would never die.

Finally the tankard did fall. First it swayed this way and that and then gave a slow totter. Bill moved with acrobatic desperation to save it but it pitched away, struck his right shoulder, hit the chamber pot with a loud donk ! and then drenched Matters in a fountain of beer below.

Officers everywhere fell about themselves in chronic disorder. Some groaned because they couldn't laugh. Others wept because they couldn't laugh any longer. One young pilot officer actually fell off the balustrade and into the rose-bud below, sereing the air with loud blue oaths. From the lake came a sudden splash as if someone had fallen into that too but hardly anyone took any notice of an incident of such triviality.

Matters' reaction to the fall of the beer tankard was merely to look casually up, as if the business of being struck by strange falling objects on mountainsides was an everyday occurrence,

46

and then replace the chamber pot more firmly on his head. His hands were steady as steel and he moved slowly upwards with what seemed cool indifference, as if by means of steps cut into the brick-work.

'Excuse me, madam. Been looking for you everywhere. Compliments of Flying-Officer Devlin, miss.'

A mess orderly in white jacket stood by my side, holding a salver with two glasses on it. I hadn't the faintest idea who Flying-Officer Devlin was. It might have been that he was one of the officers who had kissed me casually in passing. It didn't really matter in that crazy moment and I simply picked up another glass of punch and Splodge picked up another glass of beer.

'Cheers,' we said to each other. 'Good show.'

To a great concert of cheering Bill reached the level of the stone cornice above the third floor window. In a moment of half-hysterical excitement I suddenly shouted 'That was my nursery up there! That window! My nursery!' and a young officer turned and gave me a stare of such blank astonishment that I might have been a baby crying in the night.

On the cornice Bill momentarily lost a footing. A lump of stone as big as a cricket ball broke off and struck the chamber-pot with yet another hollow donk! below. Unmoved, Matters continued to climb up, holding on, as it seemed, to nothing at all.

Finally Bill pulled himself up the last foot or so to the cornice and then sat there, brushing a casual hand across those vast moustaches in acknowledgement to the cheering gallery below. The fact of his having climbed to the very edge of my nursery window once again excited me absurdly and I danced up and down, cheering like mad. The stars danced too and in a ridiculous flush of hero-worshipping hysteria I was suddenly immensely proud of Bill and longed to be with him there, in the dizzy, starry heights.

Then Bill pulled Matters up the last foot or so by the rope and they both sat there on the cornice, grinning and waving. Then Matters took the rope off and started to lower it down the wall.

At this moment a very young, very dripping, very unsteady figure groped past me, muttering, not to anyone in particular but merely to the night air :

'Thought the bloody thing was concrete. Thought I was on the bloody apron. Bloody good show.'

Solitary in rumination he disappeared, dripping lake water, into the night.

I looked up to see two quart bottles of beer being slowly hauled heaven-wards by rope. When Matters and Bill had finally pulled them up the two officers stood smartly to attention, raised the bottles and drank.

'One, pause, two !' a wit shouted and a momentary tremor ran through Bill as he tilted the bottle.

'God,' a voice said, 'shakes me to the tits.'

'Good show !' we shouted. There was much raising of glasses and tankards. 'Good show !'

My innocuous glass was empty, but it was too late to wonder how and when I had emptied it. Suddenly the terrace, the house, the officers and the stars above the chimney pots started to go round and round me in a spiral I couldn't stop. For a moment Bill was no longer on the cornice and then suddenly was there again, amazingly duplicated. Then Matters disappeared and came back again and there were two of him too.

'Easy,' a voice said, 'easy,' and I found myself leaning unsteadily on the balustrade. A thousand officers were suddenly milling about the terrace but Bill and Matters and the Count were nowhere among them. I groped wildly and caught a uniformed arm.

'Bill,' I said. I wanted Bill to be with me very much. 'Oh ! there you are.'

'It isn't Bill.'

'No ?'

'It's Splodge.'

'Oh ! Splodge – Splodge, dear –'

I was vaguely aware of being taken by Splodge to the lake-side. I was even more vaguely aware of lying on the lake-side, on cool damp grass, and of Splodge holding my hand as I tried desperately to halt the rampant spiral of the stars in their courses. How long I was there I shall never know but later, I think long,

long later, I heard the sound of singing and I still remember the song:

> *Isn't it a Pity*
> *She's only got one Titty*
> *To Feed the Baby on —*

And at long last, to the far echo of that sad ballad someone — it might have been Bill or Matters or Splodge or Uncle Harry or all four of them for all I know — carried me away and gently put me to bed in the summer dawn.

5

IF that was the strangest dawn of my life up to that time an even stranger one, and far more important, was to begin some two weeks later. The party and the gay time were over; that morning the reality, or at least some part of it, began.

As I walked across the garden after breakfast there was nothing to show that that morning was any different from any of the many exquisite ones that presently were to make up that long summer. It was to be one of those summers when nearly every day is pellucid, when the weather is never too hot and when the bloom on the ripening wheat becomes an almost burnished golden-brown and is never tarnished by rain.

That morning many of the first roses, the blood red *Etoile d'Hollande* and that old pink variety *Caroline Testout*, were in bloom on the house wall. A tree of white lilac was in full blossom under the walls of the dove-cot. The sky was pure and very blue. There was hardly a breath of wind to swing the weather-cock on the dove-cot roof and if the roof had been crowded with white doves — and by that time we no longer kept any — the scene could hardly have been more peaceful in its pastoral calm.

I lingered about the garden for perhaps ten minutes or so, thinking of Bill and wondering if I would see him that day. We hadn't met except for a brief lemonade at *The Olive Branch* since the night of the party. It once or twice occurred to me that he might just possibly have deserted me for the little blonde two-engined job and there were days when I felt angry and jealous because of it. But most of all I missed the particular brand of exhilaration he gave.

I had just decided to turn and go back into the house when I caught sight of Uncle Harry striding across the paddock that lay in front of the house. He was carrying a thick red-brown thorn stick and now and then, in his usual blundering fashion, he took savage swings at the heads of moon-daisies, cutting them off as clean as with a knife.

'You've heard the news, I suppose?' he said. 'We're going to lose an army. A whole damned army.'

So much had I been shut away in my own crazy private world that I had only the very vaguest idea of what he was driving at.

'See that?' he said. 'Can't you smell it?'

The only answer to this doubly contradictory question, which struck me as quite nonsensical, was to stand and stare.

'Over there!' He pointed savagely eastward, towards the climbing sun. 'Down towards the coast there. It's been thickening up for the last half hour or more.'

'Oh! I see what you mean. It's clouding over already.'

'Clouding over my Aunt Fanny. Look at it. Smell.'

The cloud that I now saw had gathered all along the eastward horizon, well below the sun, suddenly struck me as being very curious. It wasn't an ordinary cloud. In colour it was somewhere between snuff-colour and grey and it occurred to me that it might have been a sea-mist drifting in. We get that sort of sea-mist on this coast sometimes and when it blows in there's a sharp chill in the air.

'You know what that is?' He slammed the little wicket gate leading into the garden with such force that a rusty nail actually dropped out of it. He picked it up, swore and threw it into the field. 'You know what? I'll give you a thousand to one that's oil. Burning oil?'

'Burning where, do you suppose?'

'France. You weren't up early enough to hear the news bulletin.' There was a note of aggrieved shame, as well as anger, in his voice. 'We're going to lose an army. A whole damned army. Those poor blighters are being pushed into the sea. They've asked for every craft, yachts, paddle-steamers and God knows what, to go over there and take 'em off. God, what a shambles, what a God-awful shambles.'

I stood sniffing burning oil, having no idea what to say, and watching the slow uprising of that strange brown-grey cloud towards the region of the sun.

Suddenly he turned on me as if I were directly responsible for the defections of strategy that were now about to be visited upon us.

'I'll tell you something, young lady,' he almost shouted at

51

me. 'I'll tell you something. The damned Frogs have let us down. They've shopped us, my girl, lock, stock and barrel. I said they would. They live too well. They think too much about women and wine and their damn bellies.'

Before I could speak again I caught the sound of a squadron of fighters going over, pretty high up, and he heard it too.

'Your friends,' he said. 'What are they mucking about up there for? Why aren't they damn well over the other side in France, helping our chaps? That's where they're needed, aren't they?'

I said that perhaps it might be that some were needed in England too.

'Oh? Why? Why? Tell me why. If we lose the damn thing over there we've lost it here, I tell you. That's as sure as eggs.'

I opened my mouth to speak, but he shot me down, all guns firing.

'You know what will happen next? That other bastard'll be here. Invading us. After the Frogs, the Huns. God, what a shambles. What a God-awful shambles. It makes you sick.'

For the first time I started to feel a little sick too. The upper edges of that curious cloud, a few moments later, rose to the sun and there was a strange feeling of an approaching total eclipse in the air.

Harry stumped indoors and I followed him. In the sitting-room my grandmother was sitting by the window, knitting long white socks with her customary imperturbable calm. Harry strode up to the radio set, switched it on and, when it yielded no sound after a mere second or two, struck it a savage blow with his fist, almost as if to say 'That'll damn well teach you to answer when I speak to you!'

Presently popular music came forth and Harry snarled.

'That's all you ever get!' he said. 'Music. Damn cater-wauling.'

'Is something troubling you, Harry?' my grandmother said.

'We're losing an army!' he shouted. 'And I'll tell you something else. If we don't damn well watch out we'll lose the war.'

'Really.'

'Look over there.' He strode to the window and pointed eastward, where that strange cloud seemed at last about to eclipse the sun. 'See that? I've been watching it for an hour.'

My grandmother looked at the cloud and said, rather as I had done, that it was a pity the day was clouding over so early.

'Clouding over, my foot! That's oil. You can smell it. Burning on the French beaches.'

'I suppose that's possible.'

'Possible, possible? – it *is*. And you know what that means don't you? Invasion. I'll lay you a thousand to one we'll be invaded. Sure as eggs. Sure as tomorrow's Thursday.'

'It happens to be Friday.'

'Well, whatever it is! It's a damn job to know what day it is any day nowadays.'

None of this conversation had any visible effect on my grandmother's calm. Indeed as she took one further glance at the cloud which by now had completely eclipsed the sun she looked positively complacent.

'Why don't you go fishing or something?' she said.

'Fishing? My God. At a time like this? I tell you what, though.' Suddenly Harry jerked to a pause and a second or two later we were aware that a great brain-wave had gone through him. 'I tell you what –'

'Well?'

'I'll get my guns cleaned. At least I can get them ready.'

'You feel they would be of much use?'

'You never know,' Harry said. 'You never damn well know,' and suddenly made an almost triumphal departure.

For the next ten minutes or so I mooched about the house, half lost, not knowing what to do with myself. In my typically English fashion I didn't want to show my feelings but my sympathies were rather with Harry. Many emotions were bubbling about inside me and one of them, if I'd been honest enough to admit it, was fear; but the worst of them was uncertainty and I was both relieved and delighted when suddenly the telephone rang.

I rushed to it in the hope that it might be Bill on the line. Instead a piercing soprano demanded 'Are you all right, darling? It's me.'

It was my mother.

'Are you quite sure you're all right, Elizabeth darling? I dreamed you'd been bombed. It was all horribly clear. They were carrying bodies out of the house on a gate. They laid you out in the church. You and grandmother and Edna. It was really real, not like a dream at all. Are you quite, quite sure you're all right?'

'Absolutely. Everything's perfectly all right.'

'You sound tense.'

'It's early, that's all. You know I don't rouse up very easily.'

'I'm worried for you. I think you should come to Malvern. You feel it's absolutely safe here. You don't know there's a war on.'

'Is that a good thing?'

'Well, it's comforting, it's comforting. At least you can sleep well.'

'I sleep splendidly.'

'Yes, but you must admit you're sort of in the front line, aren't you? I mean with all those air-fields and so on. I mean that's where it's going to be fought, isn't it?'

'Where what is going to be fought?'

'Well, I mean we'll have to fight somewhere, won't we?'

'I suppose we will.'

'Is Mother there? I feel I must try to persuade her to come down here. You seem so terribly far away. Oh! by the way – before you go – there's something. I'm thinking of becoming a Catholic.'

'Good gracious, why?'

'Well, one's got to do something, hasn't one? One's got to do something.'

This conversation with my mother had the effect of restoring all my calm. I even felt a little smug. To be in the front line – well, perhaps there was nothing wrong with that. Perhaps it was no bad thing for morale.

'Well, one's got to do something, hasn't one?' I said to my grandmother when she had finished on the telephone, 'one's got to do something,' and added that I supposed she had heard about my mother becoming a Catholic.

'Oh! yes. But she'll soon get over that. There was a time when she was going to become a Theosophist. Unfortunately she hadn't the vaguest idea what it meant. She simply thought it sounded rather nice.'

'Actually I meant the bit about one must do something,' I said. 'I feel terribly lost this morning. I feel I must do something.'

'In that case you can walk as far as the glasshouses and get more cucumbers.'

We both laughed at that; our persistent cucumbers were always something of a joke with us.

'I suppose we *will* get through this tiresome thing some day, somehow,' she said. 'Well, if we do we can always say it was the cucumbers.'

'Yes, I suppose in a way you could say they were sort of symbolic of something – you know, cool –

'Tut, tut. Now don't get pompous, dear.'

Thus dismissed, I started to walk to the glasshouses, going the longest way round, by what we called the back road, first by *The Olive Branch* and then down by the church, where my mother had seen me so vividly laid out in her dream, and back through our village street of three shops, two more pubs, *The Welcome Stranger* and *The Pomfret Arms*, a couple of dozen houses, a Baptist chapel and a horse trough. One of the shops was also the post office and outside it a horse was actually tethered to the front railings. We hadn't even a petrol pump in those days.

It might in fact have been any morning in any peaceful year except for one thing. The cloud of smoke-haze that had earlier darkened the sun had now shut out most of the sky completely. The effect, as in a total eclipse, was a strange and eerie one. The earlier morning had been full of bird song but now the birds had stopped singing, with the result that you felt you were walking in an uncanny haunting vacuum.

As I walked down the street two army trucks went through, full of soldiers, who all waved and whistled madly. This time I waved in reply, a gesture that positively convulsed them with joy. 'Tonight?' one actually yelled and I grinned and waved again in answer.

After buying stamps at the post office I stopped to speak to Charley Bailey at the forge, half in the hope that Tom Hudson might turn up too. Charley, who actually touched his cap to me, was heating a long iron bar in the fire and while waiting for it to hot up said he thought that things looked bad and what did Harry feel about it all?

I said Harry thought they looked bad too.

'Does he think we'll be invaded?'

'He's sure of it.'

'I'm blessed if I ain't with him at that.'

Suddenly a crackle of machine-gun fire split the air very high up, far above that pall of cloud. The effect was to send both of us foolishly running into the street, where we stood for some minutes staring up, also rather idiotically, since there was nothing to be seen. When a second and longer burst of fire cut across the sky – it was a thrilling and exciting sound rather than one of portent or alarm – Charley nodded his head with approval and said something about 'they were the boys.'

'Well, it's nice to know they've got *some* friends.'

'My youngest boy's in that outfit. Bombers, though. Rear gunner.' In the pride of the moment he suddenly forgot himself. 'Arse-end Charlie. Oh! sorry, miss.'

'It's all right. I know all the words.'

'I expect you do. I've seen you a time or two with that officer in that little yellow car.'

'Yes.'

'Might be him up there.'

'Could be.'

Suddenly, from a mile or two away, there was the most appalling crump: I couldn't tell whether it was a bomb or a plane bouncing and simply said:

'Shaky do.'

'Sounded near,' was all he said.

It sounded, to me, even nearer than that. It sounded dead in the centre of my heart. I knew it could have been Bill or Splodge or Matters or the Count or anybody else I knew and the fact that I knew equally well that it couldn't did nothing to lessen the tension of my fear.

Charley went back into the forge and I stood by the open door, watching him. I had the feeling for a moment that he was going to say something more about his son but instead he took up his pincers and gripped the red-hot bar with them and turned it slightly and then worked the bellows, so that the coals glowed white-blue with heat.

'Know what?' he said. 'I'd like to run this bar through that blasted Hitler. Slow.'

I hadn't time to say anything before I heard the snarl of a sports car coming up the street. I joyfully rushed out of the forge, knowing Chloe's voice, and sure enough there she was, coming like a bomb. I started waving frantically and in seconds, brakes wailing, she pulled up twenty yards beyond me.

'Bill!' I called. Then I saw that in the driving seat sat not Bill but Splodge.

'Splodge!' I said. 'Whatever on earth are you doing in Chloe? Bill – Heavens above, he'll cut your ears off.'

'Lent it to me for five minutes. I left my gas-mask at the Mess and had to go back for it. The Wing-Co. tore me off a terrible strip.'

'How's Bill? Where have you all been?'

'Oh! things. Busy.'

'Bill hasn't rung me up or anything.'

'We're all so busy we hardly get time to shave. Give you a lift? I've got to go.'

'No, thanks all the same. I'm walking. Give Bill my love. Tell him I'll give him the old one-two if I find he's been with that blonde job.'

'No fear of that.'

'Tell him to ring me.'

'Good-bye, Liz. Simply must dash.'

'Must you? Well, you can give him this for me.'

I bent down quickly and kissed him lightly on the cheek. He grinned and the painfully young eyes glowed.

'Wizard. Absolutely made my day.'

In another moment I was waving good-bye and Chloe was far up the street, splitting the air with her waspish snarl.

All through the rest of that day I was restless and troubled. I kept recalling the crackle of machine-gun fire. My constant fear that it might have been Bill up there was counteracted by the equally constant irritation that he might have abandoned me for the little blonde two-engined job. And every half an

57

hour or so, just to make things worse, Harry would barge into the house, switch on the radio for news, bark at it when there was none and then repeat the fretting catechism that I had heard so often before :

'First Poland, then Norway, then Belgium, then Holland and now France, by God. What a sell-out. By God, do you realize we're on our confounded own ?'

About half past nine I could bear it no longer. I picked up the first book I could lay my hands on and was just about to say good night to my grandmother when Harry came in from the garden and said, with heavy innuendo :

'I suppose the yellow sports car out in the road wouldn't be waiting for anybody, would it ?'

I ran out of the house, down the garden path and into the road, where Chloe was waiting, only to be brought up sharp by a repetition of what had happened in the morning.

'Bill –'

Again it wasn't Bill in the driving seat, but Splodge.

'But Splodge – where on earth's Bill got to ? I haven't seen him for such ages. He's just abandoned me.'

At first he didn't answer. Suddenly a dark fear ran over me and I seemed to feel all my skin shrink and tighten and grow cold and deadly dry. My disembodied voice was cold and dry and shrunken too.

'You're not trying to –'

'Oh ! no. Good God, no. Actually he's been posted, that's all. Him and the whole ruddy squadron. Two days after that party. They had about two split seconds to pack their gear.'

I didn't know whether to weep or shout with joy. I was trembling all over and for some moments I couldn't say a word. And when at last I did manage to form a sentence it was rather an acid one.

'I think someone might at least have had the decency to tell me.'

'Terribly sorry, Liz. But thing's have hotted up like hell lately. Nobody's had a minute to spare.'

All my fears and misgivings suddenly came rushing back.

'Splodge, you're not trying to tell me Bill's been killed, are you ? Please, for God's sake, if he has –'

'Good God, no.' He actually laughed at me. 'You can't kill blokes like Bill. He's not the type.'

Though I hadn't very much to be happy about I laughed too. An image of Bill standing to attention, beer-bottle in hand, under my nursery window, on that evening of early summer madness, made me recall my fond notion that he was immortal and my faith was restored.

'I suppose you're right – but my nerves have been on edge all day. Ever since –'

'Ever since what?'

'Just before I met you this morning there was the most awful bang. Bursts of machine-gun fire and all that and I couldn't help wondering –'

Splodge didn't say anything. He just sat very still, staring over the car-wheel, at some far-off distance.

'Did anything happen this morning?' I said. 'Was someone killed?'

'Yes. I'm afraid so. Devlin.'

Devlin? I couldn't for the life of me think who Devlin was.

'Who's Devlin?'

'Well, he isn't now. But you remember him.'

'No.'

'The Irish type.'

I couldn't remember any Irish type either.

'At the party,' Splodge said. 'You and he had a bit of an argument. I think you misunderstood something he said about England. I think you had an idea he didn't like England or something and you said well, if he didn't like it why did he bother to come over and fight for it? or something like that.'

The incident, which until then I had utterly forgotten, now came back to me.

'He was terribly cut up about it. Thought he'd put up a terrible black. His fault and all that,' Splodge said. 'That's why he sent you that drink.'

'Drink?'

'That enormous punch. Must have been a treble. The one that put you out.'

'God, what a stupid fool I must have been. Getting into an argument like that.'

'Just one of those things.'

It was just one of those things. The young Devlin, whom I hardly knew, was dead. And his face, which I could barely remember, suddenly started haunting me far more than if I had known it well. I felt I owed him a deep apology and was full of nagging and wretched reproaches that it was too late to make it now.

'Talking about a drink,' Splodge said, 'could you use one?'

'I might use two. Or even three.'

'You sound depressed.'

'I am.'

'About Bill?'

'Not so much. It's hard to explain. I sort of feel I haven't any right to be here.'

I got into the car and we drove up to *The Olive Branch* without another word. Inside the pub, in the public bar, several soldiers were drinking beer and two R.A.F. sergeants were playing darts with a couple of young farm hands. Splodge and I walked through to the private bar and I knew the sergeants and the soldiers were staring after me.

'Cheers,' Splodge said.

'Cheers.'

Splodge had bought a whisky for himself and a shandy for me.

I bitterly wanted to cry into that shandy. It may sound slightly heavy now, but that evening I felt as if I were being deeply reproached by the dead. It isn't a pleasant thing to hate yourself and it's even less pleasant when you don't quite know why.

'Cheers,' Splodge said. 'You look as if the end of the world had come.'

'I could jump in the lake,' I said.

At this he put his arm gently on my shoulder and looked at me so earnestly with those painfully young eyes of his that it merely made things worse and I could have wept aloud.

'You'll get over it,' he said.

And presently I did get over it, enough at least to ask about Chloe.

'How,' I said, 'do you come to have Chloe?'

'Bill sold her to me for thirty quid. With strings.'

'Strings?'

'I've got to sell her back to him for twenty-five when he gets back to England.'

'So he's gone to France after all.'

'God-awful clot. I shouldn't have said that. You didn't hear me.'

'France,' I said. 'He's happy now.'

After that, in some curious way, I set Bill aside. We didn't talk of him any more and we didn't talk about Devlin either. The summer dusk came slowly and after a time Splodge got hungry and Mrs Croft, the landlady, made us a plate of corned beef sandwiches and brought a pot of mustard to go with them.

While Splodge was digging into the blue mustard pot and spreading mustard on to his first sandwich Mrs Croft, a pleasant, pale, elderly body who at no time looked either very well or strong, started asking after my family. Was it true my mother had gone away?

'Yes. She's at Malvern. She's been trying her best to get us to join her there.'

'And will you go?'

'Not on your life.'

'Funny,' she said. 'That's how I feel. Anybody who wants me out of here will have to cart me out on a pitchfork.'

It was this remark of Mrs Croft's that finally restored my self-confidence. Then as we were finishing the last of the sandwiches Splodge said :

'You wouldn't like to hear some music, I suppose?'

'Music? Where?'

'I've got my portable gramophone in the bus. I thought we might listen to a few records. That's if you'd like to.'

'I'd love it.'

We finished up the last of the drinks and the sandwiches and said 'Good night' to Mrs Croft and went out and got into Chloe. Just before he started up the engine Splodge asked me if there was anywhere I'd particularly like to go to and I said :

'Let's drive up to the Devil's Spoon. I'll tell you the way.'

From the Devil's Spoon, a big grassy hollow on the crest of the downs where in spring great numbers of cowslips grow, you can look out on a great wide quilt of orchards and woodland and little villages and cornfields and pastures to a point where the smoke stacks of ships are just visible on the line of sea. On days of westerly wind big cloud shadows come sweeping in across it and on spring days the cowslips are tossed about like silent golden bells. They say that Caesar's legions camped here. Chaucer's pilgrims skirted through the big beech-wood lower down the hill, the very beech-woods where Bill and I had sometimes sat and listened to the sound of incoming planes, but that night there were neither legions nor pilgrims, wind nor cowslips to disturb a silence so vast that it was exactly as if, as someone later remarked, an entire nation was holding its breath. It was all deathly, ominously still.

'Don't put on the music yet, Splodge. I'd just like to sit and listen to the night.'

'Sort of music of the spheres?'

'Something like that.'

We didn't, as it turned out, put on any records at all. We simply sat listening, as I said, to the night. The sky was perfectly clear and there were a great many stars. Almost the only sounds we heard were an occasional call from an owl, a clock striking quarters from a village down below and once the sound of a plane stooging away in the west.

We didn't talk much either. Splodge put an arm round my shoulder and I felt a great sense of tenderness in the air. With Bill there really hadn't been any tenderness. With him it had all been a marvellous game, a sort of emotional helter-skelter. Perhaps that was why, though I had been dismally sure that my heart would break if Bill were taken from me, alive or dead, it now showed no sign of any such disaster.

Presently Splodge brushed his mouth across my hair and then, without a word, drew my face towards him and kissed me. I don't know why but I got the strange impression that this was the result of a solemn promise given long, long ago. I suppose I am really trying to say that it had in it a feeling of great inevitability. If there is a pre-ordained pattern to life, and there are times when I'm not at all sure that there isn't, this was the most pre-ordained thing that had ever happened to me. I knew I had been born for that particular moment in time and I accepted it with wonder.

And also with calm and joy. Curiously enough I felt a good

deal older. I suppose I grew up quite a bit that day but one thing at least is certain: I didn't ask any questions. The moment and its blossoming were enough.

Splodge didn't ask any questions either but at last simply said, very quietly:

'I like it here.'

'We must come again.'

'Yes.'

'By July there will be wild strawberries.'

'Wild strawberries? I've never tasted one in my life.'

'You're going to this year.'

And with these words I felt, for some reason, that summer had really begun.

6

In France, by this time, the battle had raged forward to inevitable doom with a swiftness and ferocity that couldn't escape even a girl like me. By June 9th German Panzers had reached the lower reaches of the Seine and Oise; presently they were on the Marne and in another week, on the 16th, had reached Orleans and the Loire. Paris had fallen even before this, on the 14th, and a great gap opened southward, past Dijon and Besançon, almost to the Swiss frontier.

The effect of all this on my Uncle Harry was to spur him to a frenzy of tireless activity in an endeavour to turn our little house into an armed fortress. A great pile of yellow sand arrived, together with several hundred sand-bags, and for days Harry and the two remaining gardeners, Baxter and Lines, laboured strenuously to fill the sandbags and then pile them four or five feet high about such strategic places as the steps leading to the coal-cellar, the windows of the gun room, the still room and the larder. Baxter, fearful that none of us would be able to have an egg for breakfast or a pie for dinner, begged to be allowed to go to market to remedy this desperate state of affairs and did so, coming back with a cockerel and a dozen Rhode Island Reds, six Khaki Campbell ducks and two Belgian hares. The hares, a buck and a doe, were duly hutched and a few spare sandbags piled over and about them too. The Khaki Campbells ranged freely about the meadow. From somewhere Baxter got an old baker's van, housed the hens in it and surrounded it with wire-netting, which was partly sand-bagged too. The sun-flaked words *Geo. Oakley Family Baker Finest Bread and Cakes*, still visible on the side of the van, were a great and curious comfort to us all.

It was as if we were preparing for a long siege. This impression was further strengthened by the fact that Harry also deemed it necessary to turn the house into an armoury. Baxter and Lines were fitted up with 12 bores. Of Harry's two pairs of guns one pair was kept in the gunroom; another gun he kept by his bedside and sought to insist that my grandmother keep another one by hers.

She would hear of no such thing.

'And what do you propose that I should shoot at? Owls?'

Harry pointed out that it wasn't of owls that he was thinking of but of Nazi parachutists, who would surely be upon us, at the least expected moment, any time now.

'What would you do if one of them dropped in the garden, eh?'

'Give him a whisky-and-soda and telephone the police.'

'And be raped meanwhile.'

'I cannot conceive even remotely that a man dropping from several hundred feet by parachute in enemy territory would have uppermost in his mind any such thing as the pleasures of intercourse.'

'People do strange things,' Harry said darkly, 'under pressure.'

'I've little doubt they do. In which case you'd better keep one gun on one side of the bed and one on the other. Then you can fire on both flanks.'

'All right. But you'll be very sorry if you look out of your bedroom window one fine morning and see an armed Hun floating down.'

'We will meet that eventuality,' she said, 'when it comes.'

In the middle of these crises, one military and one domestic, another and smaller one occurred, seemingly quite trivial in itself but in reality of great importance to me.

At the big house we had kept eight servants : two cooks, two housemaids, a sort of secretary housekeeper and three gardeners. In addition there were the bailiff and two game-keepers, one of whom acted also as river-keeper, but since my grandmother was inclined to be impatient, if not actually contemptuous, in her dealings with men, these three came under Harry's jurisdiction rather than hers. Of these servants the two cooks, the housekeeper, one housemaid, one gardener and the two keepers had been dismissed for the duration. We now had only Edna, who washed, ironed, darned, cooked, swept, waited at table and still starched Harry's stiff collars after the fashion of 1910, and the two gardeners, who ran the gardens and glasshouses of the big house on a commercial plan, sending produce to shops and markets.

A few days after the fall of Paris, at which time a stunned nation was still holding its breath, Edna came into the sitting-room one afternoon to announce that Rose had called and would Mrs Cartwright be good enough to see her?

Rose was the elder of the two cooks and presently was shown in, harassed if not actually haggard, visibly quaking and, as it presently turned out, on the verge of tears. Rose, sixtyish and always rather fragile, had taken a post as cook in a boys' school and had now met disaster in the form of a storming headmaster who, temper much-frayed by events, had accused her of stealing sugar. Everybody's temper was in fact frayed by events and people were apt to take it out on each other in a variety of disloyal and petty ways.

The infamy of being accused of theft had been too much for Rose, to whom honour and loyalty were as fundamental as breath. We all loved her and indeed my mother and grandmother had openly shed tears at her departure.

'If only I could come and assist part-time, ma'am. At weekends, say, or when you wanted to give a little dinner party or a luncheon party for some friends.'

'I don't think that would be a very good arrangement, Rose. It's much too haphazard.'

'Then perhaps I could come and live in again, ma'am. I would come for less wages than I had before.'

'It's very kind of you to offer, Rose.'

'It must be a lot of hard work for Edna.'

'Indeed it is a lot of hard work for Edna. But the truth is we just haven't a spare bedroom.'

'Oh! this awful war,' Rose said and promptly burst into tears, as if not having a spare bedroom were the worst evil of the lot.

While Rose was stemming her tears I stood at the window, staring at the garden, over which the June heat was quivering like a hovering dragonfly. The nights had been very hot that week and I now recalled coming downstairs the previous night, about midnight, unable to sleep, to get myself a drink of cold water, only to find Edna still ironing in the kitchen.

Edna had a great fear of being bombed in her bed and had taken to working late in order to avoid the terrors of sleeping. As a result she had started to look haggard too and dark and heavy-eyed.

'Edna was working till after midnight last night,' I said. 'It isn't good. We'll have her crack up on us. And then what?'

'I know it isn't,' my grandmother said. 'But short of slinging a hammock up in an apple tree we just haven't another bed.'

'Edna and me could sleep two in a bed,' Rose sobbed.

'I've just thought of something,' I said. 'I could sleep in the dove-cot. I could turn that upstairs floor into a room for myself. It would be fun. I should love it.'

'There's no electric light there.'

'What's wrong with candles?'

'Nothing, I suppose.'

'Then why don't I? It's the simplest thing. The easiest solution.'

'Won't you find it rather lonely at night?'

'If I do I'll borrow one of Harry's guns and fire distress signals every half hour.'

'Oh! Miss Elizabeth, I'll come and help you flit!' Rose said and promptly burst into another flood of tears.

So it came about that, in the very centre of that early summer's bewilderment, cynicism and humiliation, I was once again insulated – but now it was to be for the last time – against the raw-edge of war. Just as I suppose we all think of ourselves as immortal so in the same way I never really thought, up to that time, that war could do anything even of merely unpleasant consequence to me.

I was like a child with a new dolls' house. My dove-cot was my very own and as I carried curtains and chairs and rugs and tables and mattresses and candlesticks and so on up to it I felt sometimes quite giddy with excitement. Unaware of its effect of insulation – that was to come rather later – I felt instead almost a feeling of jealousy, of being defensively in possession, so much so that I even remarked at breakfast one day, half-seriously, half-mocking :

'Visitors to the dove-cot are requested to ring three times.'

'And ask for Charlie, I suppose,' Harry said.

'*Not,*' I said, 'very funny.'

I thought the moment a good one, however, in which to ask my grandmother a question and I said :

'Would you object if I sometimes had a few friends in? Even a little house-warming party?'

'We are not sending you to a nunnery.'

'Thank you.'

'No late night stuff, though,' Harry said. 'I need my beauty sleep. I know these fellers.'

'I wonder,' my grandmother said.

Meanwhile, across the Channel, in France, despair and capitulation were presently complete. Somewhere, and I still wasn't even aware enough to guess where, Bill was among the Hurricanes being shot down at the rate of two hundred and fifty in ten days or two in every daylight hour. Soon a Frenchman blessed with great clarity of vision was announcing that within three weeks England would have her neck wrung like a chicken. To be friends with us, according to a certain Pétain, was merely 'fusion with a corpse'. It would be better, someone else said, to be a Nazi province and in answer, at Churchill's behest, men of all creeds, ages and classes started to form themselves into a volunteer defence corps and at last my Uncle Harry, gas-mask, shot-gun and haversack at the ready, was really happy as he crawled about church-yards, hedge-rows, rick-yards and woodlands in deadly serious and clumsy manoeuvre through summer night-times.

One evening about this time I walked as far as *The Olive Branch* in the hope of seeing Splodge or Matters or the Count or perhaps even Tom Hudson with the idea of inviting them to my first party. The little bar with its dartboard, pots of old bulrushes on the shelves and out of date notices about slate clubs stuck about the walls was almost empty : empty, at any rate, of Air Force men. Two surprisingly young farmhands, drinking shandy, stood talking, of all things, about cricket; the local road-man, whose left ear had been shot off in the first world war and who in consequence bore a kind of angry pink mouse-hole in that side of his head, sat in a corner alone, morosely contemplating a half empty tankard. Fragile Mrs

Croft, the landlady, stood behind the bar, polishing glasses and looked rather withdrawn as she called me 'Miss Elizabeth'.

It was some time before an army sergeant came in, together with a private and a corporal, and started a lot of beef about things across the Channel. 'Was we there? I'll say we was bleedin' there. And a few thousand other unlucky bastards too. Like sitting on a wasps' nest and no bleedin' swatters. Oh! yes we was there. And where was they? The old posh wallahs. The jolly old prang brigade. Them up there. Not a bleeder in sight. Not a blue-arsed fly.'

I stood as much of this as I could, with the corporal saying in garrulous agreement 'S'right, mate, S'right, mate, S'right,' until I could stand it no longer and at last said:

'And what kind of outfit are you supposed to be? Do you need nursemaids?'

The sergeant gave me a very sergeant-like look and then surveyed me slowly up and down as if I were some stale half-baked tart or something and finally said:

'And who are you supposed to be fighting with? And, if I might say so, for?'

'God only knows,' I said. 'And if He does, He hasn't told me.'

'You're dead right.'

'So many Brown Jobs,' I said.

With this, in a state of near fury, I swept out. Someone, the corporal I think, blew me a raspberry, but I made no sign of having heard. It was all typical of the confused, contagious, groping bitterness of the time.

I walked almost blindly down the road in the evening sunshine. I didn't then know about those Hurricanes dissolving in the heat of battle at the rate of two every daylight hour, or that Spitfires, which we were being rousingly exhorted to help make by surrendering our aluminium kettles, were too precious to replace them. In my divine young ignorance I had some sort of idea that not only did Spitfires reproduce themselves, like mysterious galaxies of stars, but that also, as in galaxies, there were limitless thousands of them to reproduce themselves.

It is always a bad thing to be bitter about something without knowing quite what you are being bitter about, and this was as true of the sergeant as it was of me. Thankfully I ran into Tom Hudson at the bottom of the hill and I had never been quite so glad to see that heavily bronzed, blue-eyed face of his.

'I've just come from your house,' he said. 'I brought you a half-chip of cherries.'

Pleased though I was to see him I was still only half there. The rest of me was still arguing bitterly with the sergeant and some of my caustic confusion must have shown in my face, because Tom said :

'Well, you might look pleased. I thought you were so passionately fond of cherries.'

'I'm awfully, awfully sorry, Tom. It's just that –' and I went on to tell him of the dust-up with the sergeant.

'Everybody's bitter and on edge,' he said. 'I had a devil of a flare-up with my father the other night. We've never quarrelled before.'

'I'm sorry I wasn't there when you called. Did my grandmother tell you about the dove-cot ?'

'Dove-cot ?'

I told him, in my excited fashion, about the dove-cot, adding : 'I'm glad I saw you because I'm planning a little house-warming party. Probably next Sunday. I want you to come. Just you and some of the Air Force boys. They're a wizard crowd.'

It was now his turn not to be there. He suddenly seemed, I thought, both withdrawn and embarrassed. Nor did he say anything for quite some moments and those intensely blue eyes of his, which in very bright light had sometimes the look of being quite incandescent, now had a curious dilation about them behind his spectacles, as if they really were weak after all.

'I don't think I can manage Sunday,' he said at last. 'I've promised to drive over to Stanhurst to fetch Aunt Midge. She's been living all on her own there. She's scared of what might happen now and she's coming to live with us.'

It was a poor excuse, I thought, and I suddenly felt vexed and hurt. I couldn't for the life of me think why I should be hurt by Tom Hudson, for whom I felt nothing but ordinary neighbourly friendliness, and I tried not to show it in my face. But long afterwards Tom confessed :

'I know I hurt you that night when I said I couldn't come to your party. I could see it in your face. I wanted to come no end. But I felt it was like barging into a club when I wasn't a member.'

But all he said as we stood there at the end of the village street was :

'The cherries are very early this year. We've cleared a lot of trees already. I've known years when they'd hardly started by now.'

'There would have to be a war in a summer like this.'

'I know. That's another thing that gets people down.'

How long we might have continued this desultory conversation I don't know but suddenly I heard Chloe's musical roar and there she was, snarling up the street, with Splodge's squashy blue cap cocked to one side of his head behind the wheel. If you know anything about the arrival of heroes within the drab confines of ordinary mortals you will know how frantically I waved my hand.

Splodge pulled up Chloe with several explosive bangs and when the last of them had settled down to a mere rattle I heard Tom Hudson say :

'Good-bye, Elizabeth. I must go now.'

'Oh ! don't be silly, Tom. Of course you're not going.'

'I really must.'

'If you do I'll never speak to you again.'

After that peremptory threat he stayed and I introduced him to Splodge. Not the least of Splodge's constant and more endearing virtues was his infinite modesty but it almost seemed, that night, as if he might have been carrying some sort of blatant banner with him, so oddly embarrassed did Tom look. To say that he looked suddenly like a man carrying the burden of an enormous inferiority complex is too facile. The strange thing is that that look of acute embarrassment made him look positively aloof. I suppose he might have thought that Splodge, in uniform, wings up and all that, might have looked down on him. Whereas it was exactly the other way about. It was almost as if he was looking down on Splodge.

'Well, let's all three have a drink,' Splodge said, at last switching off Chloe and so creating an enormous silence.

71

'Thank you very much,' Tom said, 'but I really must go. I've got all the locking up to do.'

'Tom's a farmer,' I said. 'He's just taken a big basket of cherries to the house.'

'Wizard. I adore cherries. Nicest fruit of all.'

'I'll bring you some if you like,' Tom said. 'They're pretty good this year.'

'By jove, really? Wizard.'

'Where can I bring them?'

'Oh! to the Mess.'

'Oh! yes. Is one allowed in?'

'Allowed? It's our home, old boy.'

'All right. I'll be along tomorrow.'

It sounds like the most ordinary and simple of conversations but because of it I felt my latent affection for Tom Hudson stir very deeply inside myself, turn over and then go completely to sleep again, exactly like a warm kitten.

After that Splodge and I went into *The Pomfret Arms* for a drink. This is rather more of a hotel than a plain pub. Its lounge bar has red carpets and oak settles and its walls flash with brass, battle-axes and copper. It occasionally puts on luncheons for shooting parties and on Boxing Day the Hunt meets outside. It isn't quite the place where embittered army sergeants incite women to fervent protestation and I was both relieved and glad simply to be able to sit on one of the oak settles, by a window, and stare at the roses in the back garden and drink sherry.

But my relief didn't last long. I sensed — quite correctly, as it later turned out — that there was something on Splodge's mind that night, but what it was I couldn't tell and didn't probe to discover. Splodge in turn seemed to sense that I suspected this and we hadn't been sitting there more than three or four minutes before he said :

'How would you like a surprise?'

'Wizard. I always go for surprises.'

'I got you a little present.'

'But it isn't my birthday or anything.'

'It's just a little something.'

Then he put his hand in his tunic pocket. Things must have been in a rare state of boyish untidiness in there because out came a handkerchief, a cocktail stick, a box of matches, a small green leather box and, of all things, a rabbit's foot. I stared at this last object for some moments in infinite astonishment before Splodge, looking very like a small boy who has been caught smoking in bed or something of that sort, shoved it back into his tunic pocket again.

'A rabbit's foot,' I said. 'Is that the surprise?'

'Oh! no. Good Lord, no.'

'What have you got it for?'

'I sort of carry it about.'

'But why?'

'Oh! it's a sort of thing. You know.'

Tom Hudson's painfully acute embarrassment was a mere shadow of the torturous blank that I now saw on the face of Splodge and I didn't improve it by laughing briefly and saying:

'You're like a squirrel, hoarding things.'

'No,' he said. 'No. This is the present.'

He then put the little green box in my hand. If up to that moment I had always thought of him as heartbreakingly young I now experienced a passionately ridiculous moment when I wanted to take him in my arms and hold him against myself like a child.

'Do open it,' he said. 'Perhaps you won't like it. I don't know.'

I opened the box and inside was one of those old-fashioned Edwardian gold lockets on a thin gold chain. I remember thinking for a moment that it looked rather painfully provincial and then he said:

'Turn it over. Look on the back.'

'My initials. Did you have them put on?'

'They were already on. That's what made me buy it.'

I simply looked at him in silence. He stared back at me in painfully solemn and tender adoration, not speaking a word either. There is always a great pain about first love, especially in moments when there is no way of expressing it, and I felt my lips tremble and my throat tighten with an unbearable longing for him.

'Don't look at me like that,' he said at last. 'I can't bear it.'

'I can't bear it either.'

I gave a sort of half smile and bit my lips and he said :

'Do you like it?'

'The locket? Awfully.'

Then I could bear it no longer and looked quickly round the room and said in a half whisper :

'I want to kiss you very, very much but as I can hardly do it in the lounge of *The Pomfret Arms* will you please take me somewhere where I can?'

We drove up to the Devil's Spoon. We lay on the grass and looked up, during long silences, at the early stars. He kissed me over and over again and at last when he started to run his finger-tips over my breasts I did nothing to stop him. Finally he undid my dress and took out my breasts, one by one, and kissed them.

I wanted to cry with happiness. That was the first time I ever went to eternity. I was to go on a good many other occasions later but that night I went farther into the outer spaces of joy than I had ever been before or had remotely dreamed was possible.

We must have lain there till well past midnight and at last I said :

'You never really told me about your rabbit's foot.'

'No.'

'Tell me.'

'It's just one of those things.'

'Why do you carry it?'

'It's a sort of —'

'Do you carry it when you fly?'

'Yes.'

'A sort of good luck thing?'

'I suppose so.'

'A sort of talisman.'

'That's it.'

A moment later I came back from my eternity of joy to hear a voice hammering out in dead level tones inside me : 'You'll never kill him. You'll never, never kill him. He'll never die,' and so came, at last, to the naked revelation that from now on I too had to believe in the rabbit's foot.

7

So far was I lost in happiness that it wasn't until we were driving home that I remembered the party. Nor had I said a word about the dove-cot.

'Bring some good types,' I said.

'Don't know any. All bad.'

'Bring some really gay ones. I want it to be gay.'

'Let me think. Who could I bring?'

'Matters, of course. And the Count.'

'Don't think the Count could make it. He's gone on leave to find himself a Countess. Terrible, terrible type.'

'What's so terrible about finding himself a Countess?'

'He has three wives already.'

'Pull the other leg.'

'True. He married his way out of Poland and down through Roumania, then into Greece and over into Turkey and then here. Loved 'em and left 'em at every frontier.'

'Fickle man. Perhaps it's just as well he isn't coming.'

'I'll ask MacKenzie and Fitz, for two. Just for contrast.'

I asked who MacKenzie and Fitz were and he said MacKenzie was a Canadian from Winnipeg and Fitz was stinking rich. MacKenzie had a personal war on his hands – it was a case of him against Goering and the Fuehrer. Fitz on the other hand was a man of such delicate and fastidious constitution that he revolted at the mere thought of Mess food and had his lunch sent down by train from the Ritz every day.

'What about girls?' he said. 'Will you need some girls? Mac's got a nice red popsie at the moment. And I think Matters knows a few.'

'Not more than three,' I said. 'I can't have rivals.'

In this happy mood he drove me home, finally kissing me good night while I still sat in the car.

'I love you very, very much,' he said.

I said I loved him too. Then I went on to say that of course he'd heard of people being wildly in love or desperately in love or madly in love or hopelessly in love and all that sort of thing but that wasn't the way I was in love with him.

'What way are you in love with me?'

'Eternally.'

Perhaps it was an over-solemn thing to say but that was the way I felt about it. It was just the way it was.

The following Sunday evening they all drove up to the house in three cars, Chloe, Flight-Lieutenant John Cavendish Fitzroy's dark green Bugatti and a strange yellow and black Rolls Royce whose roof had been sliced off to convert it to an open car. There were six officers altogether and three girls: Splodge, Matters, MacKenzie, Fitz, an Irish boy named O'Connor who reminded me a little bit of Devlin and to my great surprise the Count, together with his Countess. The other two girls were a blonde, heavy-boned hearty named Babs and a sensational copper-haired beauty named Stephanie blessed with a glorious bust, clear green eyes and, as it subsequently turned out, hollow legs.

The Countess was young, dark-eyed, slender, electrifyingly full of nervous energy and altogether very striking. In my innocence I simply couldn't believe that the Count had married her but Splodge said:

'He solemnly assures us he has.'

A few moments later the Count was graciously kissing my hand with no sign of either tension or embarrassment and saying with elegant solemnity:

'My dear Miss Cartwright, I would dearly love to introduce you to my wife, Elaine.'

In the subsequent round of introductions it was John Cavendish Fitzroy who really struck me down. I had never seen anything quite like John Cavendish Fitzroy. If the Count was elegant, Fitz was a piece of impeccable theatrical band-box, all superior six foot something of him. I fully expected him to burst into operatic song. There was a sort of aloof rehearsed poise about him that made you think he was vain, soft, hopelessly spoilt and artificial. His fingers were long and white, the nails so scrupulously manicured that it wouldn't have surprised me at all to have found them tinted too. His hair, a light gold, looked almost as if ironed into place. His neckerchief, pure silk

76

and in a pattern of blue-and-white stripes, was more meticulously knotted than anything a woman could have done and when once he raised a hand to touch a single golden hair into place I caught a glimpse of the inner lining of his tunic sleeve. It was pure silk too and a bright rich scarlet.

I trembled, as I looked at him, at the mere thought of the food Rose had prepared for us. The man who had his lunch sent down by special envoy every day would surely never touch a crumb of our humble tit-bits.

Then, just as I had made up my mind that this impossible piece of male splendour was altogether too much for my mortal world, he did a charming thing. In a voice so unaffected, modest and engaging that I could hardly believe my ears he said :

'I hope you won't greatly mind, Miss Cartwright, but I brought along a small offering to the feast. Will you excuse me while I fetch it from the car?'

Before I could utter my barely audible and astonished word of thanks he was gone and Splodge was introducing me to MacKenzie.

'Joe MacKenzie. Mac to all and sundry.'

'Great to know you, Miss Cartwright. Heard all about you from Squire here.'

MacKenzie, it seemed, called all Englishmen Squire.

'*All* about me?'

'Well, all the best things. You know. Not exaggerated at that.'

I was engulfed in a prodigious smile. My ears were lapped in great muscular waves of laughter. MacKenzie's enormous barrel of a chest expanded with such power that I fully expected to see every tunic button shoot undone. His squashy cap, far more squashy than any other, was stuck far back on his head with a belligerence that was casual, impudent but somehow very muscular too.

I had just finished shaking hands with everyone – the Irish boy O'Connor was so shy that he faded himself out of the picture and had to be dragged in again by Matters, who said 'Paddy, old boy, girls don't bite. I've told you before' – when John Cavendish Fitzroy came back from the Bugatti, carrying half a dozen bottles of champagne, three under each elegant arm.

'Champers!' somebody said. 'Damn good show. Fitz is at it again.'

'Very Ritzy, Squire,' MacKenzie said. 'Very Ritzy, old sport.'

'I do hope you won't mind my doing this, Miss Cartwright.'

'You really shouldn't have –'

'It's a great pleasure and I only hope it will be to your liking.'

After that I led the way up the outside wooden flight of steps to my room at the top of the dove-cot. I was really very proud of my room and they were all loud in their praises of it. I had kept the furnishings as simple as I could in order not to choke it and almost all I had in it were a narrow divan bed, a mahogany corner wash-stand with a pink jug and basin, an easy chair, a few books and a table with my hair brush and powder and face cream and such things on it, together with a pair of silver candlesticks.

All this the men thought was absolutely wizard. Terrific, they said, to have a room of one's own.

'And such enchanting curtains,' the Count said. I still couldn't get over the Count's marital infidelities, just as I couldn't get over a man like John Cavendish Fitzroy belonging to a fighter squadron. It just didn't seem right. 'What flowers are in the pattern?'

'Fritillaries,' I said.

'Quite delightful.'

At this point John Cavendish Fitzroy – I simply couldn't get round to calling him Fitz until some long time later – asked if he might open the champagne. I thanked him and said yes, but if he would excuse me I would go and fetch two or three more glasses.

I had been far too shy to kiss Splodge on his arrival but now the excuse about the glasses took me downstairs and I was over-joyed when he followed me. It had been one of those warm, unblemished days that were so typical of that summer and there was a deep scent of syringa in the air.

After he had kissed me and held me for a few moments I said :

'You won't go when all the rest go, will you?'

'No.'

'Stay with me a long time.'

By the time I got back upstairs again everybody except Splodge and John Cavendish Fitzroy and myself had full glasses in their hands. When ours too were full I raised my glass and said:

'Well, cheers and welcome, everybody, to the dove-cot.'

'Cheers. Good show. Jolly good show. Thank you for asking us, Miss Cartwright.'

'And that's another thing. Not Miss Cartwright, please, all of you. Liz is the name.'

They all laughed. It was all very jolly. It was going to be, I decided, a splendid little party. Very, very gay. Then suddenly I remembered that no one had ever called me Liz until Bill Ogilvy had done so and in the very same moment I recalled his longing for champagne.

'What lovely champagne,' I said. 'Bill Ogilvy would have liked this. By the way, where is old Bill? Any news?'

For a few moments there was dead silence. It didn't seem, I thought, quite one of those accidental silences that sometimes fall on a company of people when suddenly, for some reason, no one has anything to say. It seemed to me rather a shocked silence and it was Mac who broke in by saying:

'Last news we had was he'd been promoted. Air-Commode or something.' He turned to Matters. 'That right, Squire?'

'Something like that. Too elevated for types like us anyway.'

I saw Splodge give me a quick glance with those unbearably young eyes of his and look as quickly away again. An interminable time seemed to go past before anyone said another word and then the girl named Stephanie said:

'What delicious-looking eats. Somebody must have been standing over a hot stove all day.'

'Oh! I'm so sorry,' I said and hastily picked up a plate of salmon and cucumber sandwiches. 'Do please help yourselves.'

After that the tension relaxed a bit. And I needn't really have worried about the food. Rose had done her splendid best. It was absolutely wizard, the men said. Among other things Rose had managed to get hold of fresh prawns, anchovies and smoked eel and had made a special cream cheese of her own. She had also made two kinds of tartlets, both served cold, one filled with onions and tiny strips of ham, the other with white-currant jelly.

Even John Cavendish Fitzroy, the *gourmet-connoisseur*, was greatly impressed by the white-currant jelly.

'Only once in my life have I ever come across it before. And that was in France, at Chatillon, in the Loire Valley. It takes me right back there. Delectable. Absolutely delectable.'

'I'm sure Rose would find you a pot if you'd care to have one.'

'Care? I'd bless her heart till my dying day.'

Another odd little shadow went across my mind as he said this but it was gone in a moment and I forgot it completely as he said :

'Do give my warmest compliments to Rose. Tell her how divine her cooking is.'

'She'll cry if I tell her that.'

'Tell her just the same.'

Through such trivialities the evening gradually unfolded into merriment. The champagne – I forgot to say that John Cavendish Fitzroy had seen to it, in his fastidious way, that it was well chilled – made us all laugh a great deal and now and then I actually felt it rippling about in sudden cool rising scales inside me.

During the eating and drinking some of us sat on the bed, some on the floor. The Count opened one of the casement windows and sat on the sill, one leg outside and one in, that angular profile of his looking fine and very pronounced, almost god-like, in the setting sun. And perhaps it was the brilliance and angle of the setting sun that continually brought home to me how impossibly young they all looked and that the Count wasn't the only one who looked god-like either. Fresh, gay young gods – that was how I saw them, and not merely from the pleasure of being with them, sharing their company, but every now and then with that slight twinge of shadow.

Presently twilight came on and I longed to light the candles, but when I asked if I could borrow some matches someone, I think Matters, begged me to wait a little longer. 'Sure thing,' Mac said. He had the red-haired Stephanie in gargantuan embrace on the bed, both hands across her splendid thighs.

But soon it was too dark to see and I borrowed matches from Splodge and lit the candles. 'Bad show, bad show,' Mac said, 'cramps a guy's style,' and rose from the pleasantries of the bed with a long stretch followed by a frog-like leap that took him stumbling off the end of the divan. 'Christ, overshot,' he said. We all laughed at that and then he got up to draw the curtains.

There were only two windows in the room and as he drew the curtains over the second one he turned and took a long drawling sort of look at the divan.

'Well, hell's bloody bells and kiss my sweet fanny.'

The Count, undeterred by the presence of the Countess, who anyway was sitting in my one armchair on Matters' knee, had taken over Mac's position on the divan, side by side with the red-haired Stephanie, the nape of whose voluptuous neck he was gently caressing with his lips.

'You stinking chiseller. Da-da-da-da! Shoot the bastard down!' Mac said and all of a sudden was in a wild career about the room, in imitation of some crazy dog-fight, in his own personal war. 'Bandits at Angels Thirteen! Press the bloody tit! Da-da-da-da-da! Where is the bastard? Christ, missed him. Hell, where am I? Split-arse turn – watch your bloody mirror! Up! – down now, down four hundred on the clock. How are you, Squire? Watch out, the sods are coming out of the sun. Press the bloody tit – da-da-da-da-da! Brmmmm! Pull out now, pull out, Christ, pull out. You'll be in bloody trouble – watch the rev-counter – one more go – one more burst – press the tit – da-da-da-da-da – got the bastard – in the pissing drink! – piece o' cake! – whack-o!'

We lay about the room in various attitudes of convulsion. The hearty blonde, who was slightly tipsy by now, tried heavy evasive action in face of a swift MacKenzie turn and ended up on her back, legs and short skirts in air, inches of black panties and pale thighs revealed. The young Irish boy sobbed quietly in a corner. With an air of splendid disdain, now more god-like than all the rest, John Cavendish Fitzroy watched as from afar off, smoking a large cigar, leaning against the door. The object of the attack, the Count, continued unperturbed his exploration of the heavenly body on the bed and she, as if she had never known the presence of any other man, responded with the sublimest concentration.

'Hell, thirsty work, Squire. Any more champagne? Christ, don't say that's the last drop. Squeeze it, boy, squeeze it. Press the tit.'

It was in fact the last of the champagne and I was just about to announce that if anyone cared to have another drink there was gin and plenty of tonics and lime-juice when I heard John Cavendish Fitzroy say :

'Luckily I had the presence of mind to bring a little brandy. Not gin after *that* champagne, Elizabeth dear. Please. It would be like following your darling Rose's celestial jelly with fish-and-chips. Could we find fresh glasses?'

'I'll have gin,' said a voluptuous voice from the bed. 'It always makes me amorous.'

For another hour or more we sat about, drinking John Cavendish Fitzroy's beautiful brandy in the thin light of the two candles. About half way through this Mac sat cross-legged on the floor and played a few tunes on a harmonica and some of us got up and did slow shuffling dances about the floor. I danced first with Splodge, then with Matters and was about to take a turn with the Irish boy when a blonde body cut in and bore him away in savage embrace, clutching him so hungrily to herself that he simply went in silent surrender.

'Leave the man alone, can't you?' a voice said, with such frozen asperity that for a moment I didn't grasp that it was John Cavendish Fitzroy speaking.

My head whoozed a little as I looked round at the party. I had so much wanted it to be gay and now it was gay – beautifully, foolishly, marvellously, divinely gay. If the men were all young gods I felt a little goddess-like myself, my head up in the stars again, my feet dancing. And once as I danced with Matters he said :

'Liz, you look stunning. Blooming stunning. Come out and dance on the lawn.'

'Thank you, kind sir,' I said, 'but it's not on. My feet may be with you but my heart is with Splodge.'

'Bad show,' he said. 'Bad show.'

When the last of the brandy was all gone we started to disperse in varying degrees of noisy unsteadiness, the only exception being the voluptuous, hollow-legged Stephanie, who had been steadily at the gin for the past hour but who still looked as splendidly composed as if she had done nothing but sleep all that time in sober infant-like peace on the bed.

In the final moments of departure the Count kissed everybody all round, the girls on the hand and then on the lips, then the men on both cheeks. With imperturbable gravity he afforded me the special honour of kissing me not merely on hand and lips but on my cheeks and forehead too. He called me 'dearest, divinest, darling Liz,' declared there was no other like me and that he would be my fond and shackled slave for ever and ever and then departed into the night on the possessive arm of the Countess, who if anything looked more imperturbable than even he did.

At last Splodge and I were alone in my room. The candles were burning down and now and then I saw four of them instead of two. Presently I sat on the edge of the bed and shook my head to and fro and Splodge said:

'All right?'

'Just a wee bit whoozy.'

'Marvellous party.'

'Marvellous.'

Then I found myself groping confusedly back towards the beginning of the party and suddenly remembered the curious awkward silence I had caused.

'Splodge, be a sweet and tell me. Did I put up a black tonight? I mean about Bill?'

'No.'

'What is it about Bill?'

He didn't answer.

'Has he been killed or something?'

It was pretty silly, I suppose, to add 'or something' but anyway it was a long time before he said any more.

'Tell me if he's been killed.'

'The fact is we don't know.'

I asked how it was they didn't know and he said:

'They lost about two-thirds of the squadron in France. They're re-grouping somewhere over here now but a buddy of

83

Bill's, type named Maxie Spooner, dropped in on us the other day. He saw Bill's kite shot up somewhere over Arras. Looked in dead trouble. Maxie got a lump of tracer in his leg next day and went off to hospital without hearing more news.'

'Does that mean –'

'Couldn't tell where he might land, or even if he did. Panzers were coming up all over the place and there was no real line any more. Everything pretty much of a shambles. Could be a prisoner.'

'You think there's a chance?'

'There's always a chance. I told you before. You can't kill types like Bill.'

I knew you could, but all I said was :

'Let's keep our fingers crossed. Let's hope he was carrying his rabbit's foot.'

'He always carried two.'

'That settles it. He'll come back one day.'

On that self-deceiving note I kissed him good night, then showed him out into the garden and there kissed him again.

'Good night, my precious. Take care of yourself.'

'You bet.'

Finally I was alone in the garden. The gay evening of the young gods was over. The scent of syringa was overpoweringly beautiful and so were the stars. And as I stood looking up at them I listened to the last of Chloe's explosive echoes dying away down the road and it was only when the last of them had gone completely that I started to cry.

8

July came in hot and with great beauty. The rambler roses were rich deep crimson with fire. The big-leaved magnolia on the walls of the dove-cot began to show, much earlier than usual, its pointed buds of cream. Every day baskets of fruit came in from the gardens of the big house, strawberries, black, red and white currants, gooseberries and raspberries, and every evening Edna and Rose were in the kitchen, with me helping them, sometimes until midnight, topping and tailing gooseberries, plugging strawberries and making innumerable pots of jam and jelly, including the white-currant one, which in fact turns out in the making to be a pale pink shade.

'We must be sure to save a very special pot for Mr Fitzroy,' I said and Rose glowed with joy that was almost patriotic.

Some time before this, on June 24 to be precise, I had begun to keep a diary. This was directly at the suggestion of my grandmother, who after the fashion of her generation had kept a diary, written in a minute and impeccable hand, ever since her marriage.

'You really should keep a diary. You'll find it of fascinating interest later on in life.'

'Oh! diaries are a bore. Some days there's nothing to say, some days there's too much. In any case you never stay the course.'

'That's merely a matter of discipline.'

'Oh! I'd get bored stiff with it after three days.'

'Moreover we're living in very dramatic times. It seems a great pity not to record what is going on.'

'Dramatic? Going on? Don't make me laugh. What's going on? Entry No. 1, June something or other: *Rose, Edna and I made twenty-one pots of raspberry jam, bottled twelve jars of gooseberries and six pots of red-currant jelly.* Entry No. 2, next day: *Rose, Edna and I bottled twelve jars of raspberries and so on and so forth —*'

'Take my word for it. The war hasn't started yet.'

'To hear Harry talk you might think it was already over.'

Harry, having recovered a first strong flush of zeal, rather like an attack of measles, that had sent him worming enthusiastically on his belly through woods, fields and churchyards, had now entered, like a great many of his countrymen, a strange mood of complacency. Rather like a man who, having been under a dire threat of burglary, suddenly increases his insurance and changes all the locks on his house and is convinced that these emergencies will make him for ever immune, Harry seemed to think that the setting up of pill boxes and road blocks, evacuating sea-side donkeys from beaches and replacing them with mines, sacking Mr Neville Chamberlain and removing all road signs, were measures strong enough in themselves to keep us all safe in our beds for the rest of time.

He found considerable solace also in history, fondly believing that it did in fact repeat itself, and would from time to time remind us over his breakfast eggs how Drake had dealt with the Spaniards or Admiral Hawke with the Froggy fleet at Quiberon or Nelson with the Frogs yet again at Trafalgar. When my grandmother reminded him with gentle acidity of what the Romans and William the Conqueror had done to us and that both had actually camped on the hills not more than three or four miles away, he would say something like :

'Different set of circumstances entirely. No parallel at all,' as if that too solved the problem.

He even became, about this time, rather testy about Churchill, 'The feller tells us to brace ourselves. Well, we brace. And then what? Not a damn thing happens. I tell you, one gets browned off.'

'One of these fine days,' my grandmother would say with that good sense which was so characteristic of her, 'we're going to get the shock of our lives,' and once again would go on to urge me to keep my diary.

So at last, on Midsummer Day, I started the diary, with not the remotest intention of keeping it up. I entered, at first, a mass of trivia : the jams and jellies, the arrival of the first peaches from the glass-houses, the birth of a litter to the Belgian hares. I was excited because a pair of housemartins had started to nest above one of the windows in the dove-cot and I put that in. The hens were not laying quite so many eggs now and I put that in too. There was a bad accident in the village street in which a butcher's cart was in collision with an army truck and a boy was killed and I duly recorded that. I made a record of several trout, with their respective weights, that Harry caught, and even of how Rose cooked them.

One evening after tea I was making a few desultory entries in my little book, which I was holding on my raised knees as I sat in the window seat of the sitting-room, when my grandmother said :

'I'm glad to see you're persevering with your diary. I'm sure you won't regret it. May I read what you've written? Or is it all very, very secret?'

'There isn't a secret word in it. Of course you may read.'

I gave her the diary and for a few minutes she sat reading it in silence. She had a habit of lightly wetting her thumb as she turned over the pages of a book or magazine and it always gave her a rather thoughtful air. She did it automatically as she turned the pages of the diary and it seemed to make her, I thought, more thoughtful still.

Finally she handed the diary back to me and said :

'I'm surprised.'

'Surprised? Why surprised?'

'You have all those interesting friends – the young men in the Air Force I mean – and yet there isn't a single word about them. I should have thought you'd have been thrilled to record all the things they tell you.'

'They don't.'

'Don't tell you?'

'It isn't done. It's called a line-shoot.'

'I'm astonished. I thought fighting men loved to talk about their actions.'

'Only when they're old.'

'Oh? How do you know about that?'

'I don't. I just said it.'

'What did Shakespeare say?' she said. ' "Old men forget." '

'I think young men forget too. I think perhaps they want to forget. It may be the reason they don't want to talk.'

'How strange.'

A few days earlier she had felt it her duty to invite the Group Captain and half a dozen other officers for a glass of sherry before lunch on Sunday. It was a very formal, pleasantly correct party at which nothing really amusing or exceptional had happened and at which there were just occasional bursts of obedient laughter when the Commanding Officer made such remarks as 'We're trying not to break too many chandeliers in the house, Mrs Cartwright.' The officers were mostly Ad-Min types and of the seven I had met only the Group Captain and the Adjutant before.

Something now reminded her of this and she suddenly said :

'By the way I missed that pleasant young man with those very large moustaches last Sunday. Has he gone away?'

'He was shot down.'

'Oh! my dear. You didn't tell me.'

No : I hadn't told her.

'Was he killed?'

'We don't know. I think so.'

'Why didn't you tell me?'

'I think for the same reason as I said a few moments ago. I suppose I wanted to forget.'

'I see.'

'I suppose it's sort of catching. They don't want to talk and in the end you don't want to talk either.'

She didn't say anything more for a few moments and finally I got up and said :

'I think I'll go for a walk now.'

'Do. And don't forget your diary. And if anything really tremendously exciting happens you will put it in, won't you?'

'I will.'

And with that brief promise I went for my walk, totally unprepared for the fact that two days later the most tremendously exciting event of my life was in fact about to happen.

I rarely, if ever, saw Splodge before ten o'clock at night. His daylight hours were not for me. By that time the pubs were closed but sometimes I got Rose to make me sandwiches and then called in at *The Olive Branch* on my way up to the hills, just before closing time, to buy two bottles of beer, and then wait for Splodge at the Devil's Spoon, in the last half hour of daylight. I once heard a flying man say that the most exciting sound he knew was when the prop first turns and the engine roars, but for me, that hot midsummer, the most exciting sound in the world was the sound of Chloe snarling up the hill. One minute I would be sitting there lost, almost drowned, in the deep tranquillity of the hillside, where wild yellow rock-roses were dropping their petals everywhere about the chalk after the scorching day and the scent of wild marjoram was thick on the air where you crushed it, and the next I would be utterly lost, completely drowned, in Splodge's arms. Some of those long hot summer days seemed infinite and I felt like a child who thinks a long awaited party can never possibly begin.

The entry in my diary for that day is a long one and it begins like this : 'Splodge, lying flat on his back on the grass and staring up at the sky, suddenly asked me in a most off-hand way if I knew what day it was. I said I thought it was July 4th and wasn't it an anniversary or something? And he just said "Yes, Independence Day".'

He was quite quiet for about a minute after this until at last I said : 'What was all that about Independence Day? You mean America? It isn't an important day for us, is it?' and he simply said :

'I hope it will be.'

For the life of me I couldn't think what all this riddle-making was about and then he said another odd thing :

'Do you value your independence?'

'Of course.'

'Very much?'

'Of course.'

'Terrifically?'

'What *is* all this about?'

'Would you give it up?'

'Of course I wouldn't. That's what the war's about, isn't it?'

'I'm not talking about the war.'

'Then what *are* you talking about?'

'Independence.'

'And whether I'd give it up,' I said rather sharply – I don't

really care for riddles very much and I was getting slightly vexed
– 'Well, the answer's Yes, underlined.'

'Disappointing.'

Then I felt really vexed and said, quite acidly, so that I could
almost hear the echo of my grandmother's voice in my own :

'I do wish you'd stop fooling and teasing. One thing I cannot
bear is teasing. I hate it. Now please.'

'Sorry.'

For the next minute or so I turned away and tried to simmer
down a bit; then I turned my head and saw him grinning. That
made me really annoyed and I was just beginning to think that
this was the asinine way in which quarrels between lovers have
their stupid way of starting when he said :

'This is a mad war, isn't it?'

'I suppose all wars are mad.'

'But this is madder than most, wouldn't you say?'

'What does it matter?'

'People do mad things in war time, don't they?'

'Of course. They're fools enough to take part in them for one
thing.'

'Kiss me.'

'I will not kiss you. I don't like you. I may even give up
loving you.'

'Permanently?'

'Permanently.'

'Which,' he said, 'would be a pity.'

'And, if I may ask, why?'

He then turned and gave me a long, lazy smile.

'Because,' he said, 'I was going to be mad enough to ask you
if you'd marry me.'

I simply couldn't speak. I just covered my face with my hands.
How long I kept them there I haven't the slightest idea but
when I took them away at last and looked at him he was still
smiling at me very gently.

'It isn't a joke?'

'God, no.'

There was no need to say any more. He simply took me in
his arms and we lay together on the grass in absolute silence,
for a long time. When I came back at last some part of the way

to reality it was still light enough to see his face. For some reason he didn't look quite so unbearably young as he nearly always did. In fact he had become, as he sometimes did, quite solemn.

'Of course I should have to ask Groupie and he might say No. And your grandmother. Oh! good God,' he suddenly said. 'What am I saying? You haven't said Yes anyway.'

Up to that moment my heart had been too full for me to say a word. Now I just laughed and called him my precious and kissed him quickly several times and told him that was my answer.

'You're sure you don't want to think it over?'

'I'm no thinker. I never have been.'

'There's an awful lot of snags.'

'I suppose you snore or something.'

'But seriously, do you think it's mad?'

'Utterly. Absolutely. Barmy. It's the barmiest thing I ever heard of.'

Suddenly I thought that if the conversation went on in this way much longer I should simply end up in tears and I said :

'Tell me, then, about the snags.'

'There wouldn't be a long engagement.'

'No.'

'There wouldn't be any honeymoon.'

'No.'

'I might get twenty-four hours leave. Not more.'

'No.'

'And even after that I wouldn't see you very much.'

'No.'

'I don't make it sound very exciting, do I?'

'Exciting? Oh! God, it's the most exciting thing that's ever happened to me.'

After that we both laughed – I won't say uncontrollably but there was a near-hysterical touch in both of us. We kissed each other madly several times and some little time later he took down the top of my dress and ran his lips across my breasts. It was dark now and in the centre of this wild vortex I once again had the miraculously shining idea that we were both immortal. We were together for all eternity.

'I'll ask Groupie tomorrow,' he finally said. 'And your grandmother too if I can get away.'

After breakfast next morning I wanted to get these stupendous events into my diary as soon as possible and I had just started to write them down in the dove-cot when suddenly I changed my mind and decided to go over to the house instead.

My grandmother was already writing her own diary in the sitting-room. I was aware of a strong tension of inner quietness within myself that morning and I sat writing for more than half an hour without saying a word. I think she herself had been finished writing for some time when I at last looked up and saw her gazing at me with acute and rather amused attention.

'A very long screed this morning. A wholesale order for jam?'

'Read it if you like. I promised I'd put down anything of great importance.'

I gave her the diary and she took it and started to read. For a few minutes I sat nervously watching her face and then all of a sudden I was frightened to watch it any longer. I was mortally afraid she would be shocked or outraged or terribly angry. Any one of these things would have crushed me.

Finally she stopped reading and looked across at me very steadfastly. Her astonishingly bright eyes were always piercing but very rarely tender. But that morning, to my infinite astonishment, they were tender : so much so that I was the one to be shocked.

'I suppose you realize it's like being married on top of a volcano?'

'I hadn't thought of it like that.'

Perhaps my nerves or my shock showed in my face, but anyway she suddenly smiled.

'Don't worry. I'm not going to preach at you.'

'Tell me if you disapprove.'

'I don't think it's my place to approve or disapprove.'

Still nervous, I felt I had to keep to realities and said :

'In any case he has to ask his Commanding Officer's permission first. If he gets that he'll come to see you.'

'Why me ? Your mother's the one to see.'

I had utterly forgotten my mother; and now the dithering absent figure came back to shock me yet again.

'Good God,' I said, 'that's torn it.'

She was infinitely amused at that and broke into a big broad smile.

'Would you like me to cope?' she said.

At that I rushed across the room with such half blind energy that I struck my hip against a chair and actually fell into her arms, weeping copiously.

'Splendid,' was all she said. 'Splendid. I wondered when you would.'

Later that morning she had the good sense to send me out for a walk, pretending she needed stamps and a registered envelope from the post office. It was one of those splendidly soft warm mornings that were so typical of that summer and I was wearing my thinnest summer dress. The very slightest variable wind was blowing and now and then a sudden turn of it found its way into the top of my dress, warm on my skin, and I instantly went back to that ecstatic vortex of the night before, when Splodge lay kissing my breasts in the summer darkness and I knew that my conviction that we were both immortal could never, never be shaken. So far, indeed, nothing had shaken it. I was just aware of the loveliness of the summer morning but oblivious of almost everything else. Even a sharp and rather prolonged rattle of machine-gun fire from somewhere down towards the sea did nothing to wake me.

I had just bought the stamps and the registered envelope and was half way down the village street when something happened that did, at last, jolt me out of this fond daylight dream. It was John Cavendish Fitzroy's green Bugatti, standing outside *The Pomfret Arms*. I had never seen it there before.

I stood there for fully a minute looking at it and looking for a sign of Fitz in the street. It was now about half past twelve and finally I decided to look into the lounge of the hotel on the chance that Fitz and some of the boys and perhaps even Splodge might be there.

When I went into the lounge it was to find Fitz sitting at the bar, all alone, drinking whisky.

'Elizabeth.'

It was the brevity of his greeting as much as the tense, be-mused look on his face that set me wondering.

'Strange to find you here at this hour,' I said.

'My lunch hour. Didn't want any.'

His voice was brittle; he kept clipping an elegant finger nail against the side of his glass.

'All that lovely food from the Ritz.'

'I've stopped that caper.'

'Really? Why?'

'Bloody silly. Childish.'

This was so unlike the John Cavendish Fitzroy of old that my abrupt conclusion was that he was drunk. In fact he was far from drunk — unless a man can be drunk from excess of feeling, as I later discovered a woman can — and all of a sudden a glimpse of the old Fitzroy came back.

'Elizabeth, I'm most terribly, terribly sorry. I didn't ask you what you'd like. Please, what would you?'

I hesitated, not knowing quite what I wanted, and suddenly he said:

'I tell you what's nice on a warm day. Dry sherry and water and a piece of ice. Would you like that?'

I thanked him and said I would and while the bar-maid was pouring the drink I added that Rose had brought her talents to bear on the new crop of white currants and that she had the most fancy jar of jelly in special reserve for him.

To my infinite surprise he took not the slightest notice of this remark but merely ordered himself another whisky.

Then, when I was less than half way through my sherry, he suddenly struck the bar a sharp blow with the flat of his hand and said 'Blast! Sorry. I ought to get back' and was half way to the door, in his own abrupt oblivious rush, before he just as abruptly changed his mind and came back and sat down and said:

'No good. No, I won't. Sorry.'

This, it suddenly occurred to my untrammelled innocence, was the way men are supposed to behave when crossed in love and before I could think twice about it I said with fatuous stupidity:

'Fitz, you're all on edge. She hasn't jilted you, has she?'

He didn't answer. The joke, poor as it was, passed him by as completely as the remark about Rose and the jelly. Then he started rapidly clipping his finger nail against the glass again, in an acute attack of jitters, and suddenly went off at a complete tangent and said, with some violence :

'I've got this war all wrong. All wrong.'

What this was all about I could only wonder and I had no time to ask before he blurted out :

'Types like Mac have got it sewn up. They're the ones who've got it sorted out. Bing – bang – kill 'em. Blast 'em clean to Hell. No bloody aesthetic cock about them.'

Earlier on I had longed, at intervals, to tell him something of the miracle that had happened to me. I hadn't told a soul except my grandmother and I longed again, as I had done once before, to share the secret with someone of my own generation. But it was no good now and I simply sat listening, in alternate phases of mystification and amazement, while he blurted out fresh disjointed barks of savagery. One of the things that mystified me most was the quite uncharacteristic tone of his voice. It was dark, tortured and at times almost lacerated.

At last he said : 'We had a bad show yesterday. Lost a sergeant and young –'

He stopped. I'd long since learned, or at least partly learned, my lesson about asking questions, and I wasn't asking any now. There would have been no need anyway because suddenly the entire tone of his voice changed, dropping into a key not only low and quiet but completely neutral in the most dead and disturbing way.

'You remember young O'Connor ?'

'He was at the party. Yes.'

'He was a very new kid. Hadn't been with the squadron long. He went down.'

There was more than grief in his voice. The lacerated nature of its tone had completely disappeared, leaving it heart-breakingly empty. It was partly his fault, he suddenly said. Spotted him too late, going out on a dice towards France. Didn't think he used his mirror either. Minced him up in no time.

'Jesus,' he said vehemently. 'Jesus.'

Later I talked to Mac about losing friends and he said : 'It's

95

impersonal. No time to think about it. Another name crossed off the slate, that's all.'

But then Mac wasn't in love – girls for him had only one purpose, just as a Spitfire's guns had only one purpose – as I was in love with Splodge and as Fitz had been in love, as it became borne upon my innocence of mind very slowly, with O'Connor. Perhaps the fusion of male hearts is altogether a too complex one for women to understand and the rift that parts them a still greater torment. I don't know. But I inwardly wept for Fitz, in spite of all my own tormenting happiness, that day.

Strangely, as we parted, he seemed suddenly to feel rather better about things, perhaps because he'd been able to talk to me, and at the very last he said :

'Bless you Elizabeth. Splendid to see you. I think you must have thought me a bloody awful cad sometimes.'

'My love to Splodge,' was all I said.

'Great type, Splodge.'

I walked slowly home in the brilliant midday sunshine to find my grandmother drinking a peaceful glass of sherry under a plum tree in the garden and to hear this pastoral heaven broken, five minutes later, by the triumphal brass of Harry's voice, excitedly announcing :

'They got a Hun over the Heath this morning. Lines got the news in the pub. Great big fat fellow. Parachute didn't open. Made a six-foot hole in the ground, they say.'

He actually laughed uproariously but I, faced with the joyful news of the first of our enemies to fall on our village soil, had no word to say.

But my grandmother had.

'From now on, of course,' she said, typically but to my absolute astonishment, 'it's all going to be a piece of cake.'

There were two other incidents I recorded in my diary for that day. Trivial though they may have seemed at the time they have both endeared themselves to me in memory.

In the afternoon I was again overcome by the strong feeling that I wanted to talk to someone of my own generation. I felt I must tell Tom Hudson my news. I hadn't seen Tom since his refusal to join us for a drink at *The Pomfret Arms* and in all the excitements that surrounded me he seemed as remote as the Pole. So that afternoon, about four o'clock, I started to walk up to the farm by way of the river, the strip of woodland that bordered it and the meadows beyond. In one or two fields the wheat already had on it that lovely blue-green bloom that graces it in the weeks before ripening and in the woods the Spanish chestnuts were laden with long blossoming tassels of cream, the odour of them strong on the air. A kingfisher swooped low up the river like a blue and copper scimitar and once I saw a snake swimming across it, darting head just above water.

The Hudsons' big cherry orchard was already completely bare of fruit but beyond it a smaller orchard of plums was laden to the tip of every branch, the plums touched with the first flush of purple. In neither the orchards nor the meadows was there any sign of Tom but in a paddock beyond the orchard of plums I caught sight of his father looking at a foal and its mare. The long slender legs of the foal were sheer gold in the afternoon sun and it ran nervously away when it caught sight of my white frock at the gate.

'Tom's at market,' Mr Hudson said. 'Won't be back till five or after.' He was a big gentle man, one of three brothers who farmed all down the valley, and his hair and moustache were a pleasant mixture of salt and bronze. A less vindictive man it would have been hard to find but his very next words to me were :

'Expect you heard about the Jerry this morning. Just coming out to start milking when I heard this half-tidy rattle up there. So I looked up and there he was, this Jerry, fairly belting down.'

'How did you know it was a Jerry?'

'Saw the plane. Saw the crosses on the wings. I cheered my head off when that bounder came down, I tell you. I cheered my head off. You never saw it then?'

'No, I didn't see it.'

'Dawn patrol I expect,' he said. 'Might have been one of your friends got him, very likely?'

I said I didn't know about that. For some reason I badly wanted to change the subject and suddenly said something about the cherries all being finished so early but what a crop the plums were carrying and how wonderful they looked.

'Never get 'em picked. Short-handed now. Two of my young
chaps got their papers last week. That only leaves Tom and
me and old Fred and Amos. We'll never get 'em picked.'

After that I said I ought to be walking back and he said 'Any
message for Tom? He'll be sorry to have missed you.' I said
there was no message and he said:

'If you know anybody who likes a bit of plum-and-apple
they're welcome to come and help themselves about a couple of
weeks from now. I daresay Tom's mother'll bottle a few but
otherwise they'll probably rot on the tree.'

Plums and a fallen enemy: neither seemed, at that moment
of any great importance to me. I was sorry to have missed
Tom but that no longer mattered very much either. As I walked
back I hadn't a thought for anything or anybody except
Splodge and how, that evening, he would come and see my
grandmother.

He duly came, about ten o'clock, looking restrained, rather
fatigued and by no means as impossibly young as he so often
did. When he was tired it was the eyes that went old. A greyness
enamelled the blue and the focusing wasn't quite right somehow either. On these occasions the mouth might smile but the
mouth and the eyes never smiled together.

I suppose we sat for about twenty minutes talking in a polite
and not very serious fashion about this and that when my
grandmother, partly I think with the direct intention of getting
Harry out of the room for a few minutes, said:

'I think we might have a glass of champagne, Harry. Will
you go and get it? The Bollinger '29 if you can lay your hands
on it. And get Edna to ice it well, please.'

After Harry had gone out of the room my grandmother sat
for fully a minute, in complete silence, looking at Splodge. She
was always the shrewdest judge of character and I prayed that
the brevity of the meeting with him would have been enough
to crystallize her judgement. I needn't have worried, because
presently she said:

'Naturally it's not my place to give permission for Elizabeth
to marry, but I have talked with her mother.'

'Yes? Thank you.'

'And in spite of the fact that her mind isn't the easiest of minds to make up,' she said in her characteristic fashion, 'she has made it up and says Yes.'

At this point Splodge got to his feet and uttered what were perhaps the most touching words I ever heard him say.

'I should like to thank you both from the bottom of my heart.'

If my tears were very near once more it was again from sheer happiness and I was glad when Harry came back, carrying a bottle of champagne in its silver ice-bucket and followed by Edna with a tray of glasses.

'Well, that was a damn good show one of your fellers put up this morning. Sorry to have missed that. Quite a sight, they tell me.'

Splodge said he wasn't sure it had been one of their fellows but anyway they all counted.

'Oh! too bad. Rather hoped it might have been you. Get a bag today?'

'Not today.'

'Big show hasn't really started yet of course?'

'Not exactly.'

'Think we'll be invaded?'

'Odds on, I'd say.'

By now Harry had finished pouring out the first glasses of champagne. When she raised hers my grandmother simply held it up and looked first at me and then at Splodge and said:

'Bless you both. My fondest wishes for the best of everything.'

At this we all drank and then Splodge came over to kiss me, only to find himself gazing a moment later at my grandmother, on whose face there was a look I never recalled seeing there before: petulance.

'Is the Air Force always so restrained?'

Thus commanded, Splodge went over and kissed her too and she in turn shook him by the hand, her dark eyes brilliantly glowing.

The evening might well have ended on this memorable note but my cup of happiness still wasn't, as it happened, quite full. When I finally walked to the end of the garden, just before midnight, to say good-bye to Splodge I at once looked up, out of sheer habit, at the stars. Splodge looked up too and said:

'You'd better offer up a few prayers for next Friday.' Friday was the day we were going to be married.

'What for?'

'A good thick cloud base. Then all the chaps can come to the wedding.'

I laughed and said: 'You haven't told me who's going to be best man yet.'

'We'll have to take pot-luck on that. Just depends who's available.'

Then I looked up at the stars again and said, after a silence:

'So it wasn't you today?'

'No. My kite's U.S. The fitters have been working on it all day.'

'I'm glad.'

'Why?'

'I didn't want you to kill anybody today – not this particular day.'

He didn't say anything to this but I, with my never quite dormant curiosity, then said:

'I know you don't like talking about it but I've often wanted to ask you. What do you see up there?'

'See?'

'I mean the earth down below and so on. What do you see?'

'Oh! a sort of pattern. Lop-sided. Funny. You're going so hellish fast and sometimes a hell of a way up,' he said and then added the most astonishing thing:

'Of course I see you.'

'Me?'

'Always. All the time.'

'But how? Why me?'

'Oh! you're always there. You're my other rabbit's foot.'

And who could possibly have blamed me if, that night, I went to bed on even more ethereal scales of ecstasy?

WE were married the following Friday afternoon, in the village church, at three o'clock. The day was good for flying and as a consequence we were, as they say, rather thin on the ground. Besides Splodge and myself there were only my grandmother, Harry, Edna, Rose, MacKenzie and a young Pilot-Officer named Lambton, whom I had never met before. Hugh Lambton, who had his right arm in a sling, had cracked a bone in his wrist while cranking a car. My mother, mortally in fear as always of the front line, had sent a fifty word telegram, so like a replica of her own voice, and stayed away.

Mac was best man and, like Hugh Lambton, was also *hors de combat*, but not for quite the same reason. Mac had again been conducting his personal war and as a result looked to be one of the oddest best men of all time. His face seemed to have been recently and violently beaten with iron bars. His right eye was very like a ripe purple plum, mauled and vastly swollen, with a sulphur slit across the centre. The other had a livid raspberry hue. Across both sides of his face strips of pink plaster made strange and complicated patterns. His right ear looked rather like a battered lettuce heart soaked in a mixture of stale beetroot juice and oil. His mouth, the lips puffed to twice their size, seemed to have been pushed some inches across his face, giving him a sombre leer. The only other visible signs of damage were his hands, which looked rather like two big battered lobsters.

After the ceremony, when we were all back at the house, my grandmother, never one to show excessive alarm, nevertheless felt constrained to inquire about this extraordinary sight. She hoped Mr MacKenzie hadn't fallen out of his aeroplane?

'Oh! no, ma'am. Just a fight.'

When my grandmother suggested that it had clearly been fought with clubs, flat-irons or even both, Mac looked as pained as possible under the circumstances and said:

'Oh! no, ma'am. Just an ordinary fight. A plain, ordinary fight.'

'You appear to me to have been at a singular disadvantage.'

'Oh! no, ma'am. Just one of those things. One of those personal things.'

At this point I wanted to know what had happened and Mac said:

'We were just sitting in a pub, having a nice beer, me and Stephanie, when two guys started undressing her with their eyes. That had to be sorted out, sort of. That ain't in my book.'

'Your opponent,' my grandmother said, 'must have been very powerful.'

'There were two,' Mac said. 'Well, two in the beginning. And then later on three. Maybe four.'

'What happened to the others?' I said.

'I think some guys found wheel-barrows.'

'What a shocking affair, four to one,' my grandmother said. 'It must be extremely painful.'

'Oh! just a fight. Just an ordinary fight.'

'Good show,' Splodge said. 'Good show.'

'Good show,' Hugh Lambton said. 'Wish I'd have been there. Good show.'

'Just one of those things, Squire,' Mac said. 'Just one of those things.'

In the evening the six of us sat down to a very good dinner cooked by Rose and that in itself set the seal on my extraordinary wedding day. An hour before dinner was served I went across to the dove-cot to change from my wedding dress – it was a very simple one, in pale daffodil silk – into a long black evening dress, taking my bouquet of white and yellow roses with me. I put the bouquet into the water jug on my wash-basin and then slipped out of my wedding dress. I was still ethereally flushed with happiness, but for a few moments it was good to be alone. Then I kicked off my shoes and took off my slip and stood dreamily looking at the garden outside. Big clumps of white Madonna lilies were in bloom under the crimson rambler roses and on the wall of the dove-cot, just under the window the first huge chalice of the magnolia was opening, pure and smooth as alabaster.

I hadn't been standing there for more than two or three minutes when I heard footsteps coming upstairs and in a moment Splodge came in. I stretched out my arms and said simply, 'I hoped you'd come' and without a word he held me against him. Then he kissed me several times and at last slipped down my shoulder straps so that I stood there naked to the waist. Then I sat on the edge of the bed and let him one by one take off the rest of my clothes. He too began to undress and as I lay full length on the bed, watching, I said 'I thought you said there'd be no honeymoon?' but the only answer he gave to that was to come and lie down beside me and touch me with his hands and kiss my breasts.

I don't think I thought of much else except that hour all through dinner, at least until almost the end of it. It was a very odd meal, not merely because I wasn't ever really part of it – I don't think Splodge was part of it either – but because Mac looked more and more, especially by candlelight, like a strange character out of some medieval mumming play and also because Hugh Lambton had to drink left-handed and couldn't cut up his food, with the result that every few moments Mac was bolting up from his chair like some macabre nursemaid, cutting it up for him. The trout we began with didn't present much trouble but after two or three sallies at the roast duck Mac got bored and said 'Oh! hell, pick the ruddy duck up in your fingers, Squire, and the peas too if it comes to that,' and after that time slid past me in an atmosphere both dreamy and gay.

It says much for Mac that it was he and not my grandmother who dominated it all. It was he who proposed toast after toast, picking out friends both singly and collectively and heaping picturesque abuse on most of them.

'Here's to the Count. May his Mae West never blow up when the time comes.'

My grandmother, whose life had in some ways been every bit as sheltered as mine, now inquired as to the meaning of Mae West and had her innocence rewarded with a demonstration of ripe and fleshy splendour by Mac, who I fully expected any moment to beguile us all with another dog fight too.

But it never happened. We were still toasting the Count and had hardly finished laughing at the episode of the Mae West when I suddenly saw Mac look ceilingwards with an almost savage perception. A second or two later I heard a strange whistling from the sky. 'Christ! Down! Under! Down!' Mac yelled with such ferocity that in an astonishing moment I saw Harry's mouth fall open and half a dozen green peas drop with agonizing slowness off the end of his tongue. In the next second Mac dragged my grandmother clean off her chair and pushed her under the table and then almost felled me to the ground and lay half on top of me.

In another second or two the whistling was utterly obliterated by a concerto of six or seven appalling crumps that shook the house like an eruption. A glass fell from somewhere with a crash. In another astonishing moment I caught sight of Hugh Lambton, half under a chair beside me, still gnawing intently at the wing-bone of a duck. I felt myself incredibly on the verge of laughing and then furiously bit my lips to keep it back. There followed an agonized silence of what must have been mere seconds but which seemed like half the night and then there was another long wail of whistling, this time farther off, followed by another series of crumps exactly like echoes of the first still further away, and then the long agony of silence once more.

When we all finally crawled out even my grandmother had lost some of her habitual calm and Mac did nothing to restore it by suddenly raising both battered fists to the ceiling and yelling with stentorian fury :

'Don't do that again, Goering you bastard! You might get hurt. Christ, I'll even that one up with you some day!'

The thunderous frenzy of this frightened us all as much as the bombs had done and Mac, partly realizing it too I think, hastily added in comparatively dulcet tones and with sublime disregard for the presence of my grandmother :

'Enough to shake you to the tits. In the middle of dinner too.'

During all this Harry stood shaking like a piece of tottergrass and I, having somehow groped into the arms of Splodge, wasn't much better. I had never been frightened by the war before and now I was frightened less by the physical noise of it than by the impact of the first coherent thought that Splodge and I, after that solitary interval of first love, might have been separated for ever. The irony of it stunned me.

Hugh Lambton was the calmest among us. He was still gnawing away at the duck-wing, every now and then looking at it with rapt attention, eagerly searching for some further succulent morsel of roasted flesh.

'What's the odds they're trying to knock the station out?' he said.

'Christ,' Mac said, 'they could be at that.'

This had the effect of bringing my grandmother to her senses and suddenly she swept from the room, saying 'Rose, Edna – I forgot them –'

'Anybody care for a brandy?' Harry suddenly said and it immediately became obvious that all of us cared very much.

We were still standing about the dining-room sipping brandy, with my grandmother still in the kitchen comforting Edna and Rose, when the telephone rang.

'I'll get that,' Hugh Lambton said and was out of the room and back again in less than two minutes to say : 'Good guessers never get married, they say. At the double. Everybody report back.'

'Jesus,' Mac said. 'Goering, I'll personally shoot your arse off one day. There's no future for you, boy.'

The brevity of my kiss with Splodge merely intensified the agony of the question that followed it :

'You'll come back tonight, won't you? Please.'

'God knows.'

For a few seconds the air was full of words of love and thanks and then the three of them were suddenly gone and I was alone with Harry.

'God,' Harry said. 'I thought that was the end.'

'It feels not unlike it,' I said.

That, then, was my honeymoon. Four days later the entry in my diary reads : 'Made another acquaintance this morning.' But the word 'acquaintance' is crossed out and in its place is the word 'friend'.

I SPENT those next four days in the solitude of a strange grass-widowhood. The curiously disembodied voice of Splodge called me several times on the telephone, but kept his news, his movements and such future as there might have been for him an utter mystery. During this time I felt as bruised, in spirit, as if I had been in that epic struggle of Mac's; I longed not merely in a stunned way for Splodge – I longed, as I had done several times before, for some company of my own generation. I felt acutely, as never before, what it was to be young. It seemed very cruel, that week, to be young and there was no way of assuaging the pain of it.

It was Thursday morning when I was walking back from the post office after posting a long letter to my mother chronicling most of the week's excitement except the bombs – 'I've always said Providence holds a special dispensation for people like your mother,' my grandmother said, 'I'm sure she had some celestial premonition about your wedding day' – when I stopped for an idle minute or so to read the luncheon menu outside *The Pomfret Arms*.

I was just about to turn away again when I was aware of someone else reading it too.

'Don't give you a fat lot for your money, duckie, do they?' a voice said and I turned to see a big-bodied hatless girl of about twenty-five standing there. Her shoulder length hair was an odd shade of coppery blonde.

'I never think they want the custom,' I said.

'Oh! it's like that is it?' she said. 'Bit snotty. You live here?'

I said I did and she went on: 'Hope you don't mind me asking, duckie, but d'you know anybody who lets rooms?'

'They have rooms here.'

'Oh! not a hotel. Can't afford that on a sergeant's pay.'

'I rather think they have rooms at the post office. They used to. We had some workmen down from London once and they found rooms there. Or they might have something at *The Welcome Stranger* – across the street.'

'Oh! the pub. Good name for a pub, *The Welcome Stranger*.' She laughed; her voice was quick, almost slick, high-toned and friendly. It had rather a Midland accent, I thought. 'Come over and have a drink with me while I find out.'

'Well, I should really be getting back –'

'Ah! come on. Not snotty too, are you?'

The last thing I wanted to be was snotty and presently we were in the bar of *The Welcome Stranger*. It's a small, simple, comfortable pub, with a plain varnished bar, and I could see at once that she liked it.

'This'll do,' she said. 'What'll you have?'

Just as she said this an air-raid siren whined in the near distance and she said 'Here we go again. Pin your hat on,' and then asked again 'What'll it be, duckie? What'll you have?'

I remembered Fitz and said I would have dry sherry and water.

'Blimey, that's a new one. Sure it won't go to your head?' Old Mr Gilbert, the landlord – he has one of those large globular cysts on the side of his bald head – was behind the bar, and she said 'I'll have a whisky, please. Johnnie Walker. A double,' and then she asked him about a room.

Mr Gilbert said he'd have to ask the missus and after pouring the drinks asked:

'Soda or water?'

'Neat.'

When Mr Gilbert had gone out of the bar she looked me up and down a few times, said 'Cheers,' drank half her whisky at one gulp, and then said:

'Name's Doreen Smith. Everybody calls me Doll. Don't know why. Some even say good old Doll.'

I then told her my name and asked if she hadn't said something about a sergeant?

'That's right. My husband. Sergeant-pilot. Just moved with his Squadron down here. The balloon's going up.'

I saw her take a quick look at the ring on my finger and I said: 'I'm married to a pilot too. Pilot-Officer.'

'Blimey. What a life. There's no future in it, duckie. No future, I tell you. How long've you been married?'

'Four days.'

'Some hope.'

She drank most of the rest of her whisky and gave me what I later used to call one of her old-fashioned looks and said :

'Your bloke's in the outfit here too, I suppose? You know they tried to knock the station out the other night? Put three kites out of action, killed three erks, an Intelligence type and two Waafs. One of the Waafs was preggy too. But then they mostly are.'

I, who had been moving in a vacuum all the week, marvelled silently at this ready and fascinating stream of gen and then waited for what was coming next.

'You'll get used to it in time, duckie. It's a good life if you don't weaken − I *don't* think. By the way what chance of any work around here? They tell me there's a lot of fruit-picking. Got to do something to while the time away and pay for the Johnnie Walker.'

I said the strawberries and cherries were almost all finished for this year but that soon there would be plums, probably pears and then apples.

'There's a big crop of plums. And they're short of pickers, I know.'

'Must have a look-see as soon as I get myself organized.'

At this point Mr Gilbert came back, bringing Mrs Gilbert, who still had her hair in curlers and was wearing a floppy pinafore with a big pattern of blue roses all over it.

'We've got one double room free,' Mrs Gilbert said. 'Was it a double you wanted?'

'You bet. I like company.'

She gave a high forthright laugh and I believe if Mr Gilbert had been on her side of the bar she would have given him a nudge with her elbow. As it was she merely gave him a quick sideways look and said 'You bet' again in answer to Mrs Gilbert's inquiry as to whether she'd like to see the room, adding as she went out of the bar :

'Tot out again, landlord. I need it. Spent the night standing up in a train.'

'Gay sort of girl,' I said when I was alone again with Mr Gilbert.

'Think so?' I suppose men who keep pubs and run bars have a way of sizing up people more quickly and shrewdly than most of the rest of us. 'Looks sort of a bit sad to me.'

That remark, accurate though it turned out to be, surprised me so much that I wasn't ready for the next one. There was a day-by-day calendar hanging on the wall behind the bar and the date said the 9th of July.

'Feels a bit sort of tense this morning, don't it?' Mr Gilbert said.

I said I hadn't noticed it and after staring for a few moments longer at the calendar I said:

'Is it only the 9th of July. I thought it was later than that.'

'Forgot to tear it off. Forget my own name next. It's the 11th – ought to remember. It's my sister's birthday.'

I hadn't really noticed any greater tension that morning than on any other but suddenly, just as Mr Gilbert was saying 'I'm sorry, I clean forgot to congratulate you, Miss – sorry, what is your name now?' when a loud and frenzied burst of machine-gun fire broke out high above us, followed by one even harsher, louder and more prolonged.

It was the closest and loudest gun-fire I had yet heard and I felt myself go taut and cold. I don't know why, but I didn't immediately think of Splodge. I thought instead of Mac. The harsh rattle of machine-gun fire reminded me sharply of his voice yelling violent threats at Goering. It was a stark and angry sound and the third repetition of it was so close that Mr Gilbert ducked quickly under the bar and I instinctively ran and crouched under a pin-table in a corner.

'Too close,' Mr Gilbert said when he came up again. 'It's getting so they're fighting this blasted war on top of your own chimney pot.'

'Didn't I tell you?' Doll Smith, remarkably unperturbed as it seemed, was back in the bar with Mrs Gilbert, who looked ill and shaken. 'The balloon's going up. This is it.'

'That was awful close,' Mrs Gilbert said. 'It give me 'orrible turn.'

'You got to get used to it,' Doll Smith said. 'It's like

measles — there's going to be an awful lot of it about.'

She had hardly finished saying this and Mrs Gilbert was still on her groping, shaky way to somewhere at the back of the pub when an appalling crump shattered the earth only half a mile or so to the west. I actually felt the bar floor quiver. This was followed by yet another burst of machine-gun fire and then another and then by the high scream of a plane in a long low dive. It was really like a battle now and Mr Gilbert again ducked under the bar and Doll and I slid together under the pin-table in the corner. As we crouched there the plane screamed on, overhead now, scorching the roof-tops and blasting our ear-drums and then whining away somewhere over the fields. 'Somebody isn't going to pull out,' Doll said and then another shattering crump hit the earth and shook the floor of the pub again. 'Do you mind?' she said. 'I haven't had my breakfast,' and I felt my stomach turn emptily over, as if I hadn't had mine either.

By the time we crawled out from under the pin-table it was uncannily quiet again and Doll's laugh sounded twice as loud as it probably was. 'I like *The Welcome Stranger* part of it,' she said. 'That's ruddy good.'

She took a quick swig at her whisky and said 'All right, duckie?' and I said 'Yes,' completely unconscious as to whether I was or wasn't. From the door of the bar Mr Gilbert said there was smoke all over the place and for the next few moments it drifted over, a dark ugly brown, against the already thin sunlight. Once more I had that uncanny, unhappy impression of a total eclipse but there was no time to linger over it now. The clang of a fire bell was the next sound to shatter us and then the camouflaged truck itself went belting down the street closely followed by two ambulances with red crosses on the side.

'There go the blood-wagons,' Doll said and this seemed as good a moment as any in which to ask her if she would have another whisky.

'You bet.'

I now decided that Fitz's sherry and water wasn't quite strong enough for this occasion and at the same time I ordered myself a brandy. As we stood drinking it the silence was so unreal that I felt it couldn't be anything but an ominous lull before another storm. No summer morning had in fact ever seemed as unreal as that one and when a frantic woman with two children went running past the open door Doll said :

'Panic stations. That reminds me – I left my suit-cases at the station. I'll have to go and fetch them. That's the back of beyond, that is.'

Our little one-line station, with its wooden box of a ticket office and three oil lamps, was a good mile away and I said :

'I'll come and help you with them if you like. It's a long way.'

'Thanks, duckie. Rather wait till the all-clear goes, though. Not that there's going to be much all-clear from now on if you ask me.'

It was another quarter of an hour before the all-clear went and we set off to the station for the suit-cases. The smoke had dispersed a lot by now but the morning wasn't in any case as clear as many we had had and there was a dampness in the air. Strange as it may sound I didn't think of Splodge as we walked down the road and Doll said nothing about the fighting either. The thing that really remains uppermost in my mind is of how glad I was to have her with me. If Providence had held a special dispensation for my mother on my wedding day it had certainly saved a good one for me in the shape of that warm-hearted, candid, big-bodied Doll Smith.

We were about half way back from the station, each carrying a suit-case and sometimes stopping for a minute to sit on them, when the air-raid siren wailed a second time.

'Hell's bells,' Doll said. 'Here we go again.'

'Shall we take shelter?'

'Where?'

It was a sensible question because there was, as a matter of fact, no shelter to take. We were on one of those straight stretches of road bordered by low hedges topped by honey-suckle and wild roses and ditches filled with willow-herb, meadow-sweet and long, seeding grasses. There were two or three short oak-trees dotted about and an old rusty binder stood abandoned in a gate-way. A couple of hundred yards away across a field stood a tin-roofed shed and this was about all there was to succour us.

'If anything starts,' Doll said, 'we'll hide under a daisy.'

Something started three or four minutes later. A crackle of machine-gun fire hit a long hole in the air just above us and with a good round blasphemous yell Doll pushed me into the ditch and then fell on top of me, bringing one of the suit-cases with her. This moment remains more vividly in my mind than any other because, as I lay there half buried in meadow-sweet, hands over my head, I actually heard the abrupt metallic clatter of empty shell cases falling on the tin roof of the shed and then the scream of a pheasant getting up in fright from somewhere further down the hedgerow.

We lay there for what again seemed to be half the day but was probably no more than a minute or two and then Doll at last pushed the suit-case away and sat up. I think it was the sound of a train whistling down the line that really brought me to my senses and at last I sat up too.

'If this goes on much longer I shall wet my trousers,' Doll said. 'It's enough to shake you to the nellies. Did you say plum-picking? Don't make me laugh.'

At that we both did start laughing, in that peculiar strained way one does after fright, when for some reason the whole thing seems to have been a frantic joke. Strangely enough the sky was empty and whatever had been up there had melted away, leaving once again that curious illusion of a pastoral canvas utterly untouched by war.

'What they call baptism by fire, I suppose,' Doll said. 'Told you there was no future, didn't I, matey? Press on.'

After that we struggled on down the road with the suitcases. Now and then Doll stopped to pick bits of meadowsweet from my hair and now and then we laughed again, especially when Doll said:

'I'll have to see about that plum-picking. It's so damn dull here. Nothing ever happens. I've just got to get something to occupy my ruddy mind.'

No sooner had she said this than the morning was shattered yet again: this time by the glorious screaming roar of Spits taking off from the air-field down the railway line. The first kite went over us just above tree-top height but climbing fast, and this was followed by another and another and another, until the Flight was complete.

By this time we were both in the ditch again, half-laughing, half-trembling, with pride and fear.

II

THAT day the battle really began, but for me the impact of lying in a ditch with a suit-case on top of me while tracer bullets rattled a tin shed in the nearest field was nothing compared with a conversation I had that same night.

It was about ten o'clock when I decided to walk in the garden for a few minutes, for the last time, before going to bed. I seem to remember it was one of those dullish, muggy evenings when the air seems to be sapped up by oppressive summer leaves – you almost feel that the trees are crushing you – and now and then as I walked about the garden an occasional big rose would suddenly split open and silently spill its petals over the dark earth.

It was probably because of this that the sound of Chloe's exhaust coming up the road startled me far more than even the rattle of morning bullets had done. It really made me jump and I was actually trembling when Splodge walked up the garden path to meet me. I hadn't seen him for days – it really seemed more like weeks – and at first we didn't say very much to each other. Nor did I grasp at first that he was quiet from sheer weariness. It wasn't until we were in the house and I asked him if he would like something to eat and drink and he simply sat staring and made no attempt to answer me that I realized that out of absolute exhaustion he was only partly with me.

After putting the question a second time and still getting no answer I decided I wouldn't trouble him again. My grandmother and Harry had already gone to bed and only Rose was in the kitchen. When I went to ask her what food she had left she said there was cold beef and potato salad and cold mixed fruit pie. I left her to put it on a tray and then went back to the sitting-room and without saying another word mixed a big whisky-and-soda and put it into Splodge's hands. He just sat staring at it without saying anything either for fully a minute and then at last he took a slow sip or two and then all of a sudden a deep eager gulp, as if at long last he'd really woken up.

After that he stretched out a hand and simply let it lie on top of one of mine. I briefly bent down and put my face against it and in turn he rested his head against mine. Even then he didn't say anything and it wasn't until I heard Rose coming along the passage outside that he suddenly lifted his head, every bit as startled as I had been a few minutes before and said :

'What's that? Who's there?'

'It's Rose,' I said, 'bringing some supper. You'd like some supper, wouldn't you?'

'Rose? Rose? Oh! yes, Rose,' he said, exactly as if Rose were a total stranger trespassing on his life for the first time.

It didn't fully occur to me until some time afterwards that it was really he who was in fact the stranger, or equally that I might have seemed like a stranger to him. Anyway Rose came in a few moments later with the tray of cold food and set it on a card table where earlier in the evening, my grandmother had been playing double patience – the single version wasn't exacting enough for her alert mind – and then said :

'Good evening, sir. I wonder if you'd like anything to drink with your meal, sir? Mr Harry left half a bottle of hock and I put it in the fridge.'

'Hock?'

He repeated this once or twice in the same way as he had done Rose's name and I finally said :

'All right, yes please, Rose, bring the hock.'

When Rose had gone out of the room I saw him quickly drain his glass and this time I had more sense than to ask him if he needed it filling. I simply got up and filled it and again put it into his hands.

'Did you think I was never coming?'

'No,' I said, 'I never think that.'

'Sorry.'

He drank and then stared for fully another minute into his glass, rather as if his thoughts were drowned in it somewhere and he was laboriously trying to fish them out.

'How have you been?' he said.

'Quite well, thank you, darling.'

'Bit noisy today?'

'A little.'

'We really got cracking a bit today.'

I find it rather difficult to convey how laborious this was too. But soon Rose came back with the hock and two glasses and I said that I would pour the wine and that she could go to bed. She thanked me but said that there wasn't really any hurry. She really didn't sleep all that well and she'd wait to clear the tray away.

When Rose had gone he again sat sipping his whisky and staring into his glass. I was determined that I wouldn't, at any price, pester him with too many questions but suddenly I thought I'd tell him about Doll instead.

'Do you know a Sergeant-pilot named Smith?'

'Smith?' He thought for some moments and then shook his head. 'No.'

'I think his squadron's only just arrived here.'

'Oh?'

'I met his wife today.'

'Yes?'

'Big friendly girl. Outspoken and rather fun. I helped her get a room at *The Welcome Stranger*.'

'You did.'

I poured the wine. I was also determined I wouldn't be a bomb-bore and tell him of our baptism by fire in the ditch, but the conversation lagged and after taking a sip or two of the wine, which was really ice-cold by then, I said:

'She wants some work. I thought old Mr Hudson might help. So we're both going along there tomorrow.'

Suddenly, out of the blue, exactly as if he hadn't heard me, he said:

'Did you know Relf? I think you met him once. Barney Relf.'

'I can't think I did.'

'Cambridge man. Had a first in physics.' He abruptly finished his whisky and then instantly grabbed his glass of wine. 'Hellish clever. Brain like Einstein or somebody. Brilliant. No? Don't remember him? Tall and lanky. Got a Blue for golf too. Wrists like steel whips.' He drank with a certain cool ferocity. 'Bought it today.'

That was all. I didn't say anything and he started eating. I could see that the food hardly meant anything to him at all. He was just aware of certain objects on a plate. In less than another minute his glass was empty and when I filled it up with wine he was hardly aware of that either.

'We had a hell of a rasp-up. Second time out.' The ice-cold wine together with the whisky had suddenly provided him the blessed physical relief of being able to talk with a half-delirious freedom. The words came out like bullets. 'Got up to twenty thousand and a bloody great gaggle of M.E.s came at us out of the sun, screaming down like bedlam. Tore right into us and we split into a circle. Part of our plan. Then the second bunch came down on us, trying to break the segment where me and Barney were. They overshot though. Then I did a split-arse turn and, funny thing, I couldn't see a damn thing in sight. Then I could hear Barney yelling like hell's bells "There they are! There! Three of 'em! – eleven o'clock! Look at the bastards! By God, they're fast." Then he went after them. I started going too and then an M.E. came down between us and got on Barney's tail. The poor sod was going flat out and couldn't have looked in his mirror – Barney of all people. I screamed like hell for him to watch out but it was about an hour too late. He fell out like a stone – chute didn't open. Then I went stinking mad and when the M.E. peeled off I went after him – got the bastard too, all over in no time. Vengeance is mine, vengeance is mine saith the Lord, vengeance is mine! – I can hear myself yelling it now. Hell of a rasp-up. A real do.'

There was nothing I could say to this half-insane, suddenly articulate stranger. His voice, doubly intoxicated by drink and emotion, now and then rose to a pitch of stuttering frenzy. His eyes had no direction. His hands danced about like bony spiders.

The unexpected vehemence of all this quite frightened me. I felt far worse than I had ever done with Doll in the ditch. 'It was my first kill, you see. Felt like Mac all of a sudden.' The words came spluttering out in a new passionate stream. 'Personal thing suddenly. Just like Mac. God, my blood was up. I felt like raging hell inside. It was tough tit on Barney, though, the poor sod. It was tough tit on Barney.'

The peculiar nature of my fright not only prevented me from

saying a word; it also suddenly made me get up and make for the kitchen. He hardly noticed my going and in fact was still excitedly babbling when I left. The only thought in my mind was to make some coffee. Foolishly I dropped a cup in the kitchen but to my everlasting astonishment it bounced, so that I actually burst out laughing.

Rose interpreted this as an expression of unmitigated and sudden joy and with a short laugh of her own said:

'It must be wonderful to have him back for a few hours, miss.'

The words fell on me like cold stones. I felt like a benighted creature struggling for direction in the dark. All of me felt black and brittle and presently my hands started shaking so much that I knew I should never be able to carry the coffee tray. At that I said:

'I'll go back now. Will you finish the coffee, Rose, and bring it in and collect the other tray?'

'I'll be in as soon as it's ready, miss.'

I went back to the sitting-room, to find Splodge dead asleep in the chair, a spoon and fork still in his hands, a piece of fruit pie, its juice as brilliant as fresh blood, uneaten on the plate in front of him. Oblivious and released, he looked like a man both stunned and drugged and almost as if he could never wake again.

But when Rose came in with the coffee tray and set it down on a side-table a spoon jingled sharply against a cup and at the sound he shot up wildly in his chair, shouting only half-incoherently:

'Barney, you fool, you fool! Look, man, look! – for Christ's sake look! Barney – look! – for Christ's sake watch out!'

Then all of a sudden he stopped, stared with eyes incredibly dazed by exhaustion, drink, confusion and perhaps his own particular kind of fright, too, first at me and then at Rose and at last actually said:

'Where have I been? Where am I?'

'You were just dreaming,' I said and knew then that my baptism by fire hadn't been in the ditch after all.

*

When I met Doll Smith the following afternoon and walked

with her to Hudson's farm she looked more than a little baggy under the eyes. She might well have been in a dog-fight herself. As we talked, in fact, one raged above us in the far high distances, with its snowy, snaky exhaust trails.

'Feel about a hundred and twenty today. You all right, duckie?'

After my brutal divorce from unreality I felt, to say the least of it, constrained; but there was no way of conveying the rude disturbance of my feelings and I merely said:

'All right. Just.'

'Smithy didn't half give me the once-over last night. Did I say once-over? Twice-over — three times over. Turn me over and do it again. Hadn't seen me for a week. We got through nearly a bottle of whisky and then it was so warm and muggy we didn't have a sheet on the bed all night.'

We crossed the river by the little bridge, walked through the wood and came out into bright sunlight in the meadow beyond.

'What did you say they called your husband? Fudge?'

'Splodge.'

'They don't half think 'em up, don't they? Mark — that's my husband. So they call him Sparks. He's a spark, too, I tell you. A bright one. But I always call him Smithy.'

All morning I had longed, once again, to talk to someone of my own generation and to tell some part, at least, of the shattering episode of the previous night, but now my constraint wouldn't let me. I had stopped feeling grievously young. I now felt my youth had suddenly grown old.

'Has he shot any down yet?' I said.

'Five. Three probables. Two possibles. Over France. They gave him a gong.'

'You must be very proud of that.'

'Gongs? They don't butter your bread.'

There was no stupidity in Doll and this brief conversation released some of the tension in me and I said at last:

'Splodge got his first kill yesterday. For once he talked about things. Well, raved about them. He raved like a mad thing. And then had a bad dream about it. I was frightened.'

'Ah, got the fire in his belly,' was all she said. 'Well. He'll feel better now.'

We were walking, five minutes or so later, through the plum orchard. A flock of sheep, with the spring lambs already so far grown that you could hardly tell them from their mothers, grazed with silent contentment under the trees, where the fruit hung already part green, part purple, in heavy clusters. Once again my pastoral landscape was back with me, more unreal than the dog-fight – or perhaps by that time another – raging above us. I stopped once to squeeze a plum with my fingers but the pure smoky bloom on the skin was deceptive. The fruit was still as hard as stone.

'By the way,' I said, 'my grandmother asked if you'd like to come back and have tea with us. Would you? I thought I'd mention it in case Mrs Hudson should think of asking us.'

'Let 'em all ask. I could drink forty gallons of it. I feel as if I've been dragged through a hedge backwards.'

Beyond the orchard, in the farm yard, Tom Hudson's father was busy putting the finishing touches to a hayrick, clipping the edges of the straw thatch with a pair of shears, standing on the top-most rung of a ladder. He raised his cap in his typically well-mannered way as he saw us and then came down the ladder to shake hands with me and say :

'Good afternoon, Miss Elizabeth. I'm afraid I haven't had a chance of congratulating you until now. Anyway, better late than never. I think Tom's mother has something in the way of a little wedding present for you.'

'Thank you, Mr Hudson. This is a friend of mine, Mrs Smith.'

'Very pleased to meet you, Mrs Smith,' he said and again raised his cap and then shook her by the hand.

'Me too,' Doll said. 'How are you?'

After that there was some desultory conversation about the weather, together with some inquiry about my mother and my grandmother, and I was then about to ask about the plum-picking when Tom Hudson himself came round the corner of the hay-rick, hatless, in brown corduroys and a sleeveless white shirt, carrying a scythe over his shoulder. For a moment he seemed oblivious of us and was actually saying 'Just off to knock a few nettles down,' when he became alarmingly aware that we were there. A deep flush sprang into his face immediately and for a few moments he looked as if he might well drop the scythe and run. He did in fact stand it against the wall of the hay-rick before coming shyly over to us, the smile on his face one of sheer protective nervousness.

Unlike his father he didn't shake hands with us and when I introduced Doll, telling him at the same time that her husband was a Sergeant-pilot, he merely said:

'Oh! yes.'

He didn't mention my marriage either, nor did he really look at me. But once or twice I saw Doll, in her acute way, look at him, sharply sizing him up rather as he or his father might have sized up an animal at market. He responded to this by saying:

'I hope you've all been all right down at your place? Mother got worried about you the other day. Thought you were in the line of fire.'

'That,' Doll said, 'was when we were baptized. In the flippin' ditch.'

The laughter that greeted this did at least something to ease the tension I knew Tom was feeling and I said:

'Mrs Smith says it's too quiet down here. She gets bored. She really wants some work to do. I wondered if you could help.'

'Ever work on a farm?' Mr Hudson said.

'Not me. I used to work in a shoe factory.'

'I told her I thought there might be fruit-picking,' I said.

'There's fruit all right. Picking's another matter. Like I said the other day.' Suddenly Mr Hudson snatched off his cap and took a violent swat at a wasp buzzing past his head. 'These devils are early this year. They know when it's plum time.'

'I thought you were going to speak to Sam Chalmers about buying the orchard as it stands,' Tom said.

'I did. Not interested. Too busy getting rich on pig-swill. Collects it from army camps.'

'Why doesn't Mrs Smith buy it?' Tom said.

'The orchard? Don't make me laugh,' Doll said and promptly laughed uproariously. 'Me? What would I use for doh-ray-me? I want you to pay me, not the other way round.'

'You could make yourself a half-tidy profit,' Mr Hudson said.

'Oh! yes? You can see me. I start with a bike and end up with a Rolls and two minks.'

'Well, we'll never find the labour to pick them ourselves, that's for sure. Think it over. You'd have to start in about ten days.'

'Farmer Smith, eh? Land girl? Smithy'll laugh his ruddy head off.'

'We sold it once before to a gyppo,' Tom said. 'He made forty quid off it.'

'Blimey O'Reilly,' Doll said. 'I would be in the mink.'

Presently Mr Hudson said that if she could find ten pounds she could have the orchard for that. He would find boxes and a wholesaler and Tom, perhaps, would run the plums to the station in the trailer, by tractor. He begged her seriously to think it over. He hated the idea of waste in war time.

'Me and the money,' she said. 'How do we get together? Tell me.'

'I could lend it to you,' I suddenly said and she laughed again and said 'I fell among friends. What it is to be married to a Pilot-Officer,' and in that instant I saw a look of dismay and then of positive distrust flash across Tom Hudson's face, as if for a moment he thought she had said it on purpose.

Nothing could have been further from the truth; it simply wasn't in her nature. But suddenly she turned to me and said something which both surprised and touched me.

'You know about these things,' she said. 'What would you do if you were me?'

'I'd buy it,' I said, so promptly that I greatly surprised myself.

'It's a deal. I'll probably last one day and then die of sciatica.'

None of this seemed of any marked importance to either of us at the time; nor did a remark of Mr Hudson's:

'I'll get Tom to fix up a tent for you and find a load of faggots in case you want to boil a kettle.'

Then Mr Hudson remembered my wedding present and said he would go to the house and get it.

'I'll go,' Tom said and went away on long deliberate strides to the house, coming back a few minutes later with a long brown-paper parcel, which contained as it turned out a set of bone-handled carvers. He handed this to me with his mother's apologies, saying:

'Mother sends you her love and says she's terribly sorry she can't come out, but she's bottling the last of the black currants and they need to be carefully timed.' And then : 'I'm afraid I haven't got anything myself-I-I really –'

This abrupt renewal of his embarrassment made me feel suddenly and awkwardly ashamed of myself. I hadn't ever dreamed of having a present from him, nor from his mother for that matter, and I didn't know what to say. I think I managed to express some sort of thanks but a moment later he turned, said something about getting on with the nettles, picked up the scythe and walked away.

As Doll and I walked back through the plum orchard she suddenly said another thing that touched me.

'Thanks a lot for doing that for me. I'll do as much for you one day.'

'I'm only too glad to do what I can.'

'By the way,' she said, 'that's a piece of all right talent back there.'

'Talent ?'

Talent, I was about to discover, was Doll Smith's fond expression for men. Nor was there just good talent or bad talent. There was all right talent, juicy talent, ripe talent, shop-soiled talent, piece-work talent, solid talent, stray talent, chop-and-change talent – meaning fickle, I supposed – sexy old talent and all sorts of other talent besides.

Tom Hudson, it now seemed, was a piece of all right talent.

'And he hadn't half got the old peepers on you too.'

'On me ? Never.'

'Don't you kid yourself. Don't you think I know when a bit of talent gets the eye on you ? Ever been friendly with him ?'

'I've known him all my life.'

'Well, it's too late now, but if ever you're at a loose end that's a bit of all right talent, I tell you. I might be at a loose end myself one of these fine days.'

The candour of all this, I think, slightly shocked me, but what came next was really more like a rude intrusion on my deeper privacy.

'Is he the only son ?'

'Tom ? Yes. In fact he's the only child.'

'Always think that's bad. Big families, I always say. We were nine. Only seven of us left now. Ma used to say that every time Dad threw his trousers on the bed she was in the family way. Going to have a family? Kids, I mean?'

I said we hadn't even talked of it.

'Don't. Not while this lot's on the boil anyway. I had two. One lived a week. Wrong sort of heart, somehow. The other got the cord round his neck. I was broken-hearted at the time. I think I'm glad now.'

I really think it was that warm but at the same time brutal frankness, faintly touched with sadness, that most endeared her to me and with every step we took home that afternoon I felt myself draw more closely to her. If at times there were also odd inconsistencies in her they too were merely to serve as causes for fresh and still deeper affection. To my infinite surprise and satisfaction my grandmother liked her too. Candid herself, cryptically and sometimes acidly frank, impervious as steel and at the same time profound and wholly constant in affection, she was drawn to Doll very much as I was and Doll in turn, as it proved, was drawn to her.

That afternoon Rose served us tea under the cherry tree, on a bamboo table covered by a cloth of cream Madeira lace. We had the inevitable cucumber sandwiches, several sorts of jam and cake and once again Rose's excellent little tarts of white-currant jelly. I ate like a cart-horse but Doll, having blandly explained to my grandmother that she'd 'had a bit of a ripe old night of it and wasn't feeling all that hot,' didn't eat very much but drank cup after cup of highly sweetened tea.

It must have been just before six o'clock when we went back into the house because my grandmother said, looking at her watch:

'We must hear the news. We're just in time.'

But before she could switch on the radio I stopped her. There was now a new kind of fear in me. I was afraid of the news. *Three of our pilots did not return* was a sentence that now struck terror into me – and suddenly I said:

'Oh! don't let's bother with that stuff. It bores me to death. It's time for your evening Patience, anyway. You play and we'll watch you.'

She probably, in her instinctively acute way, sensed my fear. At any rate she immediately turned away from the radio, found her two packs of cards in the drawer of the little table where she always kept them and then said to Doll :

'Do you play cards at all?'

'Crib. That's about all.'

'Ah! yes, cribbage. My father taught me when I was five. He said it was the best of all card games for teaching you to count. He was right of course. It's very old, I think. I fancy it's a version of an even older game called Noddy.'

Instantly Doll gave one of her louder, riper laughs.

'And you need your noddy where I used to play sometimes, I tell you, up at The Working Men's. Biggest bunch of twisters ever. Mis-deals, mis-counts, pinching the crib and every other damn thing. You want six sets of eyes and two extra brain-boxes to beat that lot.'

'Would you care to play?'

'Now? All right, I'll have a bash with you.'

'Splendid. I haven't played for simply ages. Shall we play for a little something? I think it makes for more fun, don't you?'

You could fairly see Doll bring another brain-box into play. 'Easy meat,' you could almost hear it thinking. 'Easy meat,' but all she said, in fact, was :

'You bet. Bob a horse?'

'Bob a horse, yes. Two bob a horse if you like.'

'All right. Two bob.'

So they played, my grandmother with that firm precision that characterized all she did, the precision broken only on this occasion by the fact that she couldn't always remember the rhymes that went with the counting and had to be helped out by Doll, whose wits and eyes were every bit as sharp as her own.

'Know something? I'm going to lash you up,' she said once and a few minutes later did so.

My grandmother, accepting defeat with almost regal courtesy, thanked her for the game and then said :

'I enjoyed that so much. Another?'

'You bet. The plum orchard's got to be paid for somehow. Might as well start now.'

After that they played another four games and my grand-mother, steadily, coolly, remorselessly and relentlessly, took the skin off Doll's long-suffering back.

And also the money.

'Well for crying out ruddy softly,' Doll said. 'You'd go down well in the Working Men's.'

'And up well too, I trust.'

Half a minute later Uncle Harry, coming in dressed in his Home Guard uniform and seeking a whisky before going out on some evening exercise, found three women greeting him with gay, helpless laughter.

Not that we had very much to be gay about. I have said already that I remember that summer sometimes with joy and at others with sadness and utter dread. Now began, for me at any rate, the period of dread.

I began to dread not only the news bulletins. I began to dread the telephone, the sound of a car stopping outside the house, the scream of planes, the crackle of gun-fire. Air raid sirens wailed at us all day about this time and I began to dread their miserable whinings too. Sometimes I even dreaded meeting Doll, since it was she, for all her buoyancy and optimism, who always had the most depressing gen on things.

'Sergeant Wilson didn't come back the day before yesterday. And two officers. That makes seven gone for a Burton in the last eight days. Smithy had a shaky-do yesterday. But then, God, it's all shaky.'

I began also to dread the tedium of the long summer days and, what was even worse, the barren tedium of the summer nights. Just at that time the squadrons were hardly ever at rest; sometimes Splodge didn't appear at the house for days.

'They said it would hot up,' Doll said, 'and by God it has. Still, no use being on the ruddy moan all the time. Mustn't get the gloomies. That won't get the washing done.'

Most afternoons we walked together, sometimes along the river, mostly on the hills. Once or twice I took her as far as the Devil's Spoon and on one gloriously pellucidly clear after-noon we could actually see the dark smoke stacks of convoys in the Channel. The hard stutter of anti-aircraft artillery came up from the coast and overhead, far, far up, the air was harsh with that curiously ghostly, mocking rattle of machine-gun fire. Sometimes even in that remarkably brilliant light, which seemed as if washed to its pure crystal transparency by the nearness of the sea, you couldn't see the fighting planes and it was hard to believe that high, high up, men were fighting, screaming, yelling, shooting, bleeding and blaspheming in battle. It was equally hard to believe that down below oat-fields were already turning white, plum orchards were ripening or that on the downs where we sat the little yellow rock-roses that I so loved were now in full flower or that wild strawberries were everywhere scarlet in the sun. Whenever I stopped to pick them I remembered my promise about them to Splodge and how, that summer, he would be eating them for the first time.

One afternoon we gathered a good basket of wild strawberries and the air was so breezy and warm and strong that when we were finally tired of gathering and lay down on the open grass I dropped to sleep at once, like a child. When I woke I stared straight up to the sky and could have sworn that there, not far above me, a plane was hovering darkly. I sat up in fright, only to discover a moment later that it was merely a kestrel hovering, waiting to swoop for its prey. But for just a swift moment or two it felt as if I were the prey to be swooped upon and in my jittery state I even took it as an omen of some impending dreadful thing.

'Duckie, we shall have to do something about these nerves of yours. Got to cure 'em somehow. You can't go on like this.'

'Prescribe the cure.'

'I'm going into town tomorrow to buy myself a pair of trousers.' This seemed just about the craziest cure for nerves ever devised and I just stared at her as if it were some perverse joke of hers. 'Got to have a pair for the plum-picking. Can't very well go up ladders with my best black passion pants on, can I?'

It was never long before Doll got a laugh out of me somehow and she went on:

'You could come with me. Anyway why don't you come in on the plum-picking lark? I never asked you before. Do you good. That's it, come with me tomorrow and get yourself a pair of breeks. Girls up ladders in skirts are shocking bad for morals.'

I said I would; in fact, though I didn't say so, I had longed for her to ask me.

'Good girl. Always listen to Auntie Doll.'

That night, by no means for the first time, I slept alone and was tormented by a succession of nagging, fantastic dreams. I dreamed there were big black boars in the garden, dripping foam from their jaws, that wouldn't let me pass. I dreamed of birds of prey, first the kestrel, then of a big blue jay, its entire body transparent and of a remarkable shade of scintillating turquoise. Then both jay and kestrel were suddenly transformed to a brood of seven or eight swallows, all vividly blue too, that came and settled nervously on my hands, exactly as they do on telegraph wires before departing south for the winter. Then the boars barked, loud and evilly, scaring the swallows off, and one by one rushed to attack me. I woke moaning, in a sweat, not knowing where I was.

Next day it was my turn to look more than a little dark and baggy-eyed. And as Doll and I met outside *The Welcome Stranger* to catch the village bus to our nearest market town she took one of her characteristically swift looks at me and said:

'All right, Duckie?'

'Yes. Why?'

'I just thought.'

Then just before the bus came in she said, with her usual candour:

'Thought I was preggy the other day. False alarm, though, thank God. That would put the tin hat on. We're in a dicey business, us girls, I tell you. The wombless wonder, that's what I should have been.'

'No, it's nothing like that.'

That was another thing I dreaded: the thought that I might have a child. It may sound a curious and perhaps priggishly incredible thing to say now, but I continually felt that, in a sense, I wasn't really married. Such brief consummation as I had had up to that time had left me still remote and virginal. The thought of a child obtruding on me was another nightmare

128

that could only have deepened my already deep and jagged dislocation.

But there was no way of speaking about all this and that afternoon I laughed as much as I could at Doll's jokes about passion pants and how she was really the wrong shape for trousers and so on.

'My behind'll look like a ruddy barrage balloon. Smithy'll be shooting me down. Better keep the colour scheme a bit low. Don't want to be too conspicuous. Fancy being shot up in a plum tree. What a way to die. You're all right. You've got the figure.' We were in the fitting room at the draper's as she said all this, trying on the trousers in front of a long oval mirror. Just before this she had dropped every stitch of clothing she had on and stood stark naked, her heavily built body revealed as being very smooth, lardy and podgy. 'Look at that for a sight. All bosom, bum and belly. I don't half envy you, duckie. From behind you're just like a nice ripe plum.'

That afternoon remains vividly in my mind for another reason. The weather had grown unusually dull and suddenly, as we were waiting for the draper's assistant, a young girl of not more than sixteen, to wrap up the two pairs of trousers, Doll said :

'Know something? Funny – haven't heard an air-raid siren all afternoon.'

'That's right,' the girl said. 'There hasn't been one since about eleven.'

'Called the whole thing off for the week-end,' Doll said. 'Good show.'

'Or else they're going to invade,' the girl said. 'I thought I heard the church bells this morning. It shook me to death.'

'Well, got to make the best of it,' Doll said, 'invasion or no invasion. After all, you never know. They might bring a nice bit of come-hither talent over.'

After we had bought the trousers, mine a bottle-green colour, Doll's a farmyard shade of brown – 'So's I can sort of fade into a furrow if things get too dicey' – Doll said she'd just thought of something else we ought to have.

'Why don't we buy ourselves an oil stove, so's we can have a fry-up sometimes and make a cuppa tea?'

I said I thought it a good idea and that I too had thought of something.

'I think I might be able to borrow the car and the trailer – the one the gardeners use to take their stuff to market – for an hour or two a day. That would save Tom Hudson using the tractor. He's bound to be pretty busy.'

'Can you drive?'

'No. But Splodge could teach me. That's if –'

'If, if. They've been scrambling every blessed minute of the day. Scramble, scramble, scramble. You'll be lucky.'

'Then if Splodge can't get the time, perhaps Tom Hudson would.'

'Now, now. Danger there.'

'Doll, you do romance sometimes.'

'Danger. Bit of all right talent, that. Listen to Auntie. Funny, it don't seem right, somehow, without the air-raid sirens.'

The war, after all the racket of the several preceding days, had in fact gone suddenly quiet on us. There wasn't a single crackle of a bullet to startle us as we travelled home on the bus, nor a wail, nor a seawards thud of gun-fire. In one field that we passed I saw a farmer and three women forking out heaps of wild white clover and you could smell all the summery sweetness of it through the open windows of the bus. The hedgerows were full of yellow fingers of honeysuckle and one field of barley was as white as a child's blonde hair.

Unreality, in fact, was back with us again and as if the incredible tranquillity of the afternoon weren't enough I saw, as I walked into the garden, a far more incredible thing. Splodge, almost as if he'd dropped from a strange planet, sat on the lawn in a deck-chair in grey flannels and an open-necked shirt, reading *The Times*.

'Darling, darling, oh! my darling.'

I was so overwhelmed by this incredible event that I simply flung myself down on my knees and put my head in his lap, neither laughing nor crying and for some time not saying even another word.

When at last I did look up and speak again it was to joke feebly, merely because I couldn't trust any single one of my emotions.

'Have they thrown you out or something?'

'Discharged with ignominy. Bad type.'

'You didn't put up a black or anything?'

'No. My kite's temporarily U.S. and anyway it's been oddly quiet all day. Maybe a bit of foxing on Jerry's part. What have you got in your parcel?'

'A pair of trousers.'

He laughed aloud.

'Oh! so *you're* going to wear them from now on, are you? So that's what a man comes home to?'

I laughed too with great happiness and a few moments later we went up to the dove-cot and in that stuffy little room, which had been shut up since morning, fell passionately into each other's arms, hardly daring to say a word.

In the comparative calm that followed, some long time later, he said:

'Would you like to hear a very, very, very funny thing?'

'I'm always in the market for love and very, very, very funny things.'

'Love you have had. Now the funny thing. Listen. It's about Mac. Yesterday morning we had a very early scramble. Mac was in his trousers and shirt, and still shaving. He was in such a hurry to get to his kite he didn't put his tunic jacket on and tore off like hell, only to get shot up before he knew what was happening and finally had to bale out and land in some wretched suburb, where he got surrounded by hordes of terribly suspicious women who thought invasion had started and came at him with carving knives, garden forks, meat cleavers and friendly tools of that sort.'

'Knowing Mac. I'm sure he survived. If so, how?'

'First he called them all the Anglo-Saxon names he could lay tongue to. Then he kissed them passionately all round. They were well satisfied.'

I too was well satisfied. For the next few days Splodge taught me to drive the car and before another week was out a note came from Mr Hudson to say that the plums were ripe for picking.

12

Doll's remark that the air war had at last hotted up turned out to be not quite true. July ended in an uncanny lull. The early days of August continued it. My Uncle Harry, blundering hither and thither in his new accoutrements of battle, gas-mask, haversack, .303 rifle, ammunition belt, bayonet and a large ugly sheath knife, seemed positively disappointed at sinister rumours that a sudden peace treaty might still save the day. I believe he was keenly anxious, even if only out of sheer relief, for invasion to begin. 'Chance to show the blighters what we're made of.' One of his more active virtues was that he was a splendid shot and in his violent enthusiasm to demonstrate the fact had occasionally, in the early days of the summer, rushed out into the garden, eager to blast off, on any provocation, at sounds and movements he thought were hostile. A straggling Messerschmitt, flying coastwards at nought feet one evening at dusk and deciding that our modestly clustered village offered fair target for a parting shot or two, taught him a lesson he didn't hurriedly forget. A stream of red-hot tracer, like a furious line of morse, ripped the air over the near meadows, took a load of tiles off the church and *The Pomfret Arms* and ended up by killing two pigs in a neighbouring farm-yard, just as Harry, rifle in hand, rushed out to make reply. As if this were not lesson enough a blast from Splodge, when he heard of it, tore him off such a strip that he went almost tragically white, couldn't think of any sensible answer and was sour and mute for days.

'Do you want red hot tracer through your guts? It isn't funny, sir, I tell you. I saw a type who bought it that way. Don't be a damn fool. Keep under cover.'

Some time later he was able to take this advice with unexpected promptitude. He was peacefully occupied one afternoon in casting for trout up the river, just where it enters the upper end of the lake, when a dog fight broke out somewhere above him and a sudden hail of spent tracer shells showered harshly down on him, sending him diving for the nearest elder tree, where he lay flat on his belly watching hundreds of fish and their fry leap in an astounding silvery fountain from the lake, while at the same time dozens of moor-hens and their young scurried in frantic half-flight across the spread of water-lily leaves.

By the first few days of August Splodge was actually bored and the boredom was, if anything, less tolerable than all the previous tension had been. He found it hard to live with inaction and spent monotonous days playing poker or reading in deck-chairs by dispersal huts, coming home at night to grouse plain-tively about office hours and how bloody brassed-off all the chaps were. It wasn't until an Australian named Pierce, out on patrol over Dover, saw a solitary Hurricane get into an irretrievable situation by its pilot forgetting the golden rule about looking out of the back of your neck, that monotony was broken and morale restored. As the Hurricane's tail flew off in smithereens the Australian tore in with angry fury, hit the offending 109 to hell and went home in jubilation. A little later there was another shindy with fighters and bombers over a convoy in the Medway, as a result of which Splodge came back to say, with his own particular jubilation, that that meant a few less Huns to kill anyway.

During this last false lull – and I know that we both felt it to be false, though neither of us ever said so – Doll and I worked in the plum orchard all day and every day. Tom Hud-son had fixed up a khaki tent for us under a tree and every morning he brought us half a gallon of new milk and a big milk churn of fresh water. We had the oil stove too and some-times at midday cooked ourselves a fry-up of sausages, potatoes and eggs and always the endless, inevitable cups of tea. Two mornings a week we loaded up the trailer and I drove a load of plums into market. On the rest of the days we loaded up in the afternoons and I drove the load to the station. The trees were very heavily laden that year and as the plums got riper and riper and fell more and more thickly into the grass we lived more and more with our own private war as squadrons of wasps buzzed ceaselessly in on us from all directions.

One day Doll suffered grievously from a wasp creeping up

her trousers' leg and thereafter wore bicycle clips, remarking 'I don't mind being stung in some places, but I ruddy well draw the line at some things.' Most of the time the weather was pretty hot and most days Doll shed her shirt and worked only in her trousers and a tight black bra, in which her big breasts stood out like massive coconuts. I didn't ever strip down as far as this but preferred wearing nothing under my blouse and for extra coolness a big wide straw hat.

Again I got the feeling of living in a pastoral vacuum, one day almost exactly like another, the weather almost permanently fine and beautiful. Across the fields came the regular sound of the Hudsons' binder cutting oats and soon encampments of pink-white tents shone in the sun about the stubbles. One day Doll gave a sudden cry from a tree-top and shouted 'Blimey ! Under cover ! Heinkels !' and actually ducked into the branches as two big swans flew over very low, their wings beating with that strange sound they make. Instantly my mind went back to that evening in the winter when the swans, like me, had been imprisoned, and it seemed like a thousand years away.

On or about the eighth of August it began to be very noisy again. The sky, like a too-taut wire, snapped. Far up, angry unseen hornets buzzed. Shattering crumps began to hit the near and far distances again and on one particular thunderous afternoon Doll and I spent so much time taking shelter under the trailer that at last she half-lost her temper and said :

'What is this? I'm just about ruddy well brassed-off with this. If we're going to die we're going to die. If we're going to pick plums, let's pick plums. There's no future anyway, so what's the odds?'

So we went back to picking plums and somehow it calmed and restored us again. It was just as well that we didn't know that the Luftwaffe claimed, for the eighth of August alone, forty-nine of our fighters, including thirty-six Spits. It was equally well that we didn't know, at the time, that between the eighth and the eighteenth we lost many more than a hundred fighters in the air and nearly a hundred pilots killed or missing. But we didn't know of these things and there was no way, at the time, of our knowing these things. We were just a couple of women in a plum orchard and it was, as I say, just as well that we didn't know the cold and bloody truth about it all. It might have struck a certain chill into our youthful hearts.

But something else happened, during that time, to strike something more than a chill into our hearts and it occurred, as my diary records, on the 12th, when grouse-shooting traditionally opens : a good day, of course, for shooting.

After a warm and noisy day at market Doll and I drove back to the orchard about three o'clock, tired and rather thirsty.

'I'll go and get the stove going and make a cuppa tea. My throat feels like the underside of a ruddy star-fish,' Doll said and went away towards the tent while I drove the car some distance away to park it in the shade of a plum-tree.

Less than a minute later I heard a short, low cry and turned to see her running back to me, a strange, shocked, almost strangled look on her face, altogether so unlike her that I suddenly felt my heart hammered by the most chilling dread.

'Whatever is it?' I said. 'You look as if you've seen a ghost.'

'We'd better get the Hudsons,' she said. 'There's a stiff over there. Under that tree we finished picking yesterday.'

'A stiff?'

'A dead man. A pilot,' she said.

The pilot was lying in the grass we had trodden down the day before, flat on his back, legs straight out. His hatless face was weirdly misshapen. I remember thinking that it looked more than anything like a battered football that had split open in places and had had to be stitched up again. The longest of these stitch marks stretched from the right eye to the jaw and another, not much shorter, ran in a jagged, livid line across the left corner by the mouth. I remember briefly thinking, as the two of us stood there staring in shocked horror, how odd it was that he should have fallen there without a parachute. Instinctively I looked up into the plum-tree to see if one was hanging there, but there was nothing and when I looked at the body again I had a fresh and sharper shock of horror.

One of the legs moved; and then the other. Slowly they drew themselves up, so that the knees were fully crooked. Then the arms moved. At this point I saw that one of the arms, the left, had no hand. It simply ended in a raw, round stump.

135

Then the eyes, which seemed to be simply blank sockets, opened. All this was done slowly, almost casually; there was no sign of difficulty or pain. The eyes were quite still, staring emptily straight up, as if they were incapable of focusing properly or were trying to focus themselves out of a deep unconsciousness. Then they slowly altered direction, until at last they were looking at Doll and me.

'Oh! my God,' Doll said quietly. 'My God.'

'Jesus! Liz! My dear old darling Liz!'

There was no mistaking that voice, but I simply couldn't say a word. I just stood there, stiff as a corpse myself, while Bill Ogilvy, lacerated, moustacheless, grotesquely gay, leapt to his feet and then, a moment later, rushed over to me, embraced me with a muscular joy that almost knocked me backwards and then kissed me passionately on both cheeks and then on the mouth and then on the mouth again.

'Jolly old Liz! Wizard old Liz! Been looking all over the place for you. Wizard!'

'Bill,' was all I could say. 'Bill.'

Then he suddenly launched into a typical bit of horseplay, seizing one of my hands in his good one and gyrating round and round, rapidly swivelling my arm over my head as if we were in a country dance of some sort.

'Ring-a-ring-a-roses with old Liz. Who'd have thought it? Jesus. Bang-on, Liz, absolutely bang-on.'

All this time he was laughing. At least the sound of laughter was there. The torn mouth was really incapable of shaping laughter and simply opened in a twisted unelastic eclipse that made him look more ghastly and more grotesque than ever.

All the time Doll stood there in speechless stupefaction, never moving. 'At first I wondered who was the lunatic back from hell,' she said afterwards, 'him or me. Then I decided we both were.'

Then in the loud excitement so typical of him Bill started to make a mock proposal to me.

'Dear, loving, lovely Liz – marry me, sweetheart. I am at your feet. Marry me.'

'I'm married already.'

'I know. I heard about it. Lucky old Splodge. But who cares?
You can commit jolly old bigamy. Everybody does in war-time.'

All of a sudden he became aware of Doll and promptly
abandoned horseplay for an over-grave display of charm.

'Another fair and wondrous creature. I do apologize. The
absorbing nature of Mrs Splodge had me half-cock for a
moment. May I have the pleasure of being introduced to t'other
dear charmer?'

'Bill, this is my friend Doll Smith. Doll, this is Flight-
Lieutenant Bill Ogilvy. Doll is married to a Sergeant-Pilot.'

'Damn good show.'

'Pleased to meet you,' Doll said in an empty sort of voice.
'Would you like a cuppa tea? We were just going to make one.'

'Tea with the ladies,' he said. 'Just the job. Good show.'

'We've only two cups,' I said. 'Perhaps I could borrow
another from Mrs Hudson. I won't be long.'

'I'll go,' Doll said. 'Let me.'

'No,' I said. 'I'll go.'

I ran most of the way through the orchard and the paddock
to the Hudsons' and in fact I was wildly aware of wanting to
keep on running, into some far distant hiding place, for ever.
Mrs Hudson was in the kitchen, baking, when I arrived, her
hands all floury, her kitchen table spread out with dough and
flour and pastry board and rolling pin and trays of rock cakes
and large jam tarts, already cooked.

'Oh! you quite startled me, Elizabeth.' She then looked at
me very keenly. 'There's nothing the matter is there? There
hasn't been an accident?'

'No. Why?'

'You look as if somebody just jumped out of a bush at you.'

'No. I came to see if I might borrow a cup. That's all. Or
a mug. Any old thing.'

She looked at me keenly again and then unhooked a mug
from the dresser. I thanked her as I took it and said it was very
kind of her and how we had an unexpected visitor. Then I
started involuntarily trembling and a second or so later was
faintly aware of the floury table coming up to meet me.

The next thing I knew was that I was sitting in a chair

outside the kitchen, half-collapsed, a cup of water in my hands, and Mrs Hudson saying :

'It's all right. It's quite all right. You just went off for a minute, that's all.'

If Bill Ogilvy gave every impression of having come back from hell and the dead that was very much the way I felt too. I walked slowly back through the paddock and the orchard with a growing sense of stupendous unreality. Mrs Hudson had, in a sense, been right. A large bad dream had jumped out of a bush at me, like some hellish ogre, and had frightened all heart and senses out of me. I don't think, in fact, that I had a single coherent thought in my head as I walked back, nor any sort of question. I groped my way still half in a faint, half in the grip of a grey hypnosis, not even realizing that Mrs Hudson had given me a basket of cakes and tarts until suddenly something bounced at my feet and I saw the basket lying there. The next thing I knew was being outside the tent, inside which Bill Ogilvy was laughing with such mighty enjoyment at something or other that he even had Doll laughing on incredible scales of gaiety too. It was only when I looked into the tent that I saw what that something or other was. Bill was clasping Doll somewhere about the bust with his good hand and was kissing her with such irrepressible ardour full on the lips that she was evidently enjoying the experience equally. And finally, just to hammer home to me the fact that even the most ghastly and shattering of experiences can sometimes utterly fail to change a man, I heard him say in that off-hand debonair way of his the very words he had once used to me :

'Again? One more? Good show.'

The rest of the afternoon exists as a shadowy ruin in which occasional gaps of impossibly vivid light now and then appear. I remember him eating cakes like a ravenous schoolboy. I remember him talking more to Doll than to me. I remember him telling something of the bloody wizard miracles they'd done to him in hospital and how soon, if those types got really cracking, he was going to fly again. They were going to make him the most marvellous gadget of an artificial hand you ever saw; wizard bit of work. It meant he would be able to handle the controls again like a piece of cake. He would soon be pressing the ruddy tit again. By sheer repetition I got to know some parts of a surgical language I didn't know before and the strange words raged in my head like the utterances of a madman. There were a few confused and excited sentences about the hell of his kite pranging over France one afternoon, when he had bounced in a potato field and some peasants had dragged him, face and hands shot to hell, out of the cockpit. Irrepressibly he recounted everything with laughter. It was all a bloody wizard show.

One more thing I remember about that afternoon with great clarity and that was how, as we sat there having tea on the grass, I simply couldn't bring myself to look at him any longer, whereas Doll was looking at him all the time. It wasn't the first time it had crossed my mind that Doll was a far braver person than I ever knew how to be, nor was it by any means to be the last. She looked at him that afternoon with an intentness that was more than merely engrossed; she might have been trying to search out the truth that lay somewhere deep under that irrepressibly infectious laughter and that grotesque and twisted face of his. I've said before that Doll, for all her own brand of gaiety, was no fool and I now know that Bill was no fool either. They were in fact, in many ways, very like each other. One other thing I now know too. She was quick to sense, that afternoon, the most important thing of all about him. There was a fierce and wonderful light of living in him.

After he had finished up the last of the cakes and tarts — I myself couldn't eat a thing and half the time kept letting my tea get cold – he said :

'Got to get plenty of sun on the old face. Must harden it up. I thought I'd stay out here in the country for a bit. Have a grandstand view of the show if nothing else. Know anybody who has a room to let? The Mess is chock-a-block. They can't have me there.'

I remember Doll saying she would ask at *The Welcome Stranger* and then said :

'Don't suppose you two fair maidens need a hand – and when I say hand I mean hand – with the jolly old plums, do you? Do it for love. Always ready to oblige the fair maidens, that's the Ogilvy motto.'

'Start whenever you like,' Doll said. 'We need all the help we can get.'

'Good show. With Ogilvy on the job we'll have the whole shoot stripped bare in no time.'

After that he kissed us both in impetuous and robust farewell, said he would remain for ever our fondest and most devoted slave, asked us to *The Welcome Stranger* for a drink bang on the stroke of six and finally went swaggering happily away, humming some tune or other, under the plum-trees.

It was only some considerable time after he had gone that Doll, with that sudden reflective seriousness that was sometimes so characteristic of her, said :

'Now I know something. All this time I've wanted to get at it and now I have. You know what flying is? A damn disease.'

13

WHILE Bill motored back to Surrey to collect some civilian clothes and to let the surgeon inspect his scars again Doll and I started on the last of the plums. I don't know how many trees we gathered that summer but Doll made a profit of thirty-five pounds from the plums alone and Mr Hudson was so pleased about it that he was now about to let us have a small orchard of apples too, mostly Beauty of Bath, which were almost ready, and Worcester Pearmains, which would follow them. The weather was still very warm and beautiful and in spite of all my shocks and dreads and anxieties I had never felt or looked so physically well in all my life. I had already abandoned my long trousers for a pair of shorts and by now my bare legs, like my face and arms, were an even buttery brown. Doll refused to follow my example on the grounds that what the eye doesn't see the heart doesn't grieve over but sometimes after lunch on very hot days she used to slip off her bra completely and lie behind the tent for half an hour so that, as she put it, her bosom and the sun could get better acquainted.

'"Close bosom friend to the maturing sun",' I quoted and when she wanted to know who had said or written that I told her 'Keats.'

'I notice Bill seems to throw a few poetical bits about sometimes.'

'Yes. It's an odd habit of his.'

Then I said I was curious to know what category of talent she put him into and without any hesitation she said : 'Deep. Very deep,' and I couldn't help feeling that perhaps she was right again.

'Were you ever in love with him?' she said.

'I used to think so but now I know I wasn't.'

'Are you sorry?'

'I don't think so. When I look at him I only know one thing.'

'What's that?'

141

'I either want Splodge back whole and in one piece or not at all.'

At this she gave me one of those old-fashioned looks of hers and said :

'I wonder if you'd say that if it ever happened.'

It was now, as I have said, some few days after the twelfth of August, the Glorious Twelfth, the time of grouse-shooting, without which our calendar wouldn't be quite the same. And when in fact Bill Ogilvy came back two days later it was to be richly burdened with four brace of birds, which had been awaiting him at hospital. The grouse had been sent down from Scotland by a pilot named Forbes-Watson, of Bill's old squadron, which to its intense and irritating frustration was kicking its heels on wet moorlands, resting and re-grouping, five hundred miles from the line of fire.

'Anybody know how to cook these things?' Bill said. He had arrived for what he called the apple battle equipped with an ancient pair of once white football shorts, now much crumpled and tied at the waist with a yellow necktie, a jersey in red-and-white hoops, a pair of brown plimsolls and what appeared to be one of his sister's panama school hats. 'Never eaten one of the damn things in my life before.'

I said that of course Rose knew how to cook them and he said :

'Good show. They're yours to do what you like with, Liz. Pass them on to the dear Rose.'

I was about to say that we might make them an excuse for a dinner party when I had what I thought was a better idea.

'Why don't we have them cold, with big potato salads and all that sort of thing, at a midnight picnic? I think there's a new moon about now, isn't there?'

'You can count me out,' Doll said. 'I need my beauty sleep.'

'Nonsense,' I said. 'You'd adore it.'

'And what would my old Smithy say if he pulled up at the pub and heard I was sky-larking with officers at a midnight orgy in an orchard? He wouldn't half tan my behind.'

'Bring the dear chappie along too,' Bill said.

'Funny. He's not much of a type for parties. They make him broody.'

'Well, who shall we ask?' I said. I thought of Mac, of Fitz, of the gay Matters and the even gayer Count. I hadn't seen Matters and the Count for some time. But now when I mentioned them Bill merely said :

'Mac and Fitz could come.'

'What about Matters and the Count?'

'Oh! they're sort of tied up.'

I didn't believe him; he equally well knew I didn't believe him and I said :

'Tell me.'

'Matters went for a Burton the day before yesterday. The Count's been missing for over a week.'

I suppose the very inevitability of this piece of information kept Doll and me silent. Neither of us at any rate even looked at each other and Bill suddenly said, almost as if Doll and I weren't there and he was talking to himself :

'It's blasted well getting so's we're outnumbered all over the shop. *Et Decorum Est Pro Patria Mori*. My foot,' and I realized it was the first time I had ever heard any sort of hint of bitterness in his voice. 'I wish to hell they'd pull their fingers out and get on with that bloody gadget of mine. There's a crying need for chaps.'

'And what did that mouthful of French mean?' Doll said. 'Or whatever it was.'

I thanked God he didn't translate. He merely turned instead to a tree, snatched an apple off it and bit into it half savagely, twisting still more grotesquely that twisted mouth of his.

'Good. Very sweet. What's this sort called?'

'*Beauty of Bath.*'

'Ah! the old wife of Bath. '*Housebandes at chirche-dore I have had fyve* – the scorcher. What a gal,' and a moment later, completely his old self again, deftly swung an old empty gas-mask container over his shoulder, ready to mount a ladder and start gathering apples. 'Let battle commence. Got to do something to serve the jolly old country in its hour of need.'

Then, just before putting his foot on the ladder, he abruptly changed his mind, took off the gas-mask container and stripped off his jersey. I saw then that there were more scars on the back

143

of his neck and shoulders and three or four more big ragged scars across his ribs.

'Forgot about the old scars. Got to get the sun to 'em. Must harden 'em up.'

Finally as he went up the ladder he turned, gave a twisted but affectionate smile and said :

'When I'm as brown and beautiful as you are, Liz dear, I shall feel pretty wizard. Did I say beautiful? I don't think. Somehow I don't think this old mug of mine is going to be worth close inspection for some time.'

Quite what prompted me to do it I don't know but I looked quickly at Doll as he said this and was just in time to see her involuntarily biting her lip, but whether from uneasiness in herself or pain for him I simply couldn't tell.

That afternoon was very brilliant and the apples were warm in the sun. They came easily from the branches and were slightly waxy to the touch. From high up on the ladders I could see, across the fields, the Hudsons' binder at work in a field of barley, its red sails clattering against the sea of almost salt-white beards. Then once I thought I saw my Uncle Harry walking upstream on the near bank of the river but he was out of sight before I could tell for certain. It made me think of trout, however, and I said :

'If Uncle Harry has any luck fishing I'll beg a few trout from him and we'll have those cold too. I'll get Rose to make us some plum pie as well.'

'Flout me with trout, rouse me with grouse, plumb me with plums,' Bill was just saying, or rather half-singing, in that inconsequential and debonair voice of his when suddenly, from directly above us, a fantastically rapid and stunning burst of tracer-fire broke out of the sky, followed by a thunderous explosion that almost shook me off the ladder. Hardened though I was by now to sudden visitations by bullets and bangs I involuntarily let out a scream and Doll said 'What the perishing hell ! Come in, whoever you are, don't bother to knock !' and then Bill yelled :

'Jesus, it's a bloody Dornier. The damn thing's going to fall on top of us.'

I looked swiftly across at him, perched on the top of his

ladder, and saw him clinging with his good hand to the second top-most rung and madly waving the red-brown stump of his left hand to the sky in an almost obscene gesture of defiance.

The next thing I knew was the screaming thunder of the Dornier's engines as it came spiralling out of the sky. I just had a second or two in which to think that Bill was probably right – that the plane was going to fall dead on top of us – and then I was under the trailer, side by side with Doll, both of us having got there without quite knowing how. I suppose we must have lain there, heads buried in our arms, for fully half a minute, with the scream of the falling Dornier getting nearer and nearer and fiercer and fiercer, until at last there was the most God-awful crunch from less than half a mile away, followed by a blistering volcanic bang only a second or two afterwards.

All this time I hadn't the vaguest notion where Bill was and it was only when I finally crawled out from under the trailer that I saw to my infinite astonishment that he was still at the top of the ladder, still frantically waving his stump and yelling with frenzied hate as if at some mad football match. As a result I immediately started yelling too. I felt I also hated the Dornier and all it stood for and for some moments I danced up and down like some idiot puppet in a delirium of jibbering excitement. Then suddenly from his perch at the top of the ladder Bill stopped his incoherent yelling and shouted the fierce announcement that one of the bastards had baled out and was probably going to fall on top of us too.

'Over there! Across the field! He'll probably fall in the bloody river!'

I was so far gone in pointless delirium that I really wasn't aware of running. I was mysteriously dispatched by some mad volition or other to the end of the orchard, and it wasn't until I reached the fence there, clear of trees, that I first saw the parachute. I felt immensely elated. It looked like a big cream-white convolvulus flower floating down in the sun. It wasn't more than half a mile or so up and what astonished me very much was that the rate of its fall seemed very gentle, peaceful and slow. The grass field beyond the orchard fence was probably not more than three hundred yards wide and beyond it was the little river and then beyond that a stretch of woodland. As I started running across the field I got the impression that the parachute would fall in the open there but its course deceived me and by the time I got to the river I knew that it would probably fall in the woodland or just beyond.

The river isn't more than eighteen inches or a couple of feet deep there and I splashed into it like some blood-thirsty hound in pursuit of a fox. By that time the parachute had disappeared beyond the line of trees and as I found the path and started to run along it I was suddenly struck by the uncanny silence that enfolded everything. It was so deep that it seemed to mock me. Then some seconds later there was a sudden crash as if a tree had fallen and at last I saw the parachute again.

Like a slowly deflating balloon it lay in a clearing of young sweet chestnut saplings that had grown to five or six feet high since the previous winter's cutting. It was far bigger than I had supposed and when it had finally deflated itself and lay in wide loose enfoldments about the young trees I just stood and gaped at it like the frightened fool I was.

The body attached to the harness was clearly a dead one, I thought, and with frozen stupidity I gaped at that too. Then as I went a yard or two nearer I saw to my sickening horror that, like Bill, it was going to move. A pair of bloody hands groped for and held what I thought for a moment was an entanglement of rubber tubing and then I realized that this was all that was left of the still pulsating entrails of the dying man. His face was black from flame. Out of its scorched framework a pair of white eyeballs briefly glittered and then were stiff again. A big service revolver lay strapped across the lower part of the chest and for one horrific moment the hands moved towards it and I was struck by the wild thought that perhaps he was trying to shoot either himself or me. But nothing else happened and only a second or so later the light in the eyes was dead.

Years afterwards I came across a phrase in a book about *all the dead pilots* and whenever I think of that episode on that too-bright August afternoon it comes back to me again and I know that that is what I saw there among the young sweet-chestnuts : not one pilot, but all the pilots, *all the dead pilots, from all over the world.*

When I eventually blundered out of the wood it was to fall into the encompassing arms of somebody in the field beyond.

'Bill,' was all I could say, 'Bill.'

It was by no means the first time I had made that very same mistake and after some moments of silence a voice said with a gentleness that shattered me far more than any shot could have done :

'Not Bill. It's Tom here.'

I don't think I believed it even then and I made no attempt to look up.

'I saw you running. You shouldn't have done.'

'What did you say?'

'Don't bother about it.'

'Sometimes these things are good for you.'

'I doubt it.'

We walked slowly back across the field. I suppose if you are rescued from drowning you probably feel very much as I did that afternoon : benumbed, groping, full of a brooding sort of thankfulness shot through with bright bursts of horror. It's certain that I could collect neither my thoughts nor my emotions. My clearest impression, I fancy, was of being very close to Tom. There was a profound anchorage in Tom. There was an infinite permanency in him not to be confused with the bright, starry, eternal convictions of immortality that I so often felt with Splodge. It was almost an embalming thing and that afternoon, and for long afterwards, I was wonderfully glad of it.

When I finally got home that evening I wanted neither food nor drink, comfort nor consolation. I was going to say that by that time I felt in the grip of a sort of sober starvation; but perhaps it would be truer to say that I felt like an empty husk, bloodless and wintry. There was neither hate nor elation in me any longer.

My grandmother was taking a bath when I got home. As she always bathed before breakfast I couldn't think what this change of habit could mean until Edna said :

'The rector and his sister are coming to dinner. Your grandmother has been helping Mr Harry lift potatoes all afternoon and I suppose she felt rather grubby.'

The Reverend Hall-Williams was very strong on the subject

of cruelty to animals and his sister very active in moral welfare. I was vaguely trying to decide how I could avoid the twin impact of these fascinating subjects when the telephone rang. My old dread of that sound instantly woke in me and I let it ring for some moments in the hope that someone else would answer it. But no one did and in a growing and deepening wave of dread I at last went to it and picked it up.

'Bannerhurst three-nine.'

'Who is that? Is that you? It's me.'

It was my mother. Distantly she inquired in feathery word-flights how I was. The news was terribly disturbing, wasn't it? Well, it was disturbing in one way and not in another. We didn't think of changing our minds and joining her? Was the battle really going on over our heads? It was awful. You heard such dreadful things. She'd listened to the news at six o'clock and didn't know whether to think it good or bad. The Germans had lost a lot of planes that day but if they were losing them she could only suppose that we were losing them too. Didn't I agree?

In her funny way, as usual, she was right.

'Yes,' I said. 'And how are you?'

'Oh? busy. Busy. Terribly busy. Bridge and coffee and all that. Reading. I knit these hospital socks too now.' In the face of these absorbing trivialities I went off into a benumbed daydream, so that at last she said: 'Are you still there? You sound awfully far away.'

'Perhaps I was.'

'You were what? Where were you? How is Mother?'

'Very well indeed.'

'And your husband? I was wondering if he couldn't possibly get some leave and you bring him down here for a few days. Do you think so?'

I said he too was very busy. Pilots always were. They had a disease.

'They have what? A disease? There's not an outbreak of anything, is there? You don't mean that?'

'No, nothing like that.'

'Thank Heavens. Things are bad enough as it is, without epidemics. Do you get enough butter and sugar?'

I said that so far we did and she thanked Heaven again. We must be sure to eat as well as possible. There was no surer way of catching epidemics than being undernourished. She could think of nothing worse.

'So you don't think you can get down?'

'I'm afraid it isn't likely.'

'It's a pity, but there it is. You'd find it so much less anxious here. Ring me if you change your mind. I long to see you.'

'Yes.'

'Well, good-bye for now. My love to you all. You do take shelter, don't you? That's the thing that worries me.'

'Yes, we do take shelter. Good-bye.'

Some time later I decided to take shelter in the dove-cot, on the wall of which the big magnolia was now in its full August glory, its chalices of flower like superb classical emblems, but the decision was too late. As I prepared to retreat to solitude the Rev. Hall-Williams and his sister arrived.

My grandmother was ready to receive them and was greeted by the splendid news that the fabric of the church roof had been totally repaired.

'Charlie Shoesmith did it all in his spare time. Found all the necessary new tiles and says he won't take a penny. Of course we shall get War Damage eventually.'

'Naturally,' my grandmother said. 'That is what we pay for.'

Two evenings later we had our nocturnal picnic; and now, more than ever, it seemed to me that I had every reason to make it gay.

14

THE ingredients of our gaiety that warm half-moonlit August night were to be the cold roast grouse, big bowls of potato salad and dressed salads of mixed cucumber, tomato, cos lettuce and French beans, a large cold rabbit-and-bacon pie – Harry, not surprisingly perhaps on that catastrophic afternoon, had had no luck with the trout – loaves and butter and cheese and apples, Rose's cheese-curd and currant-jelly tarts, four bottles of Hock brought by Splodge from the Mess, another bottle of John Cavendish Fitzroy's brandy, a crate of light ale brought by Bill from *The Welcome Stranger*, a portable gramophone and, last but by no means least, the glow-worms. Oh ! yes, we were to be very, very gay.

Many lovely things repose in my mind out of that summer but among the loveliest are the glow-worms. For some strange reason you hardly ever see them now, but that year they were almost as common as night-moths. Whenever the nights were really warm you saw them everywhere, their little gas-green tails candescent in the darkness. It's a curiously unearthly but friendly glow, that light. I always feel that I could never be afraid of the dark if there were glow-worms to lighten it.

We were, I think, a good crowd that night and mercifully except for a few distant rumbles which might well have been thunder and a few even more distant searchlights, the war seemed to be far away. Besides Splodge and myself there were Bill and Doll, who after what she called 'a good old-fashioned up-and-a-downer' had made her peace with Smithy and decided that letting her back hair down wasn't a bad idea after all ; Mac and a newly acquired autumn-red lady-friend, if that's the right word, named Clorinda ; and lastly John Cavendish Fitzroy and a short-built W.A.A.F. Officer of rather uncertain age and highly tentative manner, with too large awkward brown eyes and very correct moley hair, whom everybody called, for some obscure reason, Bronzie. All of us, with the exception of Bronzie at the very beginning and John Cavendish Fitzroy throughout the entire evening were, as I say, pretty gay.

But there was no gaiety that night in Fitz and I doubt if ever there was again. I hadn't seen him for several weeks and now I saw a great change in him. Almost all the old suavity of manner had left him and the acquisition of an uncharitable air of brittle bitterness didn't suit him at all. From time to time he was so uncharacteristically rude to Bronzie that I couldn't think for the life of me why she had been dragged along to the party at all until it slowly occurred to me that he had done it for the express purpose of lacerating her and that she, in turn, out of hopelessly unspoken adoration, was lapping up every bitter syllable of it like a beaten cat lapping up milk. It wasn't until much later in the evening that she gave me a clue to this by saying:

'No, it isn't self-pity, He's simply lost every grain of faith in himself – it's commoner than you might suppose. One mistake leads to another and another and in the end it's hard to avoid a crack-up. He's desperate,' and the descending whisper of her tentative voice was almost heartbroken.

But this, as I say, was a good deal later and we started, before twilight fell, on a better note. The men all took off their jackets and ties and helped arrange the food and drink and plates and glasses on an old trestle table brought up from home. Mac put *Ain't She Sweet* on the gramophone and danced an occasional step with Clorinda, a half-can of beer in one hand, the other clasping her waist. Bill was splendidly jocular and from time to time quoted earthy scraps of Chaucer, in an early English accent, and Doll, who was wearing a thin emerald silk blouse and a black shirt, graphically re-lived for us the up-and-downer with Smithy. 'We made such a hell of a row in the bedroom the landlady thought it was another air-raid and came up to see what all the hammer was about and there we were on the floor, like a couple of all-in wrestlers. But after that we were all sweetness and light. Lovely grub.'

By half past ten it was fully dark except for the half moon which threw fragile apple-tree shadows on the grass. I don't think the temperature fell that night by more than a fraction and the air was close and balmy. I was determined to obliterate from my mind every offending trace of that desperate episode

151

in the chestnut copse and I moved among my guests with an air of effervescence that presently drew from Bill the remark :

'We're very chipper tonight, aren't we? Very chirpy.'

'I'm in that mood. Watch out. No man is safe.'

'Ah ! the old immortal longings. Good show.'

'And what about *this* bloke?' Splodge said. 'Me.'

'Oh ! Splodge, darling. Drink with me.' I held up my glass of hock to his lips. 'You out of that side of the glass and me out of this.' Then we each drank in turn and he said :

'And so I plight thee my troth.'

In return for that I kissed him and then looked him full in those profoundly young and sensitive eyes of his and felt my soul start melting.

Soon we took our plates of food and glasses of wine and split up into groups or pairs. Sometimes you saw the moon drowning in your glass and sometimes, clear even above the music of the gramophone, there was the call of an owl on the night air. During all this Fitz sat rather apart from us, solitary against the trunk of an apple tree, his nearest companion Bronzie, who by this time had taken off her service jacket too.

As we drank more and more wine I suppose we all began to perspire more freely in that humid night air and presently Doll said :

'Gosh, I must say I'm sweating hot. Anybody mind?' and promptly did her old act of removing her blouse and revealing that splendid black bust of hers.

'Do we have to be squalid?'

The voice of John Cavendish Fitzroy came coldly over from the apple tree as if some unpardonable breach of manners had been committed. But Doll was ready.

'Oh ! some come from squalid areas,' she said. 'And others, of course, are just born squalid.'

This remark at least had the effect of silencing him and Mac said :

'Jesus, I'm all for squalor. How about it, Clorinda pet?'

'Adore it,' she said and immediately stripped off her own blouse, revealing a bra of pinkish gold, so that she looked quite naked in the honey-yellow moonlight, framed against the thick mass of her coppery hair.

At this Mac smacked his lips and said 'Hell!' and gave her a trenchant and noisy kiss somewhere on the upper breast. 'Baby, you'll have me coming and going like a buck rabbit –'

'Must we?' Fitz said.

' "*When in disgrace with fortune and men's eyes*",' Bill suddenly quoted. 'Have another piece of grouse, Fitz, old boy – more grouse, eh?'

'Answer came there none,' Splodge said.

These heavy attempts at humour drew nothing from the direction of the apple tree but a silence that was as loud, in its way, as the clang of a warning gong. I abruptly sensed more than bitterness in the air. It seemed suddenly that we were on the edge of a dreadful breaking point. I could see the evening ending in miserable ruins and it made things no better when Mac said in that raw and candid Canadian voice of his:

'Hell, boy, you'll end up by being kind of a bad type.'

'Ah! the voice of colonial independence.'

'Independent? You're dead right I am. Ask 'em in Winnipeg.'

'I've no intention of asking anybody anything in Winnipeg. Thank God.'

I was just beginning to be half-terrified as to what might happen next when Bill saved everything by saying:

'Any lady care to dance with a one-arm bandit? Clorinda, may I have the pleasure? Put on something good and lively, Mac.'

'Any more for the rabbit pie?' I said. 'There's plenty.'

'Me,' Mac said. 'Hell, that's good, that pie.'

'A toast to Rose,' Splodge said and raised his glass of hock. 'Bless her.'

'Here's to Rose,' we all said. 'Good old Rose. Bless her.'

In another moment the springing notes of *Bye, Bye, Blackbird* broke on the air. There is something wonderfully and infectiously gay about that old tune and soon Mac and Doll were dancing too and then Splodge and I started and all tension was broken. Doll, Clorinda and I all kicked off our shoes as we danced and I felt the very slightest touch of dew on my stockings. Then after another moment or two I stopped dancing and took off my stockings and from then on danced in my bare feet. The sensation of dancing bare-foot on grass was exciting and delicious and presently Splodge was kissing my bare shoulders and holding me with a tension I found hard to bear.

'I can hardly wait to love you,' he suddenly said.

'Let's go and hunt for glow-worms.'

'What on earth are you talking about?'

'Hunting glow-worms.'

So we danced to the far side of the orchard. There by the hedgerow a dozen or more glow-worms shone in the grasses. Splodge, who had never seen glow-worms in his life before, knelt down and gazed at this display of night magic as if at something out of a fairy tale and kept repeating over and over again:

'What a blooming, wizard, wonderful thing.'

'And even more wizard when you think they're making love.'

'No? Gosh, it's like *Midsummer Night's Dream* or something.'

'Well, let's make it one.'

'What do you mean by that?'

'Love me here.'

I slipped off the rest of my things and lay down on the grass. How long we stayed there I never really knew but by the time we walked back across the orchard the moon was going down. The gramophone was still playing as we joined the party and Mac was going very strong with a much dishevelled Bronzie, swinging her round and round like some wild Polovitzian maiden. Bill was doing even better, dancing and prancing some kind of reel with both Doll and Clorinda, with strange barbaric cries and high-pitched laughter.

'"On such a night as this,"' I heard him say and Doll said:

'And my God, what a night! Never laughed so much in all my perishing natural. Oh! not under the arms! Please, Bill! You'll have me in a tizz!'

'Something wrong? Not enjoying it?'

'Enjoying it? And to think I nearly didn't come.' She did a sudden fantastic pirouette, skirt flying, black panties revealed, blonde hair flying out, her entire body radiant with delight. 'This is the life for Doll. I can take buckets of this!'

'What dance is this supposed to be, Bill?' I said.

'The Toothsome Reel, my child. Ah! my wild and clan-proud Scottish ancestors!'

'And where the heck have you been, Liz?' Mac called. 'All the day, all the day?'

'Hunting for glow-worms.'

'A likely story!' they all said. 'A likely story!'

'Mac! Steady!' Bronzie shrieked. 'Do you want to throw me over the moon?'

Some few moments later I became aware that the gramophone had stopped. I turned to where it stood on the trestle table, among the debris of rabbit-pie and bones and fruit skins and bottles and glasses, and to my utter astonishment saw that there were no longer seven of us but eight. A new figure had joined us. Neat in his service uniform, almost middle-aged in comparison with the faces of the young on all sides of him, he looked not at all unlike a policeman who had come to run us all in for disturbing the midnight peace. He was even carrying his brown leather gloves.

'Jeez!' I heard Mac say. 'It's Adj. Hiya, Adj? Strip off, old sport. Join the orgy. Have a beer. Get your nose-bag on. "We're going to get drunk tonight if we never get drunk no more!"'

Suddenly Bill stopped dancing and came slowly over to the table.

'Hullo, Adj., old boy. Nice of you to join us. To what do we owe this timely honour? You know Elizabeth, don't you?'

'Yes. We've met. Good evening.'

'Good evening,' I said. 'Won't you have some wine?'

'No, thanks. Is Fitz here? I'd like a word with Fitz.'

'Over here, Adj., under the apple tree. Join me in a brandy. What black have I put up now?'

The voice of John Cavendish Fitzroy seemed, I thought, a good deal less bleak than before.

'Fitz has been naughty!' Mac said. 'Naughty Fitzy. Bad type.'

Slowly also the Adjutant started to walk over to the apple tree where Fitz was sitting.

'Hell, arrest this woman, Adj!' Mac called. 'She's stealing my confounded honour.'

'Gosh, I'm thirsty,' I heard Doll gasp. She was panting like a puppy after all the wild exertions of the Toothsome Reel. 'Is there any more wine?'

'I'll see if I can find some,' Splodge said.

But by the time Splodge had found the wine Fitz had come over to the table. The Adj. was still standing under the tree.

'The Adjutant's compliments, Mrs Smith,' Fitz said, 'but would you care to join us in a brandy?'

'Burying the hatchet, Fitz?' Mac said but Fitz didn't say a word.

Nor did Doll. She simply went with Fitz over to the apple tree, where the three of them stood talking for the next two or three minutes or so. I actually saw Fitz pour her a brandy and she just stood there sipping it slowly.

Then she walked back to us.

'Has anyone seen my blouse?'

I think it was Bill who found her blouse. She took it from him without a word, put it on and slowly buttoned it up. Then she ran her hands through her fair untidy hair and said :

'Would somebody take me home please?'

That was all she said. A moment later, without any of us actually realizing it I think, she started to walk all alone across the orchard. I wanted to run after her but I couldn't and it was, I suppose, typical of Fitz that finally he was the one who ran. In my helpless way I just stared dumbly after him. Then Bronzie all of a sudden came to her senses and she went running too.

'Air-sea Rescue picked up his body off the beach near Dungeness. Just before dark,' I heard the Adj. say. 'Word's only just come through.'

I wanted to weep for Doll but I couldn't do that either. I heard Fitz's big Bugatti suddenly start up in the lane and the noise of it made me jump. And I suppose it was typical of Bill that it was he who came over to make the first gesture of comfort towards me with that one good arm of his and as his hand touched my shoulder that startled me too.

Instantly I saw the dead pilot in the wood again. He was now transfigured by an intense illumination, exactly the same colour as the gas-green glow-worm light. Then somebody started to pack up plates and I remember saying 'Oh! leave them. I'll do them in the morning,' and then I too suddenly started running.

'Doll!' I screamed. 'Doll!'

I wasn't more than half way across the orchard when I heard someone else calling. It was Splodge.

'Your shoes,' he was saying. 'You haven't got your shoes.'

I stopped. He caught up with me and bent down and started to put on my shoes. I couldn't say a word but I suppose it was the simple gesture of putting on my shoes that, more than anything else, made it easy for me to cry. The soles of my feet felt wet and cold now and I cried for quite a long time, standing there in the fading moonlight, emptily.

Not very long after that, our gay Midsummer Night's Dream over, we all went home.

15

Lack of Moral Fibre, or Flying Sickness D., as they used to call it in the old days, is the official name for the condition in which men like John Cavendish Fitzroy sometimes found themselves and it was in this condition that I too found myself the following morning, when I couldn't bring myself to go near the orchard until nearly twelve o'clock. I was certain Doll wouldn't be there and I doubted very much if Bill would be either and I dreaded the thought of being alone.

My dread was utterly unfounded. To my infinite astonishment Bill, stripped to the waist, was up a ladder, picking from one of the last half dozen trees of Beauty-of-Bath. Doll was sitting on a box outside the tent, sorting and grading apples. Still more astonishing the gramophone, which had somehow got left in the tent the previous night, was vigorously beating out some loud and brassy tune the words of which I didn't know.

When she saw me Doll got up, came over to me, put her arms round me and said simply :

'Don't say anything, duckie. Please.'

For fully a minute neither of us spoke again. We just stood there with our arms about each other and it was eventually Doll who broke the silence first.

'Brew us a cuppa tea, duckie, if you want something to do. We're both as thirsty as fishes.'

'I'm sorry I'm late. I didn't think you'd be here. I didn't sleep too well.'

'Didn't think you would.'

'Did you sleep?'

'Like a top, duckie, thanks to Fitz and Bronzie. They drove back to the Mess and roused the Doc and got me some tablets. Bronzie was a real brick. She put me to bed and didn't go until I was sleeping. Then this morning she came all the way back and brought me a cuppa tea about eight o'clock.'

'Good for Bronzie.'

'At first I thought she was a strait-lace. But she's not. She'll do.'

'I thought so too.'

'She's daft about Fitz, I suppose you know. Got it real bad.'

'I guessed as much.'

'She's worried like hell about him too. He's cracking up. Gone to pieces. Well, it's the way it is sometimes. You can't expect it to be all stiff-upper and honour and glory all the time. What price glory anyway?'

At this point Bill, who had been picking apples well out of earshot, walked over to us, stopped the gramophone, gave me an almost fatherly kiss on the forehead and said with a quietness quite remarkable in him:

'How's our tea-girl this morning? Going to brew us a cup?'

I nearly always made the tea and in another few moments I started to find mugs and fill the kettle and light the oil stove. While the kettle was boiling up Doll said:

'Might as well have a spot of lunch too while we're at it. Bill wants to get off at two o'clock.'

'Off? Where?'

'Got a bit of an appointment,' Bill said. 'Shan't be long.'

I thought it prudent not to ask questions and Doll said:

'I'm trying to sort out a decent box of apples to send to Bill's mother. I thought we'd start on the Worcesters tomorrow. What do you fancy for lunch? Boiled eggs? It's all I brought up today anyway.'

While Doll finished grading her box of apples and Bill washed and tidied himself up I boiled the eggs, made the tea and cut some bread-and-butter. Washing was always a bit of a slow and difficult task for Bill, with only one hand and his skin still tender, and it was a quarter of an hour or more before we sat down to lunch, which I'd laid out on the trestle table.

When finally the three of us sat down, Doll on an old backless kitchen chair I'd found in a loft at home, Bill and I on up-turned apple-boxes, I said:

'I think we'll keep the trestle table up here. It's handy. I don't know why I didn't think of it before.'

At this point Doll got up and went into the tent and presently came back with half a bottle of whisky in her hand.

'Who's for a drop of Scotch milk in their tea?'

Bill and I thanked her all the same and said we didn't think we would, but she poured a fairly generous dollop into her tea and said:

'Well, all the more for them as do, as my old man used to say. He used to have Scotch milk in his tea every morning for breakfast. You needed it too, up there, on those nice cold and frosty Midland mornings, I tell you. Enough to freeze brass monkeys.'

Doll, always ready to chatter, talked almost ceaselessly through lunch, while Bill and I, by contrast, were almost silent, Bill most unusually so. Then after her third cup of tea, into each of which she poured her generous tot of Johnnie Walker, she suddenly said:

'I've got something to say to you two. If you're going to mope and moon and get the gloomies about what's happened I'll give you both the sack.'

'Fair enough,' Bill said.

'I mean it. I'll not come up here every day to look at faces as long as a wet week, I tell you. So drop it now. I lost my mother when I was ten and my old man when I was fifteen. I've had this before. Are you listening, Bill? We might as well get the air clear now. You know what the chances in this bun-fight are.'

'Yes,' Bill said.

Then she turned to me with a look at once warm and candid and said:

'I'm sorry, duckie. But we've all got to face it. It's just the way it is.'

These few words, courageous in themselves, had the effect of putting at least some courage back into me. Up to that time I had nursed a grief for her which might well have been my own but now I felt an almost blessed sense of relief in the air.

'I'd rather him go like that,' she said at last, 'than be round the perishing twist for the rest of his life. And so would he.'

'Here endeth the first lesson,' Bill said. 'I'll try to think up some cracking good jokes.'

'You'd better too. Or I'll crack you one.'

During lunch the air was several times broken by the high rattle of gun-fire but on the whole the fire seemed distant and sometimes almost a desultory echo of the real thing. That day, in fact, the fighting was farther away from us and, though intense and even ferocious, as I learned later, was taking place more over the south sea-coast and the eastward estuary, so that our piece of countryside became for a few hours almost its old pastoral self again. Nevertheless whenever we heard that gun-fire I caught Bill in the act of looking up, with that peculiar hungry-angry look of longing on his face, the expression of that incurable disease Doll had diagnosed so well, his scarred lips pugnaciously tightened, the lacerations of his face, half-bronze, half-putty-coloured, more fiercely grotesque than ever.

Just after half past one he put on a shirt and tie and a dark blue brass-buttoned blazer, gave us both a rather solemn kiss and then set off, walking. It was only then, as I watched him walking across the orchard, that it came back to me that he nursed a small private grief of his own. Not only could he no longer pilot Hurricanes; he could no longer drive even the beloved Chloe. For a man of restless hunger for action, mental as well as physical – Doll was right, as usual, about his talent being a deep one – it might well have been a source of near-bitterness that the only combat he could now engage in was one with apple trees and a ladder.

It was only some time after he'd been gone and Doll and I had washed up the lunch things that I said :

'Where is this appointment? Do you know?'

'He's gone on the old, old badger again. Wants Groupie to talk the powers-that-be into putting him back on ops. Or try to.'

'He's crazy.'

'Of course. How did you guess?'

'They'll never let him.'

'Not now, perhaps, not yet. But they will. In time. They can't put him off for ever. He'll win. You'll see. Eventually.'

'I hope to heaven they won't. Apart from everything else his eyes don't look right.'

'That's just it. That's where you're wrong. He says his eyes are the best part of him. Might well be, too. The other morning a group of people stood outside the pub, staring up, like they always do, trying to pick out something up there. Not one of them could see a perishing thing. But Bill could. It was a para-chute, all of fifteen thousand feet up.'

For a brief moment I had an unaccountable vision of Tom Hudson's eyes, behind his glasses, so bright and yet not strong enough to do these things, and then she said :

'You know what he really wants to do?'

I was almost on the verge of saying 'Kill himself,' when I stopped myself in time and she said :

'He *thinks*, that man, I tell you. He really *thinks*. He isn't just thinking for now, either. He's thinking way ahead.'

'And what is it he wants to do?'

'He says if we win this battle – and God knows we haven't yet – the war may last five years, perhaps longer. And pretty soon there'll be a new battle. A lot of it at night.'

The thought of the war grinding on for another five years or longer struck a sudden new chill into my heart and I didn't say a word.

'You know they bombed London the other night? And then we bombed Berlin the next? Bill says the London bombing is the biggest mistake they've ever made. He says because of it we *will* win this battle.'

'I don't see why.'

'He says we're in for what he calls a gut-slugger. Hitler will slug our guts and we'll slug his. It might last for years. And may the best man win.'

'You still haven't told me what he wants to do.'

'It's his idea to be a night-fighter. He says we'll need a hell of a lot of 'em.'

'He'll have to eat more carrots if he's going to see in the dark.'

'The cock they put out, the ruddy drivel. Carrots, my foot. Smithy always used to say they had a special department of daft bone-heads up in Whitehall who thought up bloody silly things like eating carrots for night vision and kettles for Spitfires and iron railings for battle ships. Of all the piddling drivel.'

'So he wants to fly at night.'

'Shooting up trains, that's his idea. It seems he shot up a train near the Belgian border once. There must have been ex-plosives aboard because he says it went up like Guy Fawkes night. Wizardest prang ever, it seems. He's mad to do it again.'

Not until some long time later did it strike me as strange that whereas Bill had never talked to me of such things, Doll had somehow induced him to express himself eloquently both as to deeds and thought; but then Doll was a deep one too.

We went on talking and picking apples for another two hours or so when Doll again confessed to having a thirst like a fish and begged me to put the kettle on. The warm afternoon had made me thirsty too and I was just filling the kettle and lighting the spirit stove when I saw the oddest figure coming across the orchard. I could hardly believe my eyes.

'That's strange,' I said. 'it looks like a telegram-boy,' and suddenly my heart started racing with dread.

'Telegram-boy, my foot.'

A moment later Doll burst out laughing and I recognized the moustached figure riding towards us, no-handed, on a bright scarlet bicycle, as no other than our comedian-thinker, Bill. The red bicycle I found it possible to believe in but the old, wide, wizard and wonderful chestnut moustaches had me utterly and hopelessly floored.

Unlike Doll, I couldn't even laugh and just stood there gaping as Bill, arms in air like some circus trick-cyclist, drew up in front of us with the grandest of flourishes.

'Hail! Transport at last, ladies. Saw the jolly old gridiron outside the blacksmith's. He wanted three quid for it but he finally let me have it for thirty-five bob because his son's in Bomber Command.'

'But Bill,' was all I could say, 'the moustaches.'

'Ah! yes, the fungi. Forgot to tell you, Liz dear. Grew them overnight. Some stuff in a tube you spread on. It's the positive counterpart of what you girls use to remove superfluous hair. Pretty wizard.'

Then Doll started laughing again and said something about Bill entering the wrong profession and how he ought to have been on the halls.

'Had 'em made to measure at the barber's actually. Own specification. Thought they might hide some of the old scars and impress Groupie.'

'And did they?'

'Didn't see him. Too busy. Drew a blank I'm afraid. The chaps are having a hell of a thick day of it, it seems. Scrambling all the time, lucky bastards. Goering's kindly providing a lot of customers.'

After that he slowly and a trifle sadly took off the moustaches and stood gazing up at the sky, looking not so comic now but a little melancholy and curiously naked.

'I fear 'twas of no avail,' he said. 'No avail. Joke over. Other jokes will no doubt follow. Any tea?'

That night an unbearably tense, exhausted, fragile-looking Splodge walked slowly into the house at dusk, eyes smeared with that curious eel-coloured dilation that long fatigue brings. He might well have been drinking. His exhaustion was so great that at first he not only didn't kiss me or say a word but seemed almost completely unaware of the presence of my grandmother and myself in the sitting-room and simply sat there staring past us.

Even my grandmother, habitually so phlegmatic, was alarmed by this and intuitively sensed at least some part of the trouble. She suddenly got up and poured out a big whisky-and-soda, set it on the table in front of him and said:

'You need food. I'll go and see Rose.'

While she had gone to the kitchen he sat there in utterly exhausted silence for some minutes longer before I at last said:

'You look all in, darling. Haven't you eaten?'

'Some type shoved a bun into my hand some time this morning. About twelve I think. I think I had half a mug of tea about four.'

'You think? But I thought you had regular meal times.'

'Had six scrambles today. Just wasn't time. Goering isn't very co-operative either. Just won't arrange his ruddy raids to fit in with our grub times. Most inconsiderate.'

Up to this moment he hadn't even been aware of the whisky now at last he picked up the glass, stared at it for some moments and then drank slowly.

'But pilots can't be expected to fly and fight on these terms,' I said.

He gave me a faint, weary grin.

'Like the bumble-bee. According to aeronautical laws it can't fly. Nature says it does.'

'We'll pack up food for you tomorrow.'

'It's a question of time really. No sooner down from one sortie than we're off on another. Oh! there's food. Of a sort. Sergeant Williams and Corporal Lancaster do a pretty fair job on bacon-and-eggs, but today there wasn't even time to swallow that.'

He suddenly took a big gulp at the whisky, finishing it off. Rightly or wrongly, I got up and poured him another. He seemed a little less tense now, I thought.

'Yesterday when we had a bit more time Corporal Lancaster ran out of eggs. Then he managed to find a couple and the first one he broke into the frying pan was bad. Must have been two months old. There was a ghastly stench and Randy Mason got mad as hell and called him all the names under the sun and tore him off a strip.'

The effect of the whisky on an empty stomach was making him talk quite fast now and I was glad when Rose knocked on the door and then came in with a tray.

'Williams was terribly cut up about it. More still when Randy didn't come back today. Bad about Randy. Good type. Got seven and three possibles already. Good for a gong.'

My grandmother then came into the room.

'I got Rose to warm up some *consommé* and drop an egg into it. While you're having that she'll make you a cheese *soufflé*. They need eating straight away.'

Then she sat down and fixed those dark, keen eyes of hers on his thin, exhausted face, watching him in silence for some minutes while he sipped at the *consommé*. At last she said:

'You seem to have had a stiff sort of day. We all thought it seemed a little quieter here.'

He laughed very briefly. 'Not where I've been.'

She was sensible enough not to pursue this rather delicate matter any further and I knew that he wanted to change the subject as soon as he turned to me and said:

'What's your news, darling? Anything exciting? Coco had her kittens yet?'

This endearing question of his made me laugh too. I then

165

told him about Bill, the moustaches and the red bicycle and
how he had been off to badger authority, but with no luck.

'Typical. Good old Bill. Can't keep a good bloke down. Tell
him to lie low, though, for a bit. Groupie's got his plate full as it
can stick. Adj's half-bonkers.'

'What about Fitz? Bronzie says he's in a terrible state. Doll
told me.'

'Oh! he was flying today. Had to. Can't spare 'em even if
they're bats. What about Doll?'

I then told him about Doll and how magnificent she had been
and how she had threatened us with our lives if we got the
gloomies.

'Good show.'

After that Rose came in with the cheese *soufflé*, piping hot
and I started to spoon it on to a plate.

'Will that be all, madam?' Rose said. 'Would Mr Bannister
like a sweet? There's some stewed Victorias and cream.'

'Please, Rose,' he said. 'The *soufflé's* bang-on.'

'And Rose,' I said, 'would you pack some food for Mr Bannister to take in the morning? He'll be away quite early. I think
he ought to have breakfast by a quarter to seven.'

'And a good big one, Rose, please.'

'Yes, sir. And what sort of food to pack, miss?'

'Something dead easy, Rose,' Splodge said. 'Something I can
ram down in about half a split second.'

'Oh! sir, that's not good for your digestion.'

'Come to think of it, Rose, you're right. Still, something easy,
Rose. Like hot roast duck and cherries with new potatoes and
green peas and cauliflower and lashings of sauce. Three help-
ings. You know the sort of thing.'

Rose, lost in admiration, giggled and actually said that
only he'd have mentioned it before she'd have had the duck all
ready. After that she said good night to us all, hoped we would
sleep well and then left.

When the door had closed Splodge instantly started laughing.

'Why are you laughing?'

'The duck made me think of Fitz. You remember how he
couldn't bear the Mess food – gosh, we used to have seven
course dinners at that time, too – and always had to have his

sent down from town? Today I saw him champing on half a stale currant bun with a bit of cold fried egg on top of it. God, it seems a million years away.'

At this point my grandmother got up, smiling.

'You had Rose in such a state of ditheration about the duck that I'm afraid she forgot your sweet. I'll go and remind her. Meanwhile bless you both.' She kissed us each in turn. 'Sleep well. Good night.'

Not long after that we too went to bed. Up in my room at the top of the dove-cot he simply dropped his tunic on to a chair without bothering to fold it, then put on his pyjama trousers without troubling to find the jacket and then fell into bed. Before I had finished brushing my hair he was in a deep, stunned sleep, breathing heavily.

Hours later, some time about day-break, I found myself awake and to my astonishment he was awake too, those still painfully young eyes turned towards me.

'Some time I must take a picture of you when you're asleep. I didn't think you were quite so beautiful.'

'Oh! you didn't? Thank you, sir.'

'What I really meant —'

'Too late. Too late.'

'I meant that you *are* beautiful, but —'

'But? Wounding words, as Bill might say, very wounding words.'

'Bill? Is there more in this than meets the eye? Is there perhaps dalliance nowadays in the orchard? Is it to be supposed that you prefer my old friend to me?'

'You're suddenly wonderfully fresh after your sleep.'

'That's because I slept with a heavenly body.'

'Flattering wretch. I love you.'

With that he suddenly held me very close to him, kissing me and saying nothing for some time. The fusion of two bodies after the warmth and serenity of sleep is a wonderful thing and for the next few minutes there wasn't even the shadow of a shadow of dread in my heart or, amazingly, any sign of weariness in him. But at last he said :

'Young lady, I've something to say to you.'

'Say on. You sound very serious.'

'I thought about Doll. If anything happens to me you won't get the gloomies, will you?'

I didn't say anything.

'You won't go into purdah, will you?'

'I won't even talk about it.'

'Please do. Please listen. If anything happens to me I want you to promise me something. Promise me you'll make a new life for yourself. As soon as you can. You're very young. Don't get the gloomies and be a martyr, please.'

'Nothing is going to happen to you.'

'Famous last words.'

'Please don't talk like that. It makes me very unhappy.'

'I'm sorry. I just had to say this. And I only say it because I love you a little more every day.'

'Only a little?'

'There I go again.'

'Hold your old rabbit's foot very tight, will you?' I said. 'She feels a little shaky.'

After that we again lay very close to each other and very quiet, watching daylight grow stronger and then sunlight gradually colour the curtains with an apricot glow, until at last he said:

'Oh! by the way, can you sew?'

'Of course I can sew.'

'Good show.'

'Why? Have you lost a button or something?'

'No,' he said, starting to laugh. 'Nit that I am, I almost forgot to tell you.'

'What? That you still love me?'

He then kissed me on the end of the nose, twice, with grave tenderness.

'No,' he said. 'They gave me my gong.'

In the middle of the following afternoon I discovered, when I went to boil the kettle in the orchard, that we were almost out of tea. There was just about enough in the packet for one pot, but not enough if we worked late, and I was just about to beg Bill to go stunting on his grid-iron down to the village to buy another half pound when I had another idea.

'We're almost out of tea, Doll. I'll slip along to the farm and see if I can borrow a little from Mrs Hudson.'

The tea was exactly the excuse I needed to go to the Hudsons'. I simply had to tell somebody else about that gong, my heart was so vast with pride.

To my surprise it was Tom, and not his mother, I found in the kitchen. He too was boiling a kettle. On the table stood a basket covered with a clean white cloth and beside it a huge white tea-pot and a big blue enamel urn.

'Hullo,' he said. 'Just making tea for the harvest field. Nice surprise to see you.'

He smiled at me in a very friendly way and then started shovelling large spoonfuls of tea into the pot.

'Don't use it all,' I said. 'That's what I've come to borrow. We're out of tea. That's if you can spare it.'

'Oh! that's easy. Sorry Mother isn't here. She's gone into market with Aunt Midge. They generally go on Tuesdays.'

He then filled up the big white tea-pot with boiling water and then, while the tea was mashing, looked in the side cupboard of a big oak dresser for a new packet of tea. The kitchen at the Hudsons' was enormous, half of it dominated by a vast black coal range, which was always burning, however hot the weather.

While he was finding the tea I asked him how the harvest was and he said pretty good, the weather had helped a lot and the wheat-yield was going to be heavy, and in return he asked how things were with me? How was my husband?

'Too much on ops.,' I said. 'But it has its compensations. They gave him the D.F.C. yesterday.'

'But that's marvellous. That's really something. You must be very proud.'

'Bursting.'

'I'm sure you are. What's the score?'

'No idea. He never shoots a line.'

He then found another basket and put a wine bottle full of milk in it, with several enamel mugs and a packet of sugar.

'Why do you say too much on ops.?'

Then I started to tell him all about the scrambles and the sorties and how the squadron hardly ever got time to eat. He was so absorbed that he actually sat down at the table, chin in his brown straw-scratched palms, and just gazed at me in fascinated silence, like a small boy listening to an adventure story. When I got to the part about Corporal Williams and the bad egg in the frying pan he said :

'Dammit, that's awful. I could let them have eggs. Mother and Aunt Midge have taken on another hundred pullets and they're just coming on to lay. Let me do that. We've always got tons.'

'It's very nice of you.'

'At least they'd be sure of having fresh ones. How do they fare for bacon I wonder? What about taking a bit of real bacon for them too?'

I knew that the Hudsons always cured their own hams and bacon and there was now such a look of eager generosity on his face that I hadn't the heart to say anything but :

'Your bacon's always so wonderful but could you really spare it?'

'Oh! we've always masses. Let's go over to the malthouse and have a look.'

The Hudson farm-house was old, built in fine squared rag-stone, as all the farm buildings were, with roofs of vivid orange-brown tiles. Down one entire side of the yard stood a vast corn barn, with a high double wagon door, and on the other a row of stables. At the end opposite the house stood the old malt-house and next to it the brew-house and behind them four big circular oasts, with snow-white cowls, each crowned by a prancing white horse as a weather-vane. Fresh oat straw littered the yard and everywhere, as Tom and I walked across it, brown and white hens were clucking and pecking and scratching about in the sun.

I always got a great feeling of permanence and solidarity from the yard. The immemorial nature of that warm square stone seemed always to me as eternal as the hills and the big beech-woods that rose behind the farm. The big corn barn was almost church-like in its dignity and the four oasts were like short but splendid orange spires.

It must have been years since the malt-house had been used for malting. It was rather dark inside, with only two small windows. I hadn't ever been in there before and now I stood looking at the white-washed walls hung all about with muslined sides of bacon, hams, jowls and shoulders. There was a thick ammoniated odour in the air that was sharp on the nostrils. It too was oddly church-like and the big oblong greyish sides of bacon clothed in the thin white butter muslin hung there like plaques.

'You see, there's plenty,' Tom said. 'Dad will have it. He was brought up to know a decent bit of bacon when he tasted it and won't have any muck from any shop. He's right too. I must say you really do taste something when you get your teeth into a slice of this.'

Then he said he thought there was the better part of three quarters of a side of bacon still in cut back at the house and there was no reason why I shouldn't have half of that; but first he'd better get back to the harvest-field and take the tea and would I care to walk over with him? Then he'd come back to pack up the eggs and cut the bacon. He confessed long afterwards that this was rather a clumsy ruse to keep me there as long as possible but I had no sort of clue to this at the time except that once or twice I caught him looking at me with something more than mere steadfastness and once, as we neared the harvest-field, he said :

'You've got marvellously brown since you've been in the orchard. I've never seen you look so well. By the way, how's your friend?'

'Doll? Not too bad. Her husband went for a Burton the other day.'

'I'm sorry. Wasn't he a Sergeant-Pilot?'

'That's right.'

'I'm sorry. Tony Johnson was badly wounded last week, I hear.'

In the harvest-field Tom's father, two rather oldish labourers named Fred and Amos and a boy were building wheat stooks. When Tom and I arrived with the tea baskets they all knocked off and sat down against a long stook while Tom filled the big enamel mugs with tea and I handed round the food baskets. One of the old men, Amos, had a remarkably fruity eye for a girl and after sizing me up several times all the way from bust to calves cocked his cap saucily on the back of his head and nudged his mate with a very knowing elbow and said :

'Nice to be waited on, Fred. More still when it's a young female.'

'That is.'

'Have to offer her a job, I reckon. Think she'd take it on?'

'No bounds.'

'How about it miss? We old 'uns could do with a nice bit o' company,' he said, and actually winked at me with devilish sauciness. At which I made everybody laugh and got my own back smartly by saying :

'I'm beginning to think it's a good job I can run pretty fast.'

'You'd better get your second wind, Amos,' Mr Hudson said, laughing. 'Sharp too.'

The wheat-stooks, the old men, the harvest-field and the laughter all had their own kind of permanence too and for a little while the war was no longer near me. I don't think we were disturbed by a single burst of fire, either near or distant, as we sat there and all about us the late August fields drowsed in deceptive slumber.

When finally Tom and I got up to go the saucier of the two old men, Amos, made another fruity reconnaissance of my figure and said :

'Well, that was arf-tidy drop o' tea, Fred mate. Suppose we'd better get back on the job, eh, even if we atta force ourselves? Coming to wait on us, tomorrow, miss?'

'Who knows?'

'Ah! now she's a-talking. Now she's a-talking. Eh, Fred?'

'She is that.'

'Well, good-bye for now,' I said. 'Keep out of mischief.'

'Ah! that ain't so easy at our age,' they said. 'Not at our age.'

'Nor mine,' I said and to that quick parting shot they had no answer except renewed cackles of laughter.

As Tom and I walked out of the gate of the harvest-field he turned to me and said :

'Well, thanks for coming to help. I never dreamed you could be so flirtatious.'

'That wasn't flirtatious. It's just that this farm always makes me happy.'

Back in the big farm kitchen Tom cut off half the remaining three-quarter side of bacon and then said :

'Are you planning to work late? If you are I can cut off a few slices while I'm at it and you can have them for supper. You'll never taste anything better.'

I thanked him and he sliced off about a dozen rashers of the home-cured bacon for me. He'd already put two score of eggs in a basket and now he started to parcel up the big lump of bacon with string and brown paper, saying at last :

'It's pretty heavy. I'll carry it for you. It's too much for you with the eggs.'

So he walked back to the orchard with me, for most of the way carrying both basket and bacon, even though I several times insisted on taking the basket.

'No, no. Pleasure. It isn't all that often I get the chance of seeing you.'

When finally he had finished chatting to Doll and Bill and myself and had turned to go back to the harvest-field Doll gave me one of those slow old-fashioned looks of hers and said :

'So that's where we've been all this long time. As if I didn't know. You know what I told you. Danger there.'

'Doll, for a woman of your experience you do talk utter cock sometimes.'

'See any green in my eyes? I can tell by the look of your face you've been flirting. Don't deny it.'

'I don't deny it. I have. Vigorously and with success.'

'You want to watch out, my girl.'

'And not only with one man. With five.'

'Oh, so it's numbers now, is it? Numbers.'

'In which,' I said, 'lies safety.'

Then, having gazed into the basket at the fresh brown pile of eggs there, she wanted to know what was in the brown paper parcel. When I told her she said :

'Ah ! bringing home the bacon, too, eh?'

'Tom sent it for the squadron. At least they'll get a few decent meals.'

'Of course. Of course. For the squadron. Of course.'

'One of these days, Doll, I'll crown you.'

'I wish you could see the street where I was brought up,'

she said. 'You had to have your eyes open pretty early there.' Suddenly she laughed in that endearing and affectionate way of hers, squeezed my waist and said : 'Come on, flirty. Back to the apple battle.'

As if this brief interlude of happiness were not enough – in my heart I was certain we should never be gay again – we ended the day with Bill biking down to the pub to fetch bottles of light ale while I fried eggs and the thickish slices of home-cured bacon in our old over-worked frying pan. The bacon, and the smell of it on the air, was utterly delicious. We all mopped great lumps of bread in the warm bacon fat and Bill kept saying 'Manna, Liz dear, absolute manna. Fit for the gods.' Replete at last, we sat for a long time under the apple trees, talking, bantering, even laughing, sipping beer and all the time listening, as someone once said, to the song the summer evening sings.

Next day they buried Smithy and we hadn't much time to gather very many apples.

If it was true that Providence sometimes created a special dispensation for my mother it was equally certain, in September, that it had the goodness to arrange one for me.

As the tension of battle rose and stretched – in the first week of the month alone we lost a round gross of fighters and claimed, if over-optimistically, three hundred and seventy-five of the enemy's – so my own tension tautened in parallel. Sometimes I felt that my nerves were a tangled mess of gnawing maggots. Once again I was stricken by dreads that haunted me like ghouls : the dread of coming home at night, the dread of the telephone, the dread of some messenger coming across the orchard in the garden or knocking on the door. Even Bill's tireless jocularities couldn't lessen the shadow of these things and in fact sometimes, by some curious paradox, merely increased it. At times even Doll's breezy and faithful optimism failed to do anything but jar my already crawling nerves. Most of all, I think, I was unsure and frightened of myself : so much so that one morning, at breakfast, I did an unheard-off and unprecedented thing.

I quarrelled with my grandmother.

Harry always breakfasted long before us and that morning had already, I think, gone off with his trout rods when she came down into the breakfast room, took the little red woollen cosy off her boiled egg and said to me with great cheerfulness:

'Good morning, dear. Edna tells me that Coco has had her kittens in an old sieve in the potting shed. Isn't that nice?'

I was in a shocking mood and hid behind the morning paper and didn't answer.

'I said Coco has had her kittens.'

'I heard you. Who the hell cares about Coco?' In my impatience I slapped the paper on to the table. 'Kittens, my foot.'

For some time she said absolutely nothing to this outrageous show of temper. She merely picked up a knife, carefully sliced off the top of her egg, peered into it, sprinkled a pinch or two of salt on it, buttered herself a slice of toast and then cut it into thin fingers. She then took one of these fingers and slowly dipped it into the egg-yolk and ate it.

'Would you,' she said, 'care to pour me some tea?'

I poured out a cup of tea, clattering loudly about with spoon, cup-and-saucer and lumps of sugar. She, meanwhile, merely peered sideways at the paper's headlines with apparently all the unconcern in the world and finally said:

'If this sort of thing goes on much longer there will be only one thing for it. We shall both evacuate from here and go and join your mother.'

'Punishment I can stand. Purgatory I won't abide.'

'That was a ridiculous and bitter thing to say.'

'We live,' I said, 'in ridiculous and bitter times.'

'Nevertheless I can't help thinking it would do you a great deal of good to get away.'

'I do not need doing good to.'

She then calmly buttered herself another piece of toast and ate another spoonful or two of egg.

'I must say these eggs that Tom Hudson brings are awfully good.'

'It so happens I fetch them.'

She then took *The Times* from the side of her plate, glanced casually at the Personal Column and then as casually put it down again.

175

'I notice you haven't been eating very well lately either.'

'Oh? I'm told by all and sundry I eat like a horse.'

'Yes? Your egg sits there less than a quarter eaten and you haven't eaten a scrap of toast.'

Nothing, in that dark mood, could have pacified or sweetened me and I was almost at breaking point when she said:

'I've been thinking I'd like to take you out to lunch today. How would you like to run over to Tunbridge Wells and have lunch there?'

'How very thrilling.'

'Very well. You can take me for a drive this afternoon instead. Even half a day away from that orchard might do you a power of good. You can get stale even gathering apples.'

'Sour,' I said, 'is the word,' and sour was how I felt: sour and sharp and miserable, like some maggoty, rotten, fallen apple that nobody wanted.

But even this monstrous display of unforgivable acidity didn't provoke or perturb her and she merely said:

'I'll have my after-lunch rest and we'll start off about half-past two.'

'And where,' I said, 'do you propose we should go? Off to the jolly old sea-side? And have a stroll along the prom, prom, prom? I do love to be beside the seaside.'

'I think that's a splendid idea. I haven't seen the sea for such a long time. I shall look forward to it very much.'

In that unreasoning mood of mine it didn't occur to me that her refusal to be provoked might also be a state of understanding but later, half way to the orchard, I came to my senses at last and went back to beg her forgiveness and apologize.

'You see,' I said, 'it isn't only —'

'Only what? —'

'You see . . . well, last night Splodge came home and' — he too, more weary-eyed than ever, had been near to breaking point — 'and said something which really made my heart sink.'

'Yes? I'm sorry.'

The words Splodge had said to me the previous night had been altogether too much for my cowardice and fallibility and once again I felt infinitely saddened as I repeated them:

'You see, darling, it isn't only the kites we're losing. God knows that's bad enough. But it's the chaps. Four from 'B' Flight went for a Burton today. Then we had an intake of new boys. They were all so crashingly eager. Three of them hadn't even finished their training. And they all looked so bloody, bloody young. Heart-breaking. As Corporal Williams said, they'll be sending 'em in bleeding cradles soon. I felt like some doddering old patriarch beside them.'

Coming from him, who always looked so heartbreakingly young himself, this was more than I could bear and had finally induced the sour and festering mood in which I found myself at breakfast.

'Oh! do run back and fetch my binoculars, will you?' she said as we were getting into the car that afternoon, 'I never like to be without them.'

We duly drove due southward, towards the coast. Almost every big house we passed was sand-bagged, wired, guarded and shuttered up. The gardens of mansions were cluttered and shabby with the dreary accoutrements of war. Guns and gun carriages and tents and trucks and gas-caped soldiers, like giant greenish insects, filled the woods. By the roadside, under trees, several groups of soldiers were having brew-ups and there was much whistling as we passed. Nearer the coast, where the land was rather higher, most of the harvest was already finished and the stubbles were bare. Across a few of them flocks of hens were feeding and in others a few women were actually gleaning corn. One at least was scarred by the first furrows and I saw a team of three horses, one white, drawing a plough at the far end. At intervals, at what were held to be strategic points, there were concrete pill-boxes, some merely camouflaged in paint, others squatting there in innocuous domestic disguise as shops, hay-stacks, post-offices, pig-sties, garages and other shapes of equally stunning originality. At one point field engineers were running telephone wires along a fence and a very handsome boy looked up and blew a kiss at me. Once a blood wagon came hooting up behind us, very fast, racing to get past me, and partly out of self-protection I actually drew the car on to the sun-baked verge and stopped. A mass of late willow-herb was growing from the dyke, a few pale pink flowers still blooming on it but most of it already in seed.

Already, some time before this, all sign-posts and village names had been taken away and consequently, that afternoon, it was like driving through a half-shabby, neglected wilderness, an abandoned landscape only mockingly half-alive. Then, when we were, I suppose, only about five miles from the coast, a policeman stepped into the road at the entrance of a village street and flagged us down and I duly stopped the car.

'May I ask where you're going, madam?'

'We are going,' my grandmother said, 'to the sea.'

'Have you a good reason, madam?'

'Yes,' she said. 'I want to have a look at it.'

'I hardly think that's a good idea. There's been some very heavy goings-on down there this morning. Big convoys going through. You don't want to get shot up, do you? Are you residents of this area?'

'We are.'

'May I see your identity-cards, please?'

So we gave him our identity-cards and he slowly scrutinized them and us.

'Of course as you're residents of this area you're free to move around, madam, I know. But my advice to you is to turn back.'

'Thank you. I have a very keen desire to see the sea and that is what we are going to do.'

She then gave him a fairly formidable smile and we drove on again.

At the top of a treeless hill, by a small brick farmhouse, three miles or so farther on, there was a point from which you could get the first wide clear glimpse of the English Channel. It was far enough, she thought. I stopped the car and then, beyond the golden glitter of sunlight that lay on the near sea-distance like a scattering of crystals, I clearly saw the coast of France, the cliffs pale yellow in the sun.

I at once felt a strange excitement and jumped out of the car. Immediately she called after me 'the binoculars!' and I went back for them, at the same time asking if she wasn't coming too. No, she was quite comfortable where she was, she said, she could see quite splendidly. I then took the binoculars out of their case and stood on a high bank by a hedgerow and, with the queerest of thrills, raised them to my eyes. A moment or so later, as I adjusted the lenses, France seemed to leap out at me from the distance in a most unnerving fashion, so uncannily near that it momentarily made me gasp. At that moment she leaned out of the window and called :

'And to think that that Wretched Man may well be over there. Damnation to his soul.'

I suppose we stayed there ten minutes or more. On the hedge-row a few dewberries still hung fat and purple-bloomed in the sun and I remember gathering and eating them and thinking how sweet-sharp and juicy they were from long weeks of summer. Then a wagon loaded with barley and drawn by a big brown shire-horse came up the hill and the wagoner sitting in his shirt-sleeves on the shafts gave me a long searching look as he went past, not speaking a word. After that the wagon drew into the farm-yard, the barley sheaves rustling against the gate-posts as it passed, and a few moments later I was astoundingly assailed by a low whisper :

'Have you ever been taken for a spy?'

'Good heavens, I hope not.'

'Well, you're being taken for one now.'

I turned sharply and saw, across the farm-yard, standing against the door of a cow-barn, the wagoner, a woman and another man, the wagoner now with a pitchfork in his hand. Each man had me fixed in a low, smouldering stare.

'It might,' my grandmother said, 'be prudent to depart. Don't you think so?'

I thought so too and with she remarking in her most caustic fashion 'It's always as well to remember that there are occasions when the greatest danger comes not from your enemies but your friends,' we duly departed.

We arrived home about five o'clock, in expectation of what we hoped would be one of Rose's most excellent and refreshing teas, only to find Rose and Edna and Harry slaving away in a scene of utter chaos, sweeping and shovelling up barrow-loads and boxes and buckets of broken glass. Most unobligingly Goering had dropped a two-hundred pounder in the field beyond the garden fence and there wasn't a pane of glass left in the house or the dove-cot. On my bed, where I sometimes went to lie and read for a short while if I came home to lunch for a change, a lump of shrapnel as big as half a brick reposed on the counterpane.

A few minutes later, to my astonishment and delight, Splodge walked into the garden.

'Thank God you're all right,' he said. 'I heard you'd had a direct hit.'

'The Lord looks after his own,' Rose said.

'And you? What about you?' I said. 'Why so early?'

'They tried to knock us out again. Bomb craters all over the runways. We won't be operational again for at least a couple of days. Bronzie had a near shave. Two of her WAAFs were a write-off. Poor kids. Bad show.'

Then he grinned and took me by surprise by saying:

'Got a swim suit?'

'Of course. Why?'

'We'll swim and lie in the sun and sleep and swim and lie in the sun and sleep and swim and lie in the sun and sleep —'

I could have wept with joy; caught up in momentary delusion, I almost felt as if the war was over.

For the better part of two days we swam in the river, sunbathed in the garden, walked in the woods and slept late in the windowless dove-cot. In this heaven-sent pause I watched the strength and alertness and youth in him come back. I felt in myself the slow restoration of the confidence I'd begun to think I'd lost for ever.

When I finally went back to the orchard it was to find Doll all by herself there.

'What happened to you?' she said. 'It's beginning to get a bit lonesome in these parts.'

After I'd given her some idea of the joys and tremors of the past two days she said how much she'd missed me and then I asked where Bill was.

'Gone to Dorking. On the badger again. He couldn't get any change out of Groupie here so he's after his surgeon again. If the surgeon won't play he's off to 11 Group. If they won't play he's off to Whitehall. If Whitehall won't play he's going after Churchill. He'll win.'

'When do we expect him back?'

'Depends on how high up he gets. Of course Churchill may not be able to spare the time.'

Early that afternoon a more than dejected Bill bicycled into the orchard, trickless, laughless and infinitely sombre. His appearance wasn't merely that of a man who had been refused entry to the front gates of Heaven. It was as if the Archangel Gabriel had also given him a black eye for good measure.

'No bloody good. Wouldn't play. Behaved like a bunch of piddling clots. Wouldn't even let me go to Whitehall. They say the fist gadget thing won't be ready for a month anyway. Oh! I suppose it's a damn complicated bit of apparatus –'

Savagely he kicked at the back wheel of his bike where it lay on the grass, setting it spinning furiously.

'Now, now,' Doll said. 'No gloomies.'

'Well, who the hell wouldn't be? I tell you this thing is just about coming up to top pitch. *This is it*, I tell you, *now*. It's win, lose or bust. Now. Today perhaps. Tomorrow. Sunday. But this is it. *This is the bloody hour*.'

This savage anger seemed so remote from the careless figure who had once enraptured me in woods and climbed precariously to the window of my nursery and now amused us with handless tricks on bicycles that I simply couldn't say a word.

'God, I was at H.Q., when the bastards showed up like droves of bloody rooks. Ops. Room couldn't keep pace. They were absolutely choked. They're used to 20-plus, 30-plus and even 50-plus, but Jesus they had an 80-plus while I was there. Hell ! –'

The distortions of his face were all the more vivid because there was something more than mere savagery in his mouth. He was full of a furious spirituality.

Then Doll, more in an attempt to calm him down than anything, I think, said :

'Well, did you see Churchill?'

I simply couldn't believe my ears when in fact he did calm down and said :

'Yes. As a matter of fact I did.'

'You're kidding.'

'No. Fact. The old boy came up to H.Q. while I was there. Popped in to have a look-see for himself. They took him into Ops. Room and they had the 80-plus while he was there. Pip

Hitchens was on duty at the time. He told me about it later. Every squadron was up and still the bastards kept coming in. Then when he hadn't got another sausage to send up the old boy turned to Air Vice-Marshal Park and said "What other reserves have we?" Park looked pretty funeral and said "None, sir." Now do you see what I mean? If they conk any more air-fields out we've bloody near had it. *This is it*, I tell you. This is the bit you can tell your children about in the chimney corner. And your grandchildren after that. If you live that long.'

Suddenly he picked up a Worcester Pearmain, angrily bit a great lump out of it, spat out a piece of loose skin and chewed furiously.

'Then I saw the old boy getting into his car. He wasn't exactly dancing with joy either.'

At this moment he completely lost patience again, aimed another frenzied kick at the bike wheel and then madly threw the apple into the nearest tree.

'It wouldn't be so bad if I could be in there scrapping. But just to stand here stooging around – hell, what's that?'

He abruptly stopped, turned his head sharply and looked up. I suddenly became aware of a great sky-drone of noise from the south. It grew steadily and massively louder. Before many seconds it was like the roar of an immense endless train steam-rolling across the sky.

'Jesus, there must be a hundred-plus – Heinkels, Dorniers –'

Then we saw them: a gigantic black drove of bombers followed by a second, then a third, slugging across the sky in a vast procession. As they roared towards us, dark, orderly, not very high, I heard Doll say 'You'd think they might at least have a perishing brass-band to play them in, wouldn't you?' and Bill shouted some blasphemous mouthful in answer.

After that you couldn't hear a word. The sky was full of a continuous hammering thunder. The hot bright afternoon was darkened exactly as if by a great storm-shadow. The curious thing was that I wasn't frightened. I just stood there absolutely chilled – chilled not so much by the numbers, the noise and the shadow as by the relentless and ruthless order of it all. Then another drove came in, more to the west, followed by another and another, on the same course, all as dark and ruthless as the first.

How long it went on I don't know but when the last of them had slugged away out of sight, towards London, and you could still hear that distant maddening orderly drone in the sky I turned to look at Bill's impotent, distorted face, white as death.

'For Christ's sake, where are the Spits? It's like watching bloody murder being done when your hands are tied.'

I murmured something about the runways probably still being out of action and he simply said :

'I might have known. I might have known,' and then just stood there in violent, muted depression, impotent to add another word.

Like Churchill, I wasn't exactly jumping for joy, either, and it was Doll, never one for the gloomies even in the gloomiest of crises, who at last jolted us sensibly out of ourselves.

'I think that little lot calls for a spot of celebration.'

'Now?' Bill said with a cryptic acidity that quite matched my grandmother at her best, 'or later?'

'Both.'

With that she went into the tent, fetched her bottle of Scotch milk and poured out three glasses. Raising hers, she said :

'Well, cheers, everybody. Another joke over.'

'Cheers, blast and double-blast,' Bill said. He drank fiercely at the whisky. 'What's all this about a celebration? Celebrating what, for Christ's sake?'

'Being here.'

'Suppose you're right,' he said. 'Suppose you're right.'

'Get your finger nails cut and your hair oiled and wash behind your ears,' Doll said. 'I'm taking you all out to dinner tonight.'

'Savoy, Ritz or Claridge's?' Bill said.

'I thought we'd go into town and have a nice big fat Dover sole at *The Marlborough*,' she said, 'if we can get it. I'll pay. The old plum-and-apple lark has made me stinking rich.'

'I don't think I'm quite in the mood,' I said. 'Thanks all the same.'

'Oh! come on. We'll have a taxi and do the thing properly.

We'll have wine and get good and properly soaked. What about it, Bill?'

'Sounds to me,' Bill said, 'like a bloody good idea.'

'Let's make it a real party,' Doll said. 'Bring Splodge. We'll call for you about seven.'

'No,' I said and for once I was adamant. I had neither need nor urge to be gay. The processional thunder of the bombers had filled me with new foreboding. The only urge or longing I had was to go quietly home, perhaps wash my hair, and wait for Splodge.

When I did get home, an hour or two later, Harry had a strange little story to tell. Everybody was very tense and the talk was all of the bombers. But Harry, who had been fishing in the upper stretch of river where it runs into the lake, had had an experience all his own.

'It actually frightened me more than the bombers,' he said. 'It was about a quarter of an hour after they'd all gone. All of a sudden there was an Almighty pop! like a big cork being drawn, and then another and another. Damned odd.' He laughed loudly, in that bovine way of his. 'Jumped out of my skin. Couldn't think what the devil it could be. Nest of moorhen's eggs, addled, exploding in the sun.'

This ludicrous little episode somehow had the effect of calming us all.

That day and the next were great ones in the history of the Air Force. 'No doubt,' Churchill said, 'we were always over-sanguine in our estimate of enemy scalps,' and undoubtedly he was right, but at the time we didn't think of those things and I doubt very much if it would have mattered if we had.

Curious word, sanguine. Odd that any one word can mean both optimistic and bloody. But it too fitted the hour.

16

THE wail of an air-raid siren woke me two mornings later, but by now we were so used to these things that I simply turned over and went to sleep again. When I woke again, about ten o'clock, I was alone in the bed.

When I got to the orchard half an hour later an uncommonly weary-eyed Doll sat looking dejectedly at a pile of damp apple-logs that now and then emitted a slow wreath of smoke without a vestige of flame. Her usual greeting to me when I was late — 'What happened to you, matey?' — was delivered in a voice of husky pessimism, with no sign of a smile.

'Why the fire?' I said.

'Clean out of oil. Bill's gone to get some. Dying for a cuppa tea. Throat feels like sandpaper soaked in salt or something. You look perishing fresh.'

We were now on the last trees of Worcester Pearmain and only a dozen or so trees of Bramley were to come, but that morning I noticed that not a single apple had been gathered.

'How went the celebration?'

'Blimey, duckie, don't talk about it.'

'Something go wrong?'

'We fell among thieves.'

When I asked what this might mean and remarked that I'd understood that she and Bill were merely going out to dinner she gave me a grey sort of look and said:

'Oh! we had the Dover sole all right. And the bottle of wine. Then they started to close the restaurant up about nine o'clock, so we left and a couple of minutes later ran into Mac—'

'Fatal.'

'And Stephanie and three or four other types. Oh! yes, he's back with Stephanie. Isn't she the one you told me once had hollow legs? Well, you're wrong. She's hollow all through.'

She bent down and started to blow at the fire, but the effect was merely to distribute more low clouds of smoke while the apple branches dismally sizzled. 'He's a ripe piece of talent, that Mac of ours, I tell you. I wish to God Bill would come with the oil. Well, we finally fetched up at some pub or other, *The Saracen's Head*, I think. Or *The Queen's Head*. Or *The King's Head*. Some perishing ruddy head. Mac was drinking Irish whisky with light ale for chasers.'

'And had a fight.'

'Three, if not four. He's brassed off because he hasn't been able to get at Goering for two or three days. Bill says he's always bad when he can't keep the personal war going. Still, he's human. I'll say that for him. More than one of the perishers he had a fight with. One of those types who thinks all Australians are descended from convicts and all Canadians from gold-rush tarts. Mac was a bit loud and noisy, I admit, but when this type began to talk about the common decencies and something not being cricket and keeping the party civilized it was a bit much. Then he as good as called Stephanie a free-for-all girl, which I wouldn't mind betting she is in a nice sort of way, and Mac picked him up bodily and took him outside and sorted him out somewhere in the yard.'

Here she said she was talking too much and broke off and seemed, I thought, momentarily overcome by one of those occasional fits of sadness of hers. She swallowed hard a few times and at last said it was no perishing good, she'd have to have a whisky. While she'd gone into the tent to fetch it I blew at the fire too, but the apple boughs were altogether too sappy and my attempt to start a flame was every bit as dismal as hers.

When she at last came back she sat down and sipped slowly, for fully a minute, at her tumbler of whisky. And then she eventually looked up from her glass and stared at me solemnly.

'Want to ask you something. Am I daft? Do I look a bit daft?'

I said something about not more than usual but this enfeebled joke went past her.

'Me and Bill got a taxi home about midnight, all by ourselves. It was damn nice in the back with him. More than damn nice. Oh! I might as well tell you – I think I'm falling in love with this bit of talent. Think? I know. I am. I'm in. I've been falling for ruddy weeks if I did but know it.'

It hadn't escaped my notice, over the past weeks, that Bill

had once or twice showed more than a touch of affection for her and I said I wasn't in the least surprised.

'No? Funny, I thought you'd jaw me. I thought you'd say it was the re-bound from Smithy.'

'I hope I'm not quite so stupid. '

'He gets under your skin, this one. Did he ever get under yours? You used to be sweet with him at one time, I know, didn't you?'

'In my distant childhood.'

'Get under your skin?'

'Not really. I merely idolized him in the daftest sort of way.'

'Well, he's under mine. And it isn't the re-bound from Smithy either. I'm deep under the influence, I tell you.'

Here she broke off again and lapsed once more into a sad contemplation of her whisky and the sizzling fire. It was clear that the thoughts she was gradually expressing had been with her for some time and as I sat there I felt my affection for her deepen into a new phase. The one thing that perturbed me was that she seemed more than a little troubled and I couldn't think why. Her temporary lapses into bemusement seemed complex. It might well have been that love, as it sometimes does, had made her unhappy. Then she said a thing which greatly surprised me.

'Was I a bit rough when I first met you? Well, I've grown up a bit since then. Quite a good bit, thanks to you and Bill.'

Since I had long fondly believed the exact opposite to be true, and that the greater part of my emancipation from the innocent sublimations of late girlhood had certainly been due to Doll as much as Bill, I was more than a bit surprised at this latest confessional. I was completely astounded that anything in my excitable and sometimes wobbly nature could have had the remotest effect on hers.

'Taking my back hair down, am I? Well, got to talk to someone about it and I'd rather it was you. It's a fact — you two have been a big influence on me. I've got deeper, somehow. I've sort of become aware of myself. I hadn't before.'

'You've changed me a bit, too.'

Here she unexpectedly laughed and tossed back the rest of her whisky and water and said :

'Here, that's enough of that, matey. Getting the gloomies, that's what we are. That won't do. By the way, I forgot to tell you. Danger-man was here. Came by on his tractor.'

'Doll, I warned you before –'

'Wanted to speak to you, he said. I said could I take a message and he said no, he'd be back in less than an hour. Gone to pick up a new coupling or something from the blacksmith's.'

I had no comment to make and she went on :

'He tells me the harvest is all in. Got the last load in this morning. I had a good mind to say something about bacon, but I hadn't the cheek after all.'

A few minutes later Bill, irrepressible as ever, careered into the orchard on his red grid-iron, riding no-hands as usual, with a gallon oil-can in his good hand.

'Hail to thee, blithe spirits. Birds thou art and always were.'

'I slightly resent,' I said, 'being called a bird.'

'My sweet little goldfinches. Funny, I saw a pair in the lane just now. Delicate, pretty things.'

'The compliments aren't half flying around this morning, aren't they ?' Doll said.

'That's because you are both a thing of beauty and a joy for ever. Since there's no help, come let us kiss –'

While he was going through the customary morning pantomime of kissing us both it suddenly flashed through my mind that this was Doll's fear : that she might, after all, be taking part in nothing but a pantomime. I guessed, I think correctly, that she felt that her intuitive good sense about Bill being a deep one might well be wrong after all. She feared that he might be merely the jocular good-timer, the back-seat fondler, with nothing but superficialities to offer in return for her new-found love.

But having had my kiss I thought no more of it and turned away to fill up and light the stove and begin the mid-morning brew-up. Half way through doing this I happened to turn my head and saw Bill holding Doll's hand with his good hand and gazing with profound intentness straight into her eyes. There was more than mere fond adoration in the look she was giving him in return and I suddenly recognized the truth of her own words about herself : that she had grown much, much deeper.

'Privacy is a fine thing,' I said, but they either didn't hear or didn't want to hear.

Ten minutes later we were all three sitting round the trestle table and I was pouring out the first cups of tea when we heard the sound of a tractor and saw Tom Hudson driving across the orchard. I got up to fetch another cup from the tent and by the time I was back Tom had stopped the tractor and parked it twenty yards or so away.

'Good morning,' he said as he came over to us and then actually called Bill 'Sir'.

There was something infinitely touching about that 'Sir' and the word might well have been jarred out of him by the pure shock of seeing Bill's face. Doll and I had got more or less used to it now but there was always a danger that strangers, meeting him for the first time in a pub or passing him in the street, might be unable to restrain themselves in the face of the first violent impact of the twists and lacerations and would cry out in brief spontaneous horror. I had seen and heard it happen. And I knew that once, in a pub, Doll had been suddenly stunned by the thump of a falling body and had seen a bar-maid faint clean away.

At any rate Tom joined us for tea and tried to look at Bill as little as possible through his glinting spectacles.

'I'm glad I found you all three here,' he said. 'I wanted to ask you something. We're having our harvest supper next Saturday and we wondered if you'd all like to come. Harvest supper – that's pretty silly of me. We always used to have harvest supper before the war but we're making it lunch this year because of the black-out and one thing and another. I hope you can all come. I think there'll be plenty to eat and drink. Mother will see to that.'

'Sounds good,' Doll said. 'Thanks. Chalk me up.'

'Good show,' Bill said. 'Bring on the dancing girls.'

'Will you have it in the big barn?' I said.

'Yes, as usual.'

'There's something wonderful about that big barn, with all the candles burning on the supper tables.'

'No candles this year, I'm afraid.'

'Oh! please. Have candles. Do have candles. Even if it is

day-time. After all it's a thanksgiving. It isn't the same without candles.'

'All right. Candles it shall be. And will your grandmother and your husband and Mr Harry come?'

'I'm sure they'd all love to.'

Tom said he was glad and then turned suddenly to Bill and remarked 'Talking of thanksgiving, I think we've all got something to be thankful for. Your fellows put up a pretty marvellous show last week.'

'Quite a grouse-shoot. Quite a grouse-shoot.'

'Churchill seems vastly pleased. Think it'll stop invasion?'

'I'm inclined to think,' was all Bill said, 'that we've got the great Hermann by the short hairs.'

'Dad says he thinks it might all be over by Christmas. Do you?'

'Yes. Five years from now.'

'There,' I said, 'speaks our great optimist. You must really try and cheer him up, Tom, at the harvest-do. You're awfully good at cheering up.'

'I will,' he said and gave me the shyest of fond looks through his shimmering spectacles. 'I'll lace him with Mother's cherry brandy.'

Rather less than a week later we all sat down to our harvest supper, or rather lunch, our thanksgiving for mercies received and all things gathered in, by candlelight at noon.

The only familiar absent face on that occasion was that of Splodge, bound by duty. Otherwise I suppose there were about thirty of us sitting down that afternoon, but the names of most of them I have now forgotten, largely because I didn't make up my diary for that day. But I remember only too well that my grandmother, Harry, Doll and Bill were there; the Hudsons and Aunt Midge; Charley Bailey the blacksmith and his wife and daughter Florrie; the Rev. Hall-Williams and his wife; the two farmhands Amos and Fred and our two gardeners, Baxter and Lines.

We all sat at two long tables laid in the centre of the big barn and on the tables, as Tom had faithfully promised, there were lighted candles. A third table, holding spare plates and dishes and hams and legs of pork and so on for extra cutting, stood cross-wise at the end of the other two. The great span of oak roof, supported by massive posts not much less than a yard thick, gave the whole barn that church-like atmosphere I found so satisfying and on each post sheaves of wheat and barley and oats had been tied, creating the air of a harvest festival. At intervals down the three tables stood vases of flowers, dahlias and sunflowers and asters and cornflowers, with ears of barley tucked between. Big bowls of tomatoes and peeled boiled eggs and cold potatoes and lettuce and beetroot stood about, with jars of pickled onions and celery and green onions among them. In the centre of each table sat a large flat loaf, the crust all brownish gold, baked by Mrs Hudson in the form of a wheatsheaf and at intervals there were big jugs of beer and cider.

All the time we were eating and drinking the big tall doors of the barn stood open and sometimes a light breeze blew in on us, setting the yellow flames of the candles gently dancing. Once, about half way through the meal, an air-raid siren sounded but none of us took much notice except Harry, who as always couldn't restrain his curiosity and went out into the yard to survey the late September sky for visiting marauders. Shortly afterwards a few familiar crumps shook the earth some distance away and somebody asked casually 'Bombs or thunder?' and Amos, with slow wisdom, said:

'That's thunder, that is. Them thunder-flies bin biting me all day.'

Chance had it that I should sit next to Amos, who enlivened the occasion from time to time by resting a horny palm on my knee and making such dark remarks as:

'Nice to have a bit of real home-cured, eh, Fred? Very tender, eh?'

'That is.'

Opposite us sat Doll and Bill and it was the scars and twists of Bill's face that, even more than my knee, had Amos utterly fascinated. Every now and then he would pause with a loose pink slice of ham half way to his lips, his mouth open, and stare at Bill in horrified wonder. Sometimes the ham fell off the fork and had to be slowly picked up again. Equally he was fascinated by the fact that Doll had to cut up Bill's meat for him, so that he was inspired to brief respite from steady mastication to make remarks such as :

'Don't git no young females a-cuttin' up ourn, do we, Fred? That don't seem fair, does it?'

'That don't.'

'Must be very nice to have a young female a-cuttin' up your home-cured, eh, Fred?'

'That must.'

Now and then he turned that juicy eye of his on me, giving my figure a good earthy once-over, and on one occasion he said :

'You anything of a dab hand at cuttin' a man's meat up, Mrs Bannister?'

'One man's meat,' I said 'is likely to be another girl's poison.'

'Had you there, Amos,' Bill said and laughed so broadly that his face was stretched to even queerer shapes than normal, like red-brown india-rubber, holding Amos under a new and even deeper spell of fascination, so that Bill could bear it no longer and evidently deemed it simpler to be perfectly candid about it all.

'Got too near the baboon cage at the zoo one day,' he said. 'That's how I did it.'

'Never.'

'Made a meal of my hand too,' Bill said and held up his hand-less stump with a typical pleasurable grin. 'Still, mustn't mind. They're going to fit me up with a special knife-fork-and-spoon bit of apparatus soon. Guaranteed to do everything from picking up meat and potatoes to pinching young females.'

'Never. Hear that, Fred? Us two'll have to git one o' them, shan't us? Sounds a bit of all-right, don't it?'

'That does.'

'It's annoying,' Bill said, 'how this old hand itches when it doesn't know what the other one's up to,' a remark that was far too deep for Amos, who merely forked up a positive hand-kerchief of ham from his plate and slowly chewed it in like a cow consuming a cabbage leaf.

For once indeed he was wholly put to silence and for several minutes chewed solidly on his ham without a word, so that Fred was prompted to say :

'Gone middlin' quiet in 'ere all of a sudden, ain't it?'

'None o' your old buck,' Amos said. 'I was just a-going to propose this 'ere goodly gentleman's 'ealth.' He raised a courteous tankard of beer in Bill's direction. 'Your very good 'ealth, sir.'

'Cheers, Amos,' Bill said. 'Good show. Here's to the young females. Where should we be without 'em?'

'I be damned if I know. And that's a fact, that is. Eh, Fred?'

'That is.'

'Any more for any more?' Tom's father now called down the table. 'There's plenty of ham. Don't be stingy on the ham. Help yourselves. Tom, be a good chap and carve some more ham. Rector, another plate of ham?'

The Rector who, after the general fashion of parsons had been eating like a cart-horse, needed no second invitation and just beat Amos by a short head in the race to the end table, where Tom was sharpening the carving knife before attacking the ham. In that moment I turned to look at him and in return he gave me the most solemn and intimate of winks from behind his spectacles. It was altogether the most open gesture he had ever made to me and to my infinite astonishment I felt myself start blushing deeply.

A moment later I knew Doll was looking hard at me. She had seen it all and suddenly her lips framed, silently, the word 'danger'. This so unnerved me that I flushed even more deeply and suddenly tried to take refuge from it all by taking deep swigs of cider. In that moment the profound, amusing and homely tranquillity of the afternoon, with all the solidity so well expressed by stone and oak and corn and bread, broke into inexplicable confusion. I heard in the distance the heavy noise of a bomber. All the candles started to dance in front of me. With a sudden premonition that something dreadful was about to happen, that perhaps the corn-barn and the candles and all of us, all the good, solid English faces, were about to be blasted to pieces, I abruptly got up and walked into the yard.

I think Tom must have thought I was going to faint or something, because a few moments later he came out too and stood there with me, saying:

'Are you all right? You don't feel ill or anything?'

193

'It's nothing. Nothing at all.'

'You had me worried for a moment.'

Then I suddenly said something that I really had no conscious intention of saying at all. I looked away from him, for some reason unable to bear the flat shine of the spectacles, and said:

'It was just that I thought we all had so much to be thankful for. And then I heard the sound of that plane and I suddenly got a mad idea we were all going to be destroyed. I just couldn't bear it and —'

Then I realized how great was my attachment to that barn. It was more than a mere physical relationship between my flesh and its oak and stone. It held my heart deeply and firmly in its solid bondage. It wasn't merely that it had stood there for perhaps three or even four hundred years or that because of its age I thought it immemorial or anything of that sort. In it was enshrined all I knew and felt and loved about England. I realized, in fact, that it now held a greater meaning for me than ever our old big house had done. Strangely I no longer felt any love for that house. In detachment it had become impersonal. I hoped and in fact thought I knew that we should never go back to live in it again and that my love for it would never revive even if war left it undestroyed.

'Do you feel better now?' Tom asked me.

'It wasn't that I felt ill or anything like that. I just — Has it been a good harvest? I meant to ask you.'

'Very good. Such good weather. We start ploughing to-morrow.'

'I thought your father looked very pleased with things.'

'He loves these harvest suppers. I think it means more to him than Christmas.'

'I love them too. Shall we go back now?'

So we went back into the barn, to the good faces, the sheaves, the bread, the jokes, the beer and the dancing candles. My premonitions and fears gradually slipped away. I peeled myself an apple and helped myself to celery and cheese and drank glasses of Mrs Hudson's cherry brandy. Bill kept us continually laughing and Amos started to tell us of the young females, or at least some of them, he had known over the years. Bill fed him with promptings and Fred with beer, so that the tale and the eye grew juicier and juicier. Then the Rector, replete with food and flushed with beer, made a speech of thanks, a rather rambling one, in which he got badly entangled with the alien corn and the sowing and reaping of the whirlwind. Then Amos, not to be outdone, also made a speech, a brief, beery, pithy one, ending with something like these words :

'Blast the Jerries. Blast Hitler. Blast Goering. Blast the bombers. Blast the Nazis. And bless us all.'

With our faith in ourselves so stoutly expressed we started to disperse for home about half past four. Amos kissed the ladies all round, the younger ones more than once, and Bill kissed most of them too. Even my grandmother received the benefit of their affections. Bill also had lavish praise for the cherry brandy and had a bottle conferred on him as a parting gift. Fred was very slightly drunk and there was much laughter.

When I got home a little later, calm in mind and at last very content in heart, I walked into the garden and saw, suddenly, that I had two visitors.

Mac and John Cavendish Fitzroy were standing over by the cherry-tree, both in uniform. They started to walk towards me. Strangely Fitz looked almost imperturbably calm. It was Mac who looked both worn and desperate.

I didn't say anything and it was Fitz who said, simply :

'My dear Liz.'

'I know why you've come,' I said.

'It happened this afternoon,' Fitz said.

'God,' Mac said. His voice, though low, was near to breaking. 'Jesus.'

Curiously I felt neither confused nor shattered. I just stood there frozenly waiting.

'How?' I said.

'That's the damn funny –' Mac started to say.

'Funny?'

'God. Forgive me, Liz, forgive me. I don't know quite what the hell I'm saying. Jesus, forgive me.'

There were now tears in his eyes. I tried hard not to look at him and then Fitz took me by the hands.

'It was a stray bomb. Some damned Dornier had one left on

the way home and let it go. They were having a fry-up at dispersal when it happened. Corporal Williams too.'

For a moment I had nothing to say. I stood there in deathly silence, as securely imprisoned in my sudden bond of bitterness as the swans had once been imprisoned by their dark ring of water.

'They might at least have shot him down,' I said at last. 'They might have killed him decently.'

That was why I didn't write up my diary for that day. In fact I never wrote it up again.

Nor, for some reason, did I cry very much. Someone once said that only the strong are bad; the weak haven't the guts to be. Perhaps in the same way cowardice doesn't make for easy weeping. I don't know. I only know that I shut myself away and deliberately locked myself in a loveless straitjacket, a bitter arid purdah in which I neither wanted to see anyone nor be seen. I don't suppose I was by any means the first young widow to reject all comfort in time of grief and it's equally certain I shan't be the last one. But even grief can be, as Bill well might have said, pretty bloody-minded. No doubt it was small and stupid. No doubt it was a show of callous and even cheap ingratitude. But I did it and there was no way, as I saw it, of doing otherwise; and there it is.

Quite how long all this went on I have now no idea and the diary isn't there to help me. I know only that I didn't merely reject Bill and Doll and Fitz and Mac – Mac was killed in straight and honourable combat in early October, his ruthless personal war with Goering over at last, though no one told me of this until many weeks later – I also rejected the faithful Rose and the weeping Edna; my mother, who actually braved the rigours of the front line to come and see me; and finally even my grandmother. Strangely, or perhaps quite characteristically, she made no fuss or protest about this. Possibly, in her wise way, she recognized that excess of comfort can irritate, repel or even break the comforted.

Strangely also it was Harry who, throughout this blind and bitter withdrawal, seemed to come closest to me. If it is true that there is a strong streak of woman in the highly complex strucure of the male then perhaps this is why the blundering Harry now became more understanding and tender than the women around me. It was he who came most often to the locked door of my room in the dove-cot, bringing messages, scraps of news and so on, asking if I wanted this or that, but never in any way indulging in pleas, reproaches or appeals, or revealing any trace of those gloomies that Doll so hated. It was he also who most often wrote me letters, again with never a syllable of reproach or appeal, telling me of his luck or otherwise with the trout and once of how, early one evening, for the first time in his life, he had seen an otter.

'Elizabeth, are you there? There's a Mrs Lyttleton on the phone. She'd so much like it if you'd speak to her.'

'I don't know any Mrs Lyttleton.'

'Her maiden name was Susan James. She was at school with you.'

'Tell her "no".'

'Rather not speak with her?'

'I haven't seen her for years.'

'Her husband's an Army Captain. Got the D.S.O. at Dunkirk.'

'Congratulate her for me.'

'You'd rather not speak, then?'

'No.'

'I understand.'

Then one day the unctuous voice of the Rector came through the door. This was more than I could stand and I shouted violently :

'Curse this bloody war ! Curse it, curse it, curse it, curse it ! And curse your bloody church too ! What have you maundering idiots ever done to stop it ?'

Something had to break this anguished and unholy deadlock if I wasn't to be utterly broken myself and perhaps it wasn't so very strange that the one who at last succeeded in breaking it was the one who had himself been almost broken.

Late one afternoon in October Harry came to knock on my door and said in his new quiet way :

'Mr Fitzroy is here, Elizabeth. He really wants to see you very much. He's got some rather important news for you.'

I was so near to my uttermost point of despair, at that moment, that I simply couldn't speak. I suddenly longed desperately to see and speak to Fitz but I just hadn't the guts to say so.

'Elizabeth. I haven't appealed to you about anything all this time. But will you see Mr Fitzroy? I'm sure it's important or he wouldn't have bothered you.'

'Is he alone?'

'He's just downstairs.'

The longing to see Fitz, to make even the briefest sort of contact with someone like him, was suddenly too much for me.

'All right, all right,' I said. 'Just for a moment.'

'I know he'll be glad. I'll tell him right away.'

Only a minute later there was another knock on the door and then I unlocked the door and Fitz came in. He didn't say anything at first. He simply looked at me and then put his hands on my shoulders. A sudden recollection of him as I'd first known him, all band-box and sauve and over-elegant and scarlet-lined suddenly came into conflict with that other recollection of him when he had come somewhere near to confiding in me about his own complex breaking-point. I could see that he was greatly changed. If my own soul was black and my heart ached exactly as if it had been physically battered over and over again it was his eyes that gave the clue to his own conflict. They were negative, unloved and sterile.

I think he needed me at that moment as much as, or perhaps more than, I needed him, but all he said was:

'Come out of mourning, Elizabeth. Please.'

I still couldn't speak. If I had dared to open my mouth I believe I should have shrieked like a madwoman.

'Please. For all our sakes.'

Helplessly I stood and looked at him, still without a word to say. For a moment or two I tried to find the courage to ask him what was the important thing he'd come about but it was no use. There wasn't even strength in me to do that.

'Elizabeth, I've come to ask you something.'

There was now the faintest trace of a smile on his face but in the darkness of my tortured withdrawal I resisted even that.

'It's rather a special favour I wanted to ask you.'

I simply stared and again didn't speak.

'I think you'd like to do it. I know you would.'

He smiled a second time but I still didn't speak.

'I came to ask you if you'd like to be a bridesmaid.'

In my weeks of being locked in an emotional straitjacket had sometimes come very near to being utterly unbalanced but now those incredible words made me put my hands to my head in a sudden gesture of wild helplessness. I felt blind crazy. If this bitter joke had any meaning whatsoever it could only have been to drive me finally and completely out of my mind.

'What *are* you talking about? Is that all you've come for? Just to joke with me?'

He didn't answer. Instead he went to the door, opened it and called downstairs :

'Bill, old boy, come up now, will you? And bring the champers.'

Torn somewhere between a terror of breaking down altogether and a wild disbelief that any of all this could be real I stood in the middle of the room, cold and shaking.

And then Bill came upstairs and into the room, carrying a bottle of champagne in his good hand. I had hardly time to notice that he was again in uniform before Doll followed him. She too was carrying a bottle of champagne.

'No more gloomies now, duckie,' she said and came and put her arms round me and kissed me. 'No more gloomies, matey, please.'

I could only stare. I again couldn't trust myself to speak. And then Bill came over and kissed me and laughed in his old jovial fashion and said :

'Let me not to the marriage of true minds — Think she'll make a good bridesmaid, Doll? Shall we have her?'

I again stared helplessly from Fitz to Bill and then to Doll and then back to Bill again. Then Bill laughed again and said :

'If you wish to congratulate me on our forthcoming nuptials, my dearest Liz, you may do so by shaking me by either hand.'

At this he held up his left hand for me to see. On to the stump of his wrist had been fitted a cunning arrangement in what looked like bright silver, not at all unlike an egg-whisk.

'Pretty wizard job, eh, Liz dear? Pretty marvellous ! Know something? They're bloody well going to let me fly again ! God,

199

Fitz old boy, this is a damn wizard day. Open the champers! I can even drive Chloe!'

At that moment it didn't seem that I was listening to his voice, loud and excited though it was. Instead I was listening to the echo of it coming from a long way off, from another world, from what I sometimes called my long-lost childhood; and it was saying simply :

'Lucky bastard. Lucky bastard.'

And as I heard it my tears, both of joy and grief, broke at last.

The weather too broke at last. The autumn began to turn wet and stormy, with intermittent bursts of sunshine, and there were many rainbows. There was also another frequent but rarer phenomenon to be seen in the sky : the sun-dog, a bright iridescent circle in all the colours of the spectrum, up against the sun, an ephemeral glowing mark that might have been an imprint left by the dog-fights of the summer. Odd that I've never seen one since that year.

As I was now alone again – Bill and Doll, married now, had gone back to Dorking, where Bill was to have more treatment before going on to operational training again – I took to taking long walks by myself. I walked everywhere, on the hills, in the now smouldering orange beech-woods, in the chestnut copses, across the meadows and along the river, sometimes all day.

That autumn, in the rainy, still warmish weather, there were many mushrooms. They were especially good in the Hudsons' meadow by the river, behind the blue-bell wood, where they cropped prodigiously. I got into the way of going there almost every day to gather them and it was, I think, this meandering in complete solitude, in this gentlest of occupations, that finally did more than anything else to heal me.

Then one damp, still afternoon I walked through the blue-bell wood, carrying my basket as usual, and then, at the wicket gate that leads into the meadow beyond, came to a sudden stop.

Behind me crowds of sere poplar leaves were falling on the river in the softest of shoals, like bright yellow fish, and sometimes there was a plonk! of a sweet-chestnut husk falling on to the floor of wet chestnut leaves below. In the otherwise motionless afternoon I stood for nearly five minutes listening to these sounds and at the same time staring incredulously at the meadow beyond me.

An unprecedented, startling thing had happened to the meadow. It was completely dark with fresh-ploughed furrows. Not a vestige of grass remained.

I all at once felt a great sense of having been cheated. For the first time in my life I felt intensely vexed, almost angry, at something the Hudsons had done. I felt it to be deeply unfair; it was almost sacrilegious. All my life this had been a meadow. In a sense, moreover, it was my meadow. Now, more than at any time in my life, it was my happy hunting ground. This single field, more than anything else, had helped to restore me.

Considerably upset, I walked back through the wood and then over the little bridge that crosses the river there. Then all of a sudden I decided to go to the farm. I would see Tom about it. It was really little short of outrageous. It had, I felt, to be explained.

When I got to the farm-yard I saw that the doors of the big barn, where lately we had joked and revelled in the candle-light of noon, stood wide open. I stopped and looked inside and there was Tom, sitting on an upturned box, sorting out trays of seed-potatoes from a great pink-white pile of King Edwards.

'Hullo,' he said and at once got up to come and shake me by the hand, 'how nice to see you, Elizabeth. It's been such an awful long time.'

'I know.'

'I was most terribly sorry about it all.' He suddenly took off his spectacles and rubbed them hard with his handkerchief and there was something about his exposed eyes that was far more touching that the words he was trying to say. 'I wanted to come and see you but they said —'

'I know. I'm better now.'

'I'm glad of that.'

Then I said :

'Tom, what's this dreadful thing you've done to the meadow ?'

'Dreadful thing ?'

'You've ploughed it up. It doesn't seem right. The footpath's gone. Everything. Why?'

'Ministry directive. Got to get more acres under the plough. Got to grow more corn, more potatoes, more everything.'

'Ministries, my foot. We've got to have grass, too, haven't we? What do they know?'

'You sound angry.'

'Perhaps it's silly, but I rather think I am. There's always been a meadow there.'

'I know, but it can't be helped. When the war's over we'll put it back to grass again. It's virgin soil. It should grow things pretty well.'

'When the war's over! When! And when will that be? Years. Years.'

This sudden echo of my former bitterness shocked him, so much so that I don't think he knew what to say about it. Instead he simply turned and found another box and then asked me:

'Won't you sit down? You don't mind if I go on with the potatoes?'

So I sat down and watched him continue to sort potatoes. They were a very good sample this year, he said once. They'd come up good and dry. And gradually as I watched him in the great tranquil shadowy space of the barn I once again became aware of its embalming, timeless solidity and at last I calmed down.

'I'm glad I saw you,' he said. 'We were talking about you only yesterday. Mother was wondering if you'd care to come to lunch one Sunday.'

'I don't think so, thank you all the same.'

'Or perhaps supper one evening?'

'I don't think I'd be very good company.'

'I think you'd be very good company.'

I simply stared, completely taken aback.

'What ever made you say that? At the moment I'm just about the most unsociable person in the world.'

'I don't think so.'

He gave me a sudden bright smile and his eyes gave a series of nervous jerks behind the spectacles.

'You don't know me,' I said.

MORE ABOUT PENGUINS

Penguin Book News, which appears every month, contains details of all the new books issued by Penguins as they are published. From time to time it is supplemented by *Penguins in Print,* which is a complete list of all books published by Penguins which are in print. (There are over three thousand of these.)

A specimen copy of *Penguin Book News* will be sent to you free on request, and you can become a subscriber for the price of the postage – 4s. for a year's issues (including the complete lists). Just write to Dept EP, Penguin Books Ltd, Harmondsworth, Middlesex, enclosing a cheque or postal order, and your name will be added to the mailing list.

Other Penguins by H. E. Bates are described overleaf.

Note : *Penguin Book News* and *Penguins in Print* are not available in the U.S.A. or Canada

'I don't know.'

Nor did I know, at that particular moment in time. But I know now, and I know too that there will never be a battle like it again.

'Never forget,' I sometimes tell myself as I look at the lake, the swans, the water lilies, the big barn and the great beech-woods smouldering in the sun, 'never again.'

'Would you? Oh! I don't mean now. Not even soon. Not even perhaps next year. But in time. When you feel you can face it.'

'Face it? You make it sound like a prison sentence.'

'I didn't mean that. You know how I mean. But would you? No, you don't have to tell me now.'

I sat all of a sudden very quiet. An intolerable stillness inside me told me with unmistakable clarity that once again I had reached an important moment in time. Suddenly I remembered that winter evening when Tom had called about the snow-plough and how the swans were held in their dark prison in the snow and how for some reason I had the strange idea that I should never see him again. Then I remembered the pilots, the gay pilots, the young pilots, the unbearably young pilots, the foolhardy and the grave, the friendly and the enemy, the living and the dead. I remembered the Count and Matters Devlin and Mac, Smithy and Hugh Lambton and all the others and finally one who loved glow-worms.

'Tom,' I said, 'it means a lot to me that you've asked me this.'

'Just take time to think if you want to.'

'I said and did some pretty awful things to you earlier this year. Some pretty awful, swanky, rotten things.'

'We all do sometimes.'

'I was very young and pretty damn foolish,' I said. 'Could you bear to take me for a walk? I'd like to walk somewhere with you.'

We walked as far as the orchard. On the hills great deep orange fires burned in the beeches. Lower down, in the valley, the plough had scarred the empty stubbles. Apple leaves and plum leaves were falling everywhere from now fruitless branch-es. It was very quiet, almost intolerably quiet, and there was a great odour of autumn in the air.

'And to think,' I said, 'that this was a battle-field.'

'Was?' he said. 'Do you think it's over?'

'I don't know.'

I turned and with a sudden fondness, and again with that profound stillness awake in me, kissed his face. I suddenly wanted to say something about my own battle being over but my heart was too full and I merely said again :

'No?'

'Not the me I am now.'

'Then perhaps you'd let me try?'

'What do you mean by that?'

He had been stacking the trays of potatoes in a big pile, eight or nine high. Now he lifted another tray and rested it on top of them. Then he came back and sat down and after a good deal of hesitation and staring at the ground he at last looked at me and said:

'Elizabeth, I've got to say this now or I'll never say it for the rest of my wretched life. Slap my face if you don't like it. It's probably pretty awful and I hope you'll forgive me if you think it is.'

He broke off suddenly, in a turmoil of difficulty and indecision, and I said:

'What on earth is all this about?'

'I know it's pretty awful. I know it is. But I've got to ask it.'

'What?'

'Would you ever think of marrying again?'

'Good God, what a thing to ask.'

'I'm sorry – I know it's pretty awful –'

'Awful? You might as well hold a gun at my head.'

He didn't say a word. He simply sat there in utter wretchedness, caught in a fresh turmoil of doubt and miserable regret, and suddenly I felt intensely and unaccountably sorry for him.

'I'm sorry I spoke like that,' I said.

'It doesn't matter. It's my fault. I shouldn't have spoken in the first place.'

'Not your fault. It's me. It's the me I am.'

'I'm sorry. I know it must have been hell.'

'Hell,' I said, 'wouldn't begin to describe the outer fringes of it.'

'Oh! my God,' he said and in a totally spontaneous and trembling rush of fervour suddenly came over and put his arms round me. 'God, I've suffered like hell for you.'

In that moment the last of my bitterness broke in a suppuration that nearly choked me. I couldn't resist putting my arms about him and without another word I kissed his face. Then he kissed me in return and finally said, not looking at me: